Praise for the novels of *New York Times* bestselling author Carla Neggers

"With a great plot and excellent character development, Neggers' latest thriller...is a fast-paced, action-packed tale of romantic suspense that will appeal to fans of Lisa Jackson and Lisa Gardner."
—*Library Journal* on *Saint's Gate*

"No one does romantic suspense better!"
—*New York Times* bestselling author Janet Evanovich

"Carla Neggers is one of the most distinctive, talented writers of our genre."
—*New York Times* bestselling author Debbie Macomber

"This heartwarming tale is full of fascinating secondary characters and enhanced by plot threads involving the long-term effects of a flooded valley, a search for jewels and long-ago passion."
—*Booklist* starred review of *Secrets of the Lost Summer*

"[Neggers] forces her characters to confront issues of humanity, integrity and the multifaceted aspects of love without slowing the ever-quickening pace."
—*Publishers Weekly*

"Only a writer as gifted as Carla Neggers could use so few words to convey so much action and emotional depth."
—*New York Times* bestselling author Sandra Brown

Also by Carla Neggers

Swift River Valley

A KNIGHTS BRIDGE CHRISTMAS
ECHO LAKE
CHRISTMAS AT CARRIAGE HILL
  (ebook novella)
CIDER BROOK
THAT NIGHT ON THISTLE LANE
SECRETS OF THE LOST SUMMER

Sharpe & Donovan

KEEPER'S REACH
HARBOR ISLAND
DECLAN'S CROSS
ROCK POINT (novella)
HERON'S COVE
SAINT'S GATE

BPD/FBI Series

THE WHISPER
THE MIST
THE ANGEL
THE WIDOW

Carriage House

THE HARBOR
STONEBROOK COTTAGE
THE CABIN
THE CARRIAGE HOUSE

For a complete list of titles by Carla Neggers,
please visit carlaneggers.com.

CARLA NEGGERS

THE CARRIAGE HOUSE

Recycling programs
for this product may
not exist in your area.

ISBN-13: 978-0-373-60216-2

The Carriage House

Printed in U.S.A.

Dear Reader,

I'm thrilled to have *The Carriage House* available again in print! It's the first in a fun, loosely connected series of four books: *The Carriage House*, *The Cabin*, *Stonebrook Cottage* and *The Harbor*.

Tess and her old carriage house are near and dear to my heart. My six brothers and sisters and I grew up in an even older "carriage house" on the western edge of the Quabbin Reservoir in rural Massachusetts. Talk about a fixer-upper! What an adventurous childhood we had working on the house, climbing trees, exploring the woods and fields. As I write this note, I'm just back from a family gathering there. Tess's trapdoor is much like one we had...but we never found any bodies in our dirt cellar!

I hope you enjoy *The Carriage House*. Note Tess's friend Susanna Galway, who brings the Texas Rangers to Boston in *The Cabin* when her husband, Jack, chases a killer right to her doorstep.

Please visit my website, www.carlaneggers.com, for all my latest news, contests, recipes and photos, and to sign up for my e-newsletter.

Thank you, and happy reading,

Carla Neggers

To Robyn Carr

One

On the day Ike Grantham disappeared, he missed an appointment with Tess Haviland, a Boston graphic designer and one of the few women who didn't find him irresistible. She liked him, but over a year later, she still couldn't explain why. He was blond, handsome, a risk-taker, outgoing to a fault, egalitarian and very determined not to fit the stereotype of the serious, philanthropic-minded heir to a New England industrial fortune. He was without guilt or ambition, and there were days Tess thought he was without morals, too. Especially where women were concerned.

Except for her. "Tess," he used to say, "you have too many men with guns in your life. I'm steering clear."

She had *no* men with guns in her life. It just seemed that way because she'd grown up in a working-class neighborhood and her father owned a pub. Ike wasn't without stereotypes of his own.

He was on her mind not just because it had been over a year since he'd taken off without a word, but because she'd just received the real estate tax bill for the carriage house he'd given her in lieu of a check. It was an

1868 carriage house on a small lot practically across the street from the ocean, within walking distance of one of the prettiest villages on the North Shore. The structure itself wasn't much. The location was. This was reflected in the property's value—and in her tax bill.

Tess stared down at the Old Granary Burial Ground four floors beneath her Beacon Street office. Thin, old tombstones tilted in different directions, and tourists crept along the paths in the lush shade, the tall trees filled out with leaves now, the long hard Boston winter finally over.

It had been a nose-to-the-grindstone winter. She'd left a secure corporate job to go out on her own early last year, just before Ike had bowed out of her life as abruptly as he'd barged in. Sometimes she wondered if he'd infected her—not romantically, but in creating a sense of urgency in her, so that the "someday" she'd go out on her own became something she had to do *now*. She'd been doing work for his Beacon Historic Project on the side, and before she knew it, she was hanging out her shingle. She'd worked out of her apartment for the first six months. Then, last fall, she and Susanna Galway decided to rent an office together in a late-nineteenth-century building on Beacon Street, a prestigious address. They had one room on the fourth floor, overlooking the city's most famous cemetery.

Tess turned from the window and looked at her friend. Susanna was tall and willowy, as dark as Tess was fair, with porcelain skin and eyes as green as the springtime grass down in Old Granary. She was also a financial planner, and Tess had only just told her about the carriage house. Susanna was at her desk, Tess's tax bill laid out on her keyboard. Occasionally she'd emit a sigh that conveyed the utmost distress.

"This is why you're an artist," she said finally. "Damn, Tess. You *always* get paid in cash. It's Rule One. If I'd been around to advise the Indians, do you think I'd have let them take *beads* for Manhattan? Hell, no."

"I can sell it."

"Who would buy it? It's run-down. It's on the flipping historic register. It's on a minuscule lot. And, I might add—" She swiveled around in her expensive ergonomic chair, zeroing in on her office mate and friend with those piercing green eyes. "I might add that the place is *haunted*."

"That's just a rumor."

"And not haunted by Casper the Friendly Ghost. Your ghost is a convicted murderer."

Tess dropped into her own chair at her computer. She did a great deal of her work, but not all, by computer. She still had an easel, oil pastels, drawing pencils, watercolors. She liked to touch and feel what she created, not just see it on a computer screen. Her screen was blank now, her computer in sleep mode. Her U-shaped work area, stacked and overflowing with samples, files, invoices, work in progress, wasn't as tidy and uncluttered as Susanna's. They were yin and yang, she liked to tell her more artistic friends. That was why they could work in the same space without killing each other.

"It was a duel," Tess said. "It's just that it happened to take place in the carriage house. Benjamin Morse challenged Jedidiah Thorne to a duel after Jedidiah accused him of abusing his wife, Adelaide. Jedidiah killed him and went to prison because it just so happened that dueling was illegal in Massachusetts. If Benjamin had killed Jedidiah instead, he'd have gone to prison."

"You're splitting hairs. It was murder."

Whatever it was, it happened in the carriage house within a few weeks of its completion. Jedidiah Thorne never got to live in the estate he'd built in Beacon-by-the-Sea. The Thornes had been seamen on the North Shore for centuries, but he was the first to make any money, prospering in shipping in those first years following the Civil War. After serving five years in prison for killing Benjamin Morse, Jedidiah headed west, only to return, finally, to the East Coast just before his death. It was his ghost people said haunted the carriage house to this day. It was where he'd killed a man—it was where his spirit remained. Why, no one seemed to know.

"I don't believe in ghosts," Tess said. Susanna rocked back in her chair. She was dressed in smart, slim pants and a shirt-top, naturally graceful, her nails done, her makeup perfect. She'd left San Antonio for Boston late last summer, moving herself and her twin daughters in with her grandmother in Tess's old neighborhood. There was an ex-, or soon-to-be-ex-, husband back in Texas. Susanna didn't like talking about him.

"Let's put it this way," she said. "You're stuck. Pay the tax bill or let the town take the place and call it a day. Or try to sell it. New Englanders are pretty damn weird when it comes to old houses. Maybe someone'll buy it."

"I'm not sure I want to sell it."

"Tess! You've had this place for over a year and haven't stepped foot in it."

"That's because I kept thinking Ike would show up and want it back, or want more work for it, or his sister would. Lauren Montague is the workhorse for the Beacon Historic Project—I'm not sure Ike told her what he was up to."

"He could transfer the deed on his own?"

"Apparently. I did promise him I'd do more work—we were to discuss specifics the day he stood me up. I haven't heard from him since."

"Think he's dead?"

Tess winced at Susanna's frank question and jumped back to her feet, staring once more at the centuries-old tombstones below. There were more people buried there than had markers. Her throat was tight as she thought about Ike. He was in his mid-forties, so filled with life and energy it was impossible to believe he was dead. Yet, that was what most people assumed—that his recklessness had caught up with him and he'd gone overboard or walked off a cliff. Not on purpose. Ike would never commit suicide.

"Taking off for months at a time without telling anyone is within his pattern of behavior," Tess said. "The police haven't declared him a missing person or anything. I don't know if Lauren has sounded the alarm." She glanced over at Susanna. "It's not something I've pursued."

"Well, dead or alive, he signed the place over to you. I assume your accountant factored it into your last year's income taxes, and now obviously the property tax assessors have caught up with you. So, that cinches it. You can't avoid reality. The carriage house is yours. What you do with it is up to you."

"I've wanted a place in Beacon-by-the-Sea for as long as I can remember," Tess said quietly, watching two kids about twelve years old reading Sam Adams's tombstone. John Hancock was buried in Old Granary, too, as well as Benjamin Franklin's parents, the victims of the Boston Massacre, Mother Goose. "My mother and father and I used to have picnics there on the beach before she died. We'd walk past all the old houses, and Mum would tell me stories. She loved American history."

Susanna came and stood beside her. "Fundamentally, all financial decisions are emotional." She gave Tess a quick, irreverent grin. "Look at it this way—a run-down nineteenth-century carriage house haunted by a convicted murderer ought to make an interesting weekend project."

Tess decided to drive up to Beacon-by-the-Sea and take a look at her property that afternoon. She quit work early to get ahead of rush-hour traffic and made her way up Route One, then along the water to a quiet stretch of rockbound coast on the tip of Cape Ann. The May sun sparkled on the Atlantic, bringing back memories of driving this way when she was six, up front with her father, her mother tucked under blankets in back, telling stories of whales and lost ships until she either fell asleep or became unintelligible, making sense only to herself.

After Ike Grantham had stood her up, Tess had come to Beacon-by-the-Sea three or four times hunting for him, but to no avail. His own sister didn't seem to be worried about him. Why should Tess be? Ike had taken off without notice before, often. He was self-centered and inconsiderate, not because he meant to be but simply because he was.

Now she was on her way to the Beacon Historic Project's offices to pick up the key to the carriage house.

The offices were located in one of its restored late-eighteenth-century buildings in the village, just a short walk to the harbor. Modeled after the more famous Doris Duke Foundation in Newport, Rhode Island, the project—Ike's brainchild—bought up old houses and outbuildings all over the North Shore, gutted them, rebuilt them according to exacting standards and leased them to carefully screened tenants. In many once-decaying neighborhoods, the project's work had sparked renovation and renewal, a sense of civic pride. When she started freelancing for Ike, Tess had toyed with the idea of leasing a small early-eighteenth-century house herself. Then he'd presented her with the carriage house. Its 1868 construction put it outside the project's parameters—they preferred pre-1850 structures. Or so Ike had explained. Tess had never really understood what his motives were.

She entered the building that housed the project's offices, a pretty herbal wreath on its saffron-painted front door. Inside, the atmosphere was sedate and elegant, more like entering a home than offices. The rooms were decorated in period colors and pieces, and through a doorway to the right, a pencil-thin older woman greeted Tess in an affected nasal voice. "May I help you?"

"Hi, Mrs. Cookson." Tess smiled, walking onto the thick carpet. "I'm Tess Haviland—"

"Why, Miss Haviland, I'm so sorry. I didn't recognize you. What can I do for you?"

"I stopped by to pick up the key to the Thorne carriage house. I know it's been a while, but I thought I should take a look at it before I decide what to do." Muriel Cookson looked confused, and Tess added quickly, "Ike told me you'd have the key here."

"The key to the Thorne carriage house? I don't understand—"

"It's all right." Lauren Grantham Montague approached from an adjoining room, smiling graciously. Her resemblance to Ike was subtle, but unmistakable. "It's so good to see you, Tess. I should have called you myself long before now. Mrs. Cookson, I have the key to the carriage house. I'll get it for Tess."

"Is Miss Haviland doing work for us?"

Lauren continued to smile, but a coolness had come into her gray eyes, as if she was struggling to hide much stronger emotions. "No, I assume she's checking on her property. Isn't that right, Tess?"

Tess nodded. "I need to make some decisions."

At Lauren's side, Muriel Cookson was obviously confused. Lauren said briskly, "Before he left last year, Ike transferred ownership of the Thorne carriage house to Tess. I should have told you before now. It simply hasn't come up."

The elderly receptionist paled, but said nothing. She was a contrast to the tawny-haired Lauren and her expensive, tasteful clothes and easy manner. There was nothing naturally gracious or easy about Muriel Cookson, whom Ike used to describe to Tess in unflattering terms, taking the sting only partly out when he'd declare the project couldn't run without her. That the Beacon Historic Project interested him at all amazed Tess. Then again, Ike Grantham was a fixer-upper in his own way. It wasn't so much that he liked to help people for their sake as he believed totally in his ability to know what they needed. As arrogant and self-centered as he was, he had a charm, an energy about him, that inspired people. His enthusiasm for life and risk was contagious.

"Muriel wants to die at her desk, in her Rockports," he would tell Tess, "but Lauren wants Visionary Philanthropist written on her tombstone."

He'd said this sarcastically, the same day his younger sister had announced her engagement to Richard Montague, a domestic terrorism expert with the North Atlantic Strategic Studies Institute. Ike's ego knew no bounds. When he took off a week later, Tess half assumed he was miffed because he hadn't gotten to handpick his future brother-in-law and needed to nurse the wound to his ego. Lauren was totally dedicated to the Beacon Historic Project, wanting to take it in new directions. Ike didn't care. Tess had sensed he was bored with it, anxious to move on—and apparently he had. Lauren and Richard were married two months later, without Ike.

Lauren withdrew into the adjoining room at the back of the old, restored house. Tess waited in awkward silence with Muriel Cookson, who wouldn't like not knowing Ike had given away one of the project's properties, even if he'd done them a favor in dumping the carriage house. They'd bought it five years ago and, Ike had said, hadn't drawn up even the most preliminary plans of what to do with it. It had been one of his whims, he'd told Tess. A mistake he wanted to correct by transferring ownership to her.

Lauren returned, handing Tess a manila envelope. "There are two keys, both to the side door. There's no front-door key, I'm afraid, and no bulkhead key."

"Thank you."

"My pleasure. Let us know if there's anything we can do. We have a number of files on the carriage house's history in our archives upstairs."

Tess could feel the outline of the keys through the envelope. *Her* keys. *Her* carriage house. She was surprised at the sudden rush of excitement. If Ike came back tonight and said it was all a mistake, what would she do? She thanked Lauren, said goodbye to her and Mrs. Cookson and withdrew into the May sunshine. A cute shop across the street had a display of painted furniture in the window. Next to it was a chocolate store. Down the street, she could see boats in the harbor, bright buoys bobbing on the light surf. She breathed in the smell of the ocean and smiled. For the past year, she hadn't dared believe the carriage house was really hers. It *had* to be a mistake, never mind the papers she and Ike had signed. Maybe they weren't legitimate, wouldn't hold up in court if Lauren decided to contest the transfer. After all, Tess had promised Ike more work. As week after week went by without word from him, as she poured every minute, every dime she had, into her one-woman graphic design business, she had found herself completely paralyzed over what to do about the carriage house.

No more. At least not for the moment. She hopped into her car and headed out of the village along the ocean. The business district ended, houses thinned out. A rock-strewn beach stretched out on the ocean side of the road as it wound onto a narrow point. At the very tip of the point was the Thorne estate, a slate-blue clapboard house with gnarled apple trees, oaks and a huge shagbark hickory holding their own against the elements. The main road hooked around in front of it, intersecting with a narrow side street where the carriage house stood. Tess slowed, barely breathing, and made the turn.

The carriage house was exactly as she remembered it from last March, its narrow clapboards also painted a slate blue, its own gnarled apple tree out front. She pulled into its short, gravel driveway. Well, she thought as she stared at the small house, maybe it was a little more run-down than she remembered.

And in early spring, the lilacs weren't in bloom. They were now, the bushes growing in a thick, impenetrable border on the back and both sides of the carriage house's small lot, carving it out from the rest of Jedidiah Thorne's original estate. She could smell the lilacs through her open windows, their sweet scent mingling with the saltiness of the ocean.

She shut her eyes. "All right, so the place is haunted. What do you care? With your imagination, you'd probably invent a ghost on your own. This way, you don't have to."

But leave it to Ike Grantham to give her a haunted house—and her to take it.

Two

A ndrew Thorne was not a happy man. He tried to convey this to Harley Beckett, his cousin and the one man on the planet Andrew would trust with his life—if he didn't kill him first.

"She's not in her tree house."

Harl grunted. "Then she's chasing after that damn cat."

He was flat on his back under a 1920s rolltop desk he was working on. Harl was the best furniture restorer on the North Shore, maybe in all of New England. His skills as chief Dolly-watcher, however, were currently under suspicion. Dolly was Andrew's six-year-old daughter, and when he'd come home from work—a long, aggravating day of things not going his way—he'd found her gone. And Harl oblivious.

Harl scooted out from under the rolltop and sat up on the spotless pine floor of the outbuilding where he lived and worked. He was particular. One stray dog hair or speck of mud, he maintained, could ruin a project, a touch of hyperbole few would dare point out to him. He was a Vietnam combat veteran and a retired police detective, and he'd never taken pains to make friends in Beacon-by-the-Sea. Neither had Andrew, but he got along with people better than Harl did. Which wasn't saying a lot.

Harl pulled his white ponytail from inside his habitual POW-MIA shirt. He had a white beard, shrapnel scars, parts of two fingers missing and a manner that was gruff on his best days. He studied Andrew for half a second, then sighed. "She's supposed to stay in the yard. She knows that."

"She won't have gone far," Andrew said with conviction, ignoring the twist of incipient panic in his gut. He hated not knowing where his daughter was.

Harl got stiffly to his feet. "Let's go. Hell, Andrew. Time I realize she can do something, she's off and done it. She never used to leave the yard without asking." He shook his head, plainly disgusted with himself. "I told her to stay in the yard not five minutes ago. I swear to God."

"You go out front," Andrew said. "I'll check back here."

"We don't find her in five minutes, we call in a search party."

Andrew glanced at the ocean across the street, and his stomach clamped down. He nodded, and the two of them set off.

Her neighbors, whoever they were, actually owned the lilac hedge. Tess recalled Ike explaining that to her. She reached out a palm and let a drooping cluster of blossoms brush against her skin. They were at peak, the tight, dark purple buds opening into tiny lavender blossoms, spilling their fragrance. Surely she could pick a bouquet. The hedge was obviously neglected, the lilacs in need of pruning and thinning. A few weedy saplings even grew in their midst.

"Here, kitty, kitty. Come, kitty."

A little girl's voice rose from the middle of the lilacs, just to Tess's left. It was high-pitched and cajoling, and a moment later, its owner pushed through to the narrow strip of overgrown grass on the carriage house side of the lilacs. She couldn't have been more than six, a sturdy girl with coppery braids, freckles and blue eyes that were squinted as she frowned, hands on hips. She hadn't yet seen Tess. "Come *on*, Tippy Tail." She stamped a foot, frustrated and impatient now. "I won't bother you! I'm your friend."

Tess noticed something in the girl's hair and realized it was an elaborate jeweled crown. She also wore denim overalls and a Red Sox T-shirt. Tess still had on her clothes from work, a suit that suggested creativity but also professionalism. She didn't want to look too artsy and end up scaring off the kind of clients she needed in order to stay in business.

The girl turned and saw Tess, but she seemed neither surprised nor curious. She was obviously a girl with a mission. "Have you seen my cat?"

"No, I haven't. Actually, I just got here myself." Tess hadn't dealt with many six-year-olds. "Is someone with you? Where's your mother?"

"She's in heaven." The girl's tone was matter-of-fact, as if she were giving the time. Tess pushed a hand through her hair. Lately, she'd been fretting about too much work, Ike Grantham and his carriage house and not enough about the rest of her life. She was thirty-four, and while she wasn't sure about children she'd had damn rotten luck with men of late. "Where do you live?" she asked.

"Over there." The girl pointed through the lilacs. "Harl's watching me."

Not very well, Tess thought. "Harl's your babysitter?"

"Yep."

"My name's Tess. What's yours?"

"Princess Dolly." She gave her coppery braids a regal little toss.

"Princess? Really?"

"Yep."

Tess relaxed slightly. A six-year-old who thought she was a princess was something she could relate to. "How did you come to be a princess?"

"Harl says I was born a princess."

Whoever this Harl was, Tess wondered about his judgment when it came to kids. But what did she know? She glanced at her yard with its strip of over-grown grass. Lots of places a cat could hide. "I take it you lost your cat?"

Reminded of her mission, Princess Dolly raised her shoulders and let them fall in an exaggerated, dramatic shrug. "Yes. That Tippy Tail. She's having kittens *any day.* Harl says I should leave her alone."

Okay, Tess thought, one point for Harl. "What does Tippy Tail look like? If I see her, I can let you know."

The girl thought a moment, her freckled nose scrunched up as she concentrated. "She's gray, except for the white tip on her tail." Her features relaxed, and she giggled suddenly, her eyes lighting up. "That's why I named her Tippy Tail!"

"Makes sense. You should run along home. I imagine Harl will be looking for you."

She rolled her eyes. "He's *always* looking for me."

This, Tess didn't doubt. "I can walk you home—"

"I can go by myself. I'm six." She held up the five fingers of one hand and the index finger of the other hand to prove it.

Tess wasn't arguing. "It was nice to meet you, Dolly."

"Princess Dolly."

"As you wish. Princess Dolly it is."

The girl spun on her toes and squeezed back through the lilacs.

As independent as Princess Dolly seemed, she still was only six and shouldn't be running around on her own, crown or no crown. If nothing else, Tess knew she should make sure Dolly got back to her royal palace and wasn't lost or otherwise in the wrong place.

She started to pry apart the lilacs, but heard a crunch of gravel behind her, then a man's voice. "Just what the hell do you think you're doing?"

She whipped around, realizing she looked as if she was spying on the neighbors. "I'm not doing anything," she said, taking note of the man in her driveway. Tall, lean, dark, no-nonsense. His angular features, blue eyes and humorless look were straight out of the images she'd conjured of her nineteenth-century murderous ghost. But this man had on dusty work boots, jeans and a denim shirt, all definitely of this century. Good. A princess in the lilacs and a ghost in the driveway would have been more than she could handle.

"I'm looking for my daughter," the man said. His tone was straightforward, but laced with an edge of fear. "She's taken off after her cat."

Tess managed a smile, hoping it would help relieve some of his obvious tension. "You must mean Princess Dolly and Tippy Tail, the gray cat with the white tip on her tail who's to have kittens any day now. She was just here. The princess, not the cat. I sent her home about thirty seconds ago. She slipped through the lilacs."

"Then I'll be off. Thanks." He started to turn, but added, "This is private property, you know. But go ahead and pick a few lilacs if that's what you're after."

"It's not. I'm Tess Haviland. I own the carriage house."

Surprise flickered in his very blue eyes. "I see. Well, I'm Andrew Thorne. I own the house next door."

"Thorne?"

"That's right. Jedidiah was my grandfather's grandfather. Enjoy."

He retreated along the lilacs, not going through the middle of them the way his daughter had.

A Thorne. He'd obviously liked telling Tess that. Damn Ike. He could have warned her. But that wasn't his style, any more than telling people he was off to climb mountains, explore rivers, sleep in a hammock on a faraway beach. He was a man who lived life on his own terms, and that, Tess supposed, was why, ultimately, she liked him.

But she'd rather he'd told her the neighbors were related to her ghost.

Using one of the keys in the envelope Lauren Montague had given her, Tess entered the carriage house through the side door, which led directly into a circa 1972 kitchen, complete with avocado-colored appliances. She hoped they worked. She could do fun things with an avocado stove and fridge.

She stopped herself. What was she thinking? She couldn't afford to keep this place. She'd have to scrape to pay the tax bill, much less find any money for basic repairs and upkeep. The utilities bills must still have been sent to the Beacon Historic Project—she hadn't seen an electric or a fuel bill. She'd have to straighten that out with Lauren Montague, whether she sold the carriage house or kept it.

This was exactly why she'd dithered for a year, Tess thought. She simply didn't have the time or the money to deal with a nineteenth-century carriage house. Susanna was right. She should have insisted on cash.

She checked out the kitchen. Solid cabinets, worn counters, stained linoleum floor. Little mouse droppings. The fridge was unplugged. She rooted around behind it and managed to plug it in, smiling when she heard it start to hum. She checked the burners on the stove. They all worked. So far, no sign of Andrew Thorne's grandfather's grandfather, the infamous Jedidiah Thorne who'd killed a man here, even if it was over a hundred years ago. Tess shuddered.

There was a full bathroom off a short hallway on the same end of the house as the kitchen. She wondered when the building had been converted from housing horses and buggies to people—sometime in the past century-plus, obviously. She peered up a steep, narrow staircase, shadows shifting at the top of it.

"That's a little eerie," she said aloud, then realized she was standing on a trapdoor. She jumped back, her heart pounding. What if she'd fallen through? Balancing herself with one hand on the hall wall, she stomped on the trapdoor with her right foot. It seemed solid enough. Emboldened, she knelt in front of it, pushed the wooden latch and lifted it. It was solid wood, heavier than she'd expected, every crack and crevice filled with dust and dirt. She wasn't surprised to find there was no ladder, just a dark, gaping hole to whatever was below—furnace, pipes, spiders.

Then she realized there was a ladder, after all, hooked to the cellar ceiling, under the hall floor. She'd have to reach in through the opening, unhook it and lower it to the cellar floor. Then, presumably, climb down.

"No way."

Tess shut the trapdoor and latched it. She'd do the cellar another time. Hadn't Lauren mentioned a bulkhead? Good, she'd go in that way. If she bothered at all.

She resumed her tour, still smelling the dirt, dust and musty smells of the old cellar. She'd lived in older houses her entire life. They were no big deal to her, except they'd always been in the city—never out here on the edge of the Atlantic Ocean.

"The carriage house has tremendous potential," Ike had said. "I can feel it when I walk through it. It's one of my favorite structures. Unfortunately, it's rather new for us."

She smiled, thinking of what a contradiction he was. Scion of a New England industrial family, mountain climber, America's Cup contender, tennis player, white-water kayaker, womanizer...and lover of old houses. Conventional wisdom had him off in the Australian Outback, or Southeast Asia or Central Africa. Sometimes Tess wondered if he weren't hiding in Gloucester, watching them all.

Surely *someone* had to know where he was. An open, double doorway led from the kitchen to a long, narrow room with wide-board pine floors, attractive paned windows, a stone fireplace and the front door, probably half the size of the original carriage-width doors. As Lauren had warned, there was no outside lock, just a dead bolt latched from inside. One of the many things to be corrected, Tess thought as she stepped into the middle of the room, imagining color and fabric, music and laughter, friends, children. Dangerous imaginings. She really had no business hanging on to this place for as long as she had.

Her gaze fell on a deep, dark stain on the wooden floor just inside the front door. She walked over slowly, ran her toe over it. It could pass for blood. For all she knew, it *was* blood.

A man had died here, she remembered. Benjamin Morse, the rich wife-beater, defending his honor. Did a wife-beater have honor? Not in her book. But perhaps he was innocent. Had Jedidiah Thorne been the kind of man to make such a charge recklessly, without proof? Or perhaps he'd done so as an excuse to kill Morse, whom he would have known would challenge him to a duel? Maybe Jedidiah had been in love with Adelaide Morse.

Tess had no answers. There were two small rooms at the other end of the house that immediately presented possibilities. Tess pictured domestic things like sewing machines, library shelves, overstuffed chairs, hooked rugs—and herself, working here. She could create a design studio upstairs, put in skylights and state-of-the-art equipment, work overlooking the sea instead of an historic graveyard. The designer and the ghost of Jedidiah Thorne.

She was getting ahead of herself, and she knew it.

She returned to the main room and stood very still, listening for ghost sounds.

Nothing, not even Princess Dolly's missing cat. "Ridiculous," Tess muttered, and headed back out to her car.

As soon as he reacquainted Dolly with the rules of the house, Andrew grabbed two beers and sat out with Harl in the old Adirondack chairs under the shagbark hickory. It was a big, old, beautiful tree, probably planted by Jedidiah Thorne himself, before he took to dueling.

"Where's Dolly?" Harl asked.

"Sulking in her tree house." It was six rungs up into a nearby oak, and she'd helped Harl build it out of scrap lumber. Andrew, an architect, had stayed out of it. Some things were best left to Dolly and Harl. But not all. "She thinks if she didn't go out into the street, she didn't really leave the yard."

"She's going to be a lawyer or a politician. Mark my words."

Andrew gritted his teeth. "It's that damn cat."

"I know it. If it wouldn't break Dolly's heart, I'd wish Tippy Tail would sneak off and find herself a couple of new suckers to take her in. She's a mean bitch. Clawed me this morning." He displayed a tattooed forearm with a three-inch claw mark, then opened his beer. "I should've taken her to the pound."

But Andrew knew that wouldn't have been Harl's way. He was a soft touch with children and helpless animals. Tippy Tail was scrawny, temperamental and pregnant, but once Dolly had seen her, that was that. Harl had seen and committed more violence than most, first growing up in a tough neighborhood in Gloucester, then in war, finally in his work as a detective. Yet, he was also the gentlest man Andrew had ever known. His first and only marriage hadn't worked, but his two grown daughters adored him, never blaming him for retreating to his shop, working on furniture, staying away from people.

Sometimes Andrew wondered if Joanna would have approved of Harley Beckett taking care of their daughter. But not tonight. Tonight, Andrew accepted that his wife had been dead for three years, killed in an avalanche on Mount McKinley. She'd only started mountain-climbing the year before, when Dolly was two. Ike Grantham's idea.

"He makes me want to push myself," she'd said. "He makes me want to try something out of my comfort zone. Leaving you here, leaving Dolly—it scares the hell out of me. And excites me at the same time. I have to do this, Andrew. I'll be a better person because of this experience. A better mother."

Maybe, Andrew thought. If she'd lived. But climbing mountains, even in northern New England, had made Joanna happy, eased some of the restlessness and desperation that had gripped her with Dolly's birth. She hadn't been ready for a child. He could see that now. She'd felt, in ways he couldn't understand, that she'd lost herself, needed something that was hers, that felt daring and not, as she'd put it, "tied down." She hadn't meant Dolly in particular. She'd meant everything.

"I love Dolly with all my heart," she'd tried to explain. "And I love you, Andrew, and my job." She was a research analyst with the North Atlantic Strategic Studies Institute. "I'm not dissatisfied with anything on the outside, just on the inside."

Ike Grantham seemed to understand. Or pretended to. Andrew wasn't any good at pretending.

"Ike and I aren't having an affair, Andrew. Please don't ever think such a thing."

Andrew had believed her. Whatever would have become of their marriage if Joanna had come home from Mount McKinley no longer mattered. She hadn't, and he'd had to go on without her. So had Dolly. He didn't blame Ike for Joanna's death—that would have meant robbing her of her independence, and perhaps even denying her her love of climbing.

He drank some of his beer and listened to the birds in the hickory. Winter had finally let go of the northern coast of Massachusetts. "So, Harl, who the hell is Tess Haviland?"

"No idea. Why?"

"She says she owns the carriage house."

Harl frowned. "Lauren sold it?"

"I don't think so. Not recently. We'd have heard."

"Ike."

It was possible. Andrew said nothing, picturing Tess Haviland in front of the lilacs. Blonde, athletic build, attractive. Pale blue eyes, and a touch of irreverence in her smile and manner. It was difficult to say if she was Ike Grantham's type. Most women were.

Harl grunted. "All we need is that bastard resurfacing. Things have been quiet this past year." He settled back in his chair and stared up at the sky. "I like quiet."

"I'll find out what the story is. Ike might not have anything to do with this Haviland woman."

But he knew Harl was dubious, and Andrew admitted he had his own doubts. When most of Jedidiah Thorne's original property had come onto the market not long after Joanna's death, Andrew bought it. He'd tried to buy the carriage house as well, but Ike had refused to sell. Not that Andrew had wanted it particularly, given its sordid history, but it seemed odd to have it separated out from the rest of the property—and it meant he had no control over who might end up on the other side of the lilacs.

He finished his beer and decided he should get on with making dinner. Harl sometimes ate with them. Not always. Sometimes his cousin would fix a can of baked beans or chowder and eat out here on an Adirondack chair, in the shade—or the snow. And sometimes, Andrew knew, he didn't eat at all.

"Dolly's teacher came out today when I picked her up from school," Harl said abruptly.

"Why?"

"She's worried about Dolly's 'active imagination.'"

Andrew grimaced. He knew what was coming next. "You didn't let her wear one of her damn crowns to school, did you?"

"She likes her crowns. I told her to leave them home, but she slipped one into her lunch box. It's her favorite. What am I supposed to do, frisk a six-year-old?"

Andrew felt his pulse pounding behind his eyes. His daughter had a rich, creative mind, and it was getting her into trouble. He didn't know what was normal for a six-year-old, what was peculiar. And Harl sure as hell didn't. They'd both grown up on the wrong side of the tracks in Gloucester, in a neighborhood where there was always a fight to be had. Whether at sea, on a battlefield, on the street or in a bar, the Thornes always knew where to find a fight. The enemy didn't matter.

A lot of people in Beacon-by-the-Sea would say neither he nor Harl had any damn business raising a kid like Dolly. Any kid.

"She thinks she's a princess," Harl said.

"That's what she told Tess Haviland."

The corners of Harl's mouth twitched behind his white beard. "A princess has to have a crown."

"Jesus, Harl. What did Miss Perez say?"

He shrugged his big shoulders. "No more crowns in school."

Andrew knew there was more. "And?"

"She wants to meet with you."

"Damn it, Harl—"

"You're the father. I'm just the babysitter." He yawned, the prospect of a first-grader who liked to pretend she was a princess obviously not one of the great concerns of his life. "Any idea where this Tess Haviland's from?"

"Her car had Massachusetts plates."

"What kind of car?"

"Rusted Honda."

Harl nodded knowledgeably. "City car."

Andrew watched as a few yards off, Dolly found a rung with one foot, then the other, lowering herself out of her tree house. On the second rung, she turned herself around very carefully and leaped to the ground, braids flying, crown going askew. She let out a wild yell, ran to Andrew and jumped on his lap with great enthusiasm. She was a solid girl, sweating from her adventures, bits of leaves and twigs stuck in her socks and hair. Her crown hadn't flown off because it was anchored to her head with about a million bobby pins. She and Harl had put it together in his shop. The Queen of England couldn't have asked for anything gaudier, never mind that "Princess" Dolly's jewels were fake.

"What's up, pumpkin?"

"I can't find Tippy Tail. She won't come out."

If he were an expectant cat, Andrew thought, he wouldn't come out, either. "Did you call her in a nice voice?"

Dolly nodded gravely. This was serious business. "I used my inside voice even though I was outside. Like this." She dropped to a dramatic whisper, demonstrating. "Come, kitty, kitty, come."

"And she didn't come?"

"No."

"Then what did you do?" Harl asked.

"I clapped my hands. Like this."

She smacked her palms together firmly and loudly, which didn't help the pounding behind Andrew's eyes. "That probably scared her, Dolly," he said.

She groaned. "Princess Dolly."

Andrew set her on the grass. He was beginning to get a handle on this princess thing. "Do you make everyone call you princess?"

"I am a princess."

"That doesn't mean everyone has to call you Princess Dolly—"

"Yes, it does."

Harl scratched the side of his mouth. "You don't make them bow and curtsy, do you?"

She tilted her chin, defiant. "I'm a princess. Harl, you said the boys should bow and the girls should curtsy, that's what people are supposed to do when they see a princess."

Andrew suddenly understood the summons from her teacher. It wasn't just about crowns. He shot Harl a look. "You got this started. You can finish it. You talk to Miss Perez."

"What?" Harl was unperturbed. "She's six. Six-year-olds have active imaginations. I thought I was G.I. Joe there for a couple years."

"Six-year-olds don't make their classmates bow and curtsy."

"I don't *make* them," Dolly said.

Harl was doing a poor job of hiding his amusement. As a babysitter, he was reliable and gentle. Andrew never worried about his daughter's safety or happiness with his cousin. But Harl had a tendency to indulge her imagination, her sense of drama and adventure, more than was sometimes in her best interest.

"I'm taking a walk down to the water before I start dinner," Andrew said to her. "Do you want to come with me, let Harl get some work done?"

"Can we find Tippy Tail?"

"We can try."

She scrambled off toward the front yard ahead of him. Andrew got to his feet, glancing back at his older cousin, remembering those first months so long ago when Harl had come home from Vietnam, so young, so silent. Most people thought he'd kill himself, or someone else. Andrew was just a boy, didn't understand the politics, the limited options Harl had faced—or the low expectations. His cousin had defied everyone and become a police detective, and now an expert in furniture restoration and a keeper of six-year-old Dolly Thorne.

He and Andrew had each defied expectations, fighting their way out of that need to keep on fighting. Andrew had worked construction, forced himself to give up barroom brawls and a quick temper, met Joanna, had become an architect and a contractor. He and Harl weren't part of the North Shore elite and never would be. They didn't care.

"We're not keeping the kittens," Andrew said. "We're clear on that, aren't we, Harl?"

"Crystal. I told you. I hate cats."

That didn't mean he wouldn't keep the kittens, especially if Dolly badgered him. Harl operated according to a logic entirely his own. He hated cats, but he'd taken in a mean, scrawny, pregnant stray.

"Daddy," Dolly called impatiently, "come *on*. Let's *go*."

He headed out across the lawn, smelling salt and lilacs in the warm spring air. If finding Tess Haviland at the carriage house somehow meant Ike Grantham was back in town, so be it. Dolly was happy and healthy and thought well enough of herself to wear a crown. As far as Andrew was concerned, nothing else really mattered.

Three

Lauren couldn't get the clasp on her pearl necklace to catch. Her neck ached, and she'd lost patience. She wanted to throw the damn necklace across her dressing room.

Ike had given it to her. He'd picked it up on one of his adventures. "You should go with me next time. Beacon-by-the-Sea will get along fine without you. So will the project. Live a little."

She shut her eyes, fighting a sudden rush of tears. Too much wine. She'd already had two glasses on an empty stomach. She didn't know how she'd make it through dinner. Richard had chosen a dark, noisy restaurant in town. She could sit in a corner and drink more wine while he played terrorism expert and husband of the North Shore heiress.

God, what was wrong with her? She opened her eyes and tried again with her necklace. Richard never gave her jewelry. He liked to give her books, theater and concert tickets, take her to museum openings. No flowers, jewelry, scarves, sexy lingerie. No pretty things.

Ike hadn't understood what she saw in Richard. He

was protective for a younger brother, possibly because it had been just the two of them for so long, their parents dying in a private-plane crash twenty years ago. They'd liked Ike best, of course. Everyone did. People spoiled him, spun to his whims and wishes.

"Richard Montague, Lauren? You can't be serious!" Ike had stamped his feet, horrified. "He's one of those limp-dicked geeks who thinks he's covering up his geekiness by knowing scary things."

"He plays squash and racquetball," she'd argued. "He's run a marathon."

Her brother had been singularly unimpressed. "So?"

To Ike, Richard was the antithesis of everything he was. Ike had dropped out of Harvard; Richard had his doctorate. Ike had never worked seriously at anything, even his beloved Beacon Historic Project. Richard worked seriously at *everything.* Ike played to play, for its own sake, for the sheer pleasure of it. Richard played for self-improvement, networking, always with a greater purpose than mere pleasure.

Marrying Lauren, she was quite certain, came under that same heading. It was to his personal benefit. She was an asset. She had money, a good family name, "breeding," as he'd once let slip, smiling to cover his mistake. It didn't mean Richard didn't love her. He did, and she loved him. Not everyone operated out of the passions of the moment the way Ike did. He had spontaneity and a keen sense of fun and adventure, but no idea what real love, real commitment, meant.

"Oh, Ike."

The clasp fell into place. She ran the tips of her fingers over the pearls and managed, just barely, not to cry. She'd have to start all over with her makeup if she did. She studied her reflection in the wall of mirrors. She was tawny-haired and slender, determined not to let her body slip and sink and turn into mush now that she was forty.

Ike had teased her about turning forty. "You're on the doorstep, kid, and look at you—you haven't lived!"

She had a failed first marriage, a daughter away at boarding school, all the responsibilities of managing Grantham family affairs on her shoulders. Even the project, which he'd so loved early on, was largely her doing. She saw to the details, showed up when he didn't. She made his lifestyle possible.

He knew it. He would tell her how much he appreciated what she did, even as he teased her for doing nothing riskier than go frostbite sailing with friends, laugh too loud at a cocktail party.

"Ike," she whispered. "Oh, God."

He's dead. You know he's dead. But she didn't, not for sure. Tess Haviland wouldn't keep the carriage house. She hadn't even been up to see it in the year she'd owned it. Giving Tess the carriage house had been a stupid, impulsive thing for Ike to have done—but so like him.

When Tess put the carriage house on the market, Lauren would snap it up. Maybe they could work out an arrangement on their own, without Realtors. She had to keep her focus on that singular, positive thought and will it to happen.

Her three miniature white poodles wandered in, rubbing against her legs and making her laugh. "You lazy little rats, you've been sleeping on my bed all day, and now you want my attention? Where were you when *I* wanted to play, hmm?"

Ike had warned her against poodles. "You're playing to stereotype, Lauren. Get yourself a rottweiler or a Jack Russell terrier."

She'd threatened to knit them little vests. Suddenly unable to breathe, she ran out into her spacious bedroom. The windows were open, and she inhaled the smell of spring, stemming her panic. She didn't want to think about her brother. *Wouldn't.* He'd dominated her life for too long. He was selfish, insulting, reckless. He didn't like Richard because he was doing something important with his life and Ike wasn't. That was the truth of it. The poodles followed her into the bedroom, and she scooped them up and sank onto a white chair in front of the windows. The sun was fading, but her gardens were still bright with color. This was the house where she and Ike had grown up, built by their grandfather in 1923, high on a bluff above the ocean. She preferred her view of the gardens.

She would die here, she thought as she stroked the backs of her poodles. Fifty years from now, she would be sitting right here in her chair, perhaps with descendants of these very poodles, but otherwise alone. Ike would be gone, and so would Richard. That was her destiny, and there was no escaping it.

Richard Montague knew his wife was annoyed with him. She had poured herself another glass of wine and retreated to the back porch, knowing she couldn't do anything that might embarrass him. He had company. Unexpected company. Dinner was canceled at the last minute. He didn't understand her irritation. She hadn't wanted to go in the first place.

"Care for a glass of scotch?" Richard offered his guest.

The chief of staff of the senior senator from Massachusetts declined politely. Jeremy Carver was a very careful man. Richard had noticed that about him straight off, when they'd first met at Carver's office on Capitol Hill. He was careful, discreet, naturally suspicious, and he would destroy Richard Montague, Ph.D., if Richard gave him the slightest cause. There would be no mercy.

"I'm sorry I didn't call ahead," Carver said.

"No problem. Lauren and I both had long days. It was an easy dinner to cancel. Won't you sit down?"

They were in Richard's study on the first floor of the sprawling Grantham house. It had once been his father-in-law's study, his father's before that. Richard liked feeling a part of a tradition, even if it wasn't his own. He had no traditions in his family beyond whacks up the side of the head.

Jeremy Carver sat in the cranberry leather chair as if he owned it, yet Richard knew Carver's background was no better than his own. South Boston, six brothers and sisters, a scholarship to Georgetown. He was a natural for state and national politics.

Richard resisted pouring himself a scotch and sat opposite Carver on the plaid fabric-covered love seat. Carver, he noted, had the position of power in the room. Jeremy Carver was short, paunchy and gray-haired, five or ten years older than Richard, but he radiated self-confidence, a certainty that he was in the right place, doing the right thing.

As Carver settled back in the leather chair, Richard studied the man across from him. Richard knew he was in better condition. He worked out regularly, strenuously. He was taller, and if not handsome, not as pug-nosed and unprepossessing as Carver. He was better educated, worked in a field that gave him intimate knowledge of violent fanatics, amoral operatives. Terrorists, pure and simple, although there was little that was simple or pure about them, at least from his position as someone who studied them, tried to understand them. His work mired him in shades of gray, rationalizations, excuses, life experience, points of view and mind-sets that could justify mass murder.

Yet, despite all Richard knew, Jeremy Carver was just the sort of man who made him feel unaccomplished, as if he'd never gotten out of the faceless, middle-class subdivision where he'd grown up west of Boston.

"I'll come straight to the point," Carver said. "The senator wants to push for your Pentagon appointment."

Richard's heart skipped a beat, childishly. Of course the senator wanted him at the Pentagon. Why wouldn't he? He was the best. He was the right person for the job. "I'm grateful," he said simply.

Carver had no reaction. "Before the senator pitches his tent in your camp, he'll want to know there's nothing in your background that'll jump in his sleeping bag and bite him in the balls. Understood?"

"Of course."

The room was silent. Richard thought he could hear the creaking of Lauren's porch swing. She'd had a lot of wine already this evening. It wasn't like her. He pretended not to hear, instead watching Senator George Bowler's chief of staff. A high Pentagon appointment was just the beginning. Richard saw himself eventually as defense secretary, CIA director, perhaps even secretary of state. He was only fifty. There was time.

"So," Jeremy Carver said, rubbing the fine, soft leather with the fingertips of one hand, his hard eyes never leaving Richard, "tell me about Ike Grantham."

Four

It was chowder night at Jim's Place. By the time Tess slid onto the worn stool at the bar, her father had dipped her a heavy, shallow bowl of his famous clam chowder and set it in front of her. He had a bar towel slung over one powerful shoulder. "No beer for you tonight, Tess. You look done in."

"I am done in. It's been a long week."

The chowder was thick and steaming. Jim Haviland didn't skimp on the clams, and he didn't use canned. She watched the pat of butter melting into the milk. The good, simple fare and the old-fashioned pub atmosphere, with its dark, smooth wood and sparkling glasses, drew a diverse clientele, from construction workers and firefighters to university students and tech heads. Somerville might be on the road to gentrification, but not Jim's Place.

"You work too hard," her father told her.

"That's why I let you cook for me tonight."

"The hell it is."

He pinned his blue eyes on her, the same pale shade as her own, and she saw the jig was up. He knew about the carriage house. He had spies everywhere. Including Susanna Galway. Her grandmother's place was just up the street, and she wasn't one to miss chowder night. Tess could imagine how it went. Often she and Susanna had chowder together, and when she didn't show up, her father would have asked where she was, and Susanna would have blurted, "Tess? Oh, she's up in Beacon-by-the-Sea checking out that damn carriage house of hers."

Tess hadn't told her father that Ike Grantham had paid her in the form of a haunted, run-down 1868 carriage house. Jim Haviland liked cash, too.

"You're here to fess up about that damn place up on the North Shore. Tess. Jesus. A falling-down carriage house?"

She let her satchel slide to the floor. "Susanna?"

"No, couldn't get a damn word out of her. I knew something was up, though."

"Davey."

Her father's mouth snapped shut. Tess groaned. She should have expected as much. Davey Ahearn was on his stool at the opposite end of the bar. He was a twice-divorced plumber, her father's lifelong friend and a constant burr in Tess's side. He took his role as her godfather far too seriously. She knew he was listening to every word between her and her father. "Damn plumbers. They mind everyone's business but their own."

"Hey," Davey said. "What're you saying about plumbers?"

Tess pointed at him with her soupspoon. "I'm saying you've all got big mouths."

"This has nothing to do with me being a plumber."

So that was it. Susanna had told Davey, and Davey had told her father. Or Susanna had told her grandmother and word had gotten out that way. That was one thing Tess had learned long ago about life in her neighborhood: word got out. She'd driven straight home from Beacon-by-the-Sea, jumped in the shower and hopped on the subway. And still word of her afternoon's adventures had arrived at Jim's Place before she had.

"Somebody has to tell Jimmy here what's going on," Davey said.

"And somebody could give me half a chance to tell Jimmy myself."

"Half a chance?" Davey snorted. He was a beefy man with a huge salt-and-pepper mustache and an amazing capacity for physical labor. His friends liked to joke he would die with a plunger in his hands. "You've had this place for a year. You've had a hell of a lot more than half a chance."

This was true. Tess returned to her soup. That Davey and her father could get away with treating her as if she were eleven years old was a feat on their part. Not that she put up with it.

"You've got yourself a mess, Tess," Davey said. "A damn barn. You know what barns have? Barns have snakes."

"It's an antique carriage house."

Her father pointed a callused finger at her. "Don't move. I have to wait on a customer."

"I'm not moving until I finish my soup. I don't care what you and Davey say."

"Truer words never spoken right there," her father grumbled.

Tess spooned up plump clams, potatoes, buttery milk. She'd worry about her fat intake another day. The Red Sox were playing the Yankees on a television above the bar. It was a home game. The patrons of Jim's Place didn't like the idea of shutting down Fenway, building a new park. But that was the nature of things, Tess thought with a fresh rush of frustration. They change. Even in her father's neighborhood. Even with his daughter.

At the tables behind her, a group of about a half-dozen men was arguing over who was the greatest president of the twentieth century. "Ronnie Reagan." A dark, young construction worker raised his beer glass in solemn homage. "Bow your heads when you say his name."

"No way. FDR was the man."

"Harry Truman."

Davey shook his head and glanced back at the men, all younger than he was by two decades or more. He weighed in, deadpan. "Adlai Stevenson."

"Get out. He was never president."

"Should have been," Davey said.

A kid in dusty overalls frowned. "Who the hell's Adlai Stevenson?"

"Ignoramus," his friend, the one who'd named Reagan, said. "He was that—who the hell *was* Adlai Stevenson?"

Davey sighed as Jim Haviland came back around the bar. "Country's doomed, Jimmy. Your daughter's stuck with an old barn that has snakes, and these dumb bastards never heard of Adlai Stevenson."

The conversation shifted to baseball, an even more dangerous subject in metropolitan Boston than politics. On another night, Tess might have joined in. Good food and a good argument were part of the charm of her father's pub, a contrast to the pace and complexity of her normal routine as both business-woman and designer.

Unfortunately the last man in her life hadn't seen the appeal of Jim's Place and chowder night.

"Pop," she said, "it's not a barn, and I wasn't stupid not to take cash. This was a great opportunity. I never could have afforded something like this otherwise. It's a half block from the ocean. It just needs work."

He put together a martini, seemingly absorbed in his work. Tess knew better. It had been just her and her father for so long, she knew when he was on automatic pilot. She'd had ample opportunity to tell him about her carriage house, and she hadn't. And they both knew it. She was the daughter who'd lost her mother at six, who'd always told her father everything. Even as they'd carved out the landscape of their adult relationship, she and Jim Haviland hadn't abandoned their tendency to speak their minds. It didn't matter if the other didn't want to hear what had to be said.

But not this time.

Tess finished her soup while he pretended to concentrate on his drink-making. It wasn't that she needed her father's approval. They'd worked that out a long time ago. It was just that her life was easier when she had it.

"How much work?" he asked.

"A lot," Davey said.

Her father shot him a warning look, and Davey shrugged and finished his beer.

Tess opened a small package of oyster crackers. She never ate them with her soup, always after. "A fair amount."

He nodded. A place that needed work was something he could understand. "You've decided to keep the house?"

"I don't know. I think so. Pop, when I was up there

this afternoon, I kept thinking of all the possibilities. There's something about this place—it fired my imagination."

That he could understand. Her imagination had put them at odds before. He grunted. "Well, if you decide to hang on to it, a bunch of these bums here owe me favors."

"I'll keep that in mind." She nibbled on a cracker, and added, "But if I go through with this, I think I'd like to do as much of the work as I can myself."

Davey gave an exaggerated groan. "If there's anything I hate, it's cleaning up after some do-it-yourselfer."

"Give me a break, okay, Davey? I'm trying to have a conversation with my father. This is important to me."

"True confessions," Davey said. "You're a day late and a dollar short, Tess."

She ignored him. "I've got pictures, Pop. Do you want to see? Ike Grantham gave them to me when he signed over the property."

"Ike Grantham." Jim Haviland snorted. "Now there's a piece of work."

"Pop."

"Yeah, sure. Show me your pictures."

Tess slid off the stool and picked up her satchel. Her father's pub was one of the rare places that made her feel short. She unzipped a side pocket and removed the best two shots of the roll Ike had taken. He'd been very proud. "It's a great place, Tess. I know I can trust you with it."

She passed the pictures across the bar to her father.

He put on his reading glasses and took a look. "Tess. Jesus. It *is* a barn."

"I'm telling you," Davey said, "it's got snakes."

Davey was getting on Tess's nerves. She almost told him the place was haunted by a convicted murderer whose descendants lived next door, never mind that one of them was a six-year-old who thought she was a princess. But she said nothing, because arguing with Davey Ahearn only encouraged him.

"It's in Beacon-by-the-Sea, Pop. Remember when we used to go up there for picnics on the beach?"

"Yeah. I remember." He took off his glasses and pushed the pictures back to her. "Long commute."

"It'd be a while before I could move in, and I'm not sure I would. If business keeps up, I could keep it as a weekend place."

"Old as it is," Davey went on, as if he'd never stopped, "it's probably got asbestos, lead pipes. Lead paint."

"So? I could buy a duplex up the street with lead paint and asbestos."

Davey eased off the bar stool. "Now, why would you want to buy a place in a neighborhood with people who've known you your whole life? That wouldn't make any sense when you can fix up some goddamn barn some goddamn rich nut gave you in a quaint little town up on the North Shore where not only no one knows you, no one *wants* to know you."

"That's pure prejudice, Davey, and I earned the carriage house. It wasn't 'given' to me." Except she'd thought she'd have to do more work to really earn it, although Ike had never put that on paper. Technically, the carriage house was hers, free and clear of everything but taxes.

"You know I'm telling the truth." Davey walked heavily over to her, this big man she'd known since she was in a crib. Her godfather. "You've lost sight of who you are, where you come from."

"Davey, I'm sitting here eating clam chowder in my father's pub. I haven't lost sight of anything."

He snorted, but kissed her on the cheek, his mustache tickling her. "You need a plumber for that barn of yours, kid, give me a call. I'll see what I can do. If it's hopeless, I'll bring a book of matches. You can collect the insurance."

Tess fought back a smile. "Davey, you're impossible."

"Ha. Like you're not."

The guys at the tables ragged him about the bald spot on the back of his head, and he gave them the finger and left.

"You're thirty-four years old, Tess." Her father exhaled a long, slow breath, as if his own words had taken him by surprise. "I can't be telling you what to do."

"That's not what I was worried about. I was worried you'd talk me out of doing something before I could figure out for myself if it was something I really wanted to do."

"And since when have I done that?"

"It could have happened today."

"You want to keep this place?"

"I'm thinking seriously about it, Pop."

"Well, so be it. How 'bout a piece of pie?"

"What do you have?"

"Lemon meringue."

She smiled. "Perfect."

Davey Ahearn was smoking a cigarette on his front stoop across the street from the pub when Tess headed out into the cool evening. He walked over to her. "You take the subway?" He tossed his cigarette onto the street. "I'll walk you to the station."

There was no point in telling him she could see herself to the subway station. He'd walk with her, anyway. "Thanks."

He glanced at her as they headed to the corner. "You didn't tell him about the ghost, did you?"

Tess hoisted her satchel higher onto her shoulder. "I don't believe in ghosts."

"Tess."

"No, I didn't tell him, okay? For God's sake, I'm a grown woman. I don't have to tell you or my father that a few highly imaginative people believe my carriage house is haunted."

"Not a few people. It's in the goddamn guidebooks."

She gripped her satchel with one hand. "How do you know these things?"

He grinned at her from behind his oversize mustache. "I know everything."

"If I decide to turn the place into a bed-and-breakfast, a ghost could be good for business."

"Not that ghost."

Tess didn't respond.

Davey grunted. "No wonder you still keep your old man up nights. He wants to go to his grandkids' Little League games, and he's got a daughter wanting to renovate a barn haunted by a murderer."

"I'm not answering you, Davey. Answering would only encourage you."

They turned onto the main road, traffic streaming past them, the last of the daylight finally fading. She thought of Beacon-by-the-Sea, how quiet it would be.

Davey eased back. "Go on. Go home, Tess. If you

screw up, you screw up. You're smart. You'll figure it out."

She smiled at him. "And you and Pop will be there. Don't think I don't know that, Davey."

"Hell, no. I'm not cleaning up after this mess. You're on your own."

She laughed, not believing him. "Look, I'll invite you up for scones and tea one Sunday. Okay?"

"I'll wear garlic."

"That's for vampires."

He shrugged. "Close enough."

Five

Susanna denied all knowledge of how Davey Ahearn had learned about the carriage house. "He and your father have extrasensory perception where you're concerned." She plopped down at her computer with a tall mug of coffee she'd brewed herself. She'd once done a chart on how much she and Tess were saving over a lifetime by staying out of coffee shops. "It's creepy. I don't think I want to know that much about my kids."

Tess emptied her satchel onto her desk. She hadn't done any work last night when she'd gotten home from the pub. "Pop and Davey don't know anything about me."

"They don't *understand* anything about you. They know everything."

Susanna wanted to know all the details of Tess's trip to see her carriage house, from the avocado appliances to the trapdoor and possible bloodstains. "Sounds like a nice little shop of horrors," Susanna said.

"It's got great potential."

"That's what we say in Texas when we're about to tear a place down and put up a new one."

Tess never knew when Susanna was being serious about her Texas observations. Some days, it was like she was living in exile in Boston. Other days, she seemed very content not to be in San Antonio.

"My neighbor's a Thorne," Tess added.

"As in Jedidiah and the bloodstains by the front door?"

"So he says."

"What's he look like?"

Tess thought of Andrew Thorne's piercing blue eyes and lean good looks. "A nineteenth-century duelist."

"Your basic rock-ribbed Yankee?"

"If that's the way you want to put it."

"Okay." She tilted back her chair and sipped her coffee, which she drank black and strong. "It's going to be tough, paying rent on your apartment and office *and* keeping up this carriage house. At least there's no mortgage. Damn, you must have a good accountant—"

"I do." Tess crossed their small office to the coffeepot, filled her own mug. She added more milk than she normally would since Susanna had done the brewing. "I don't know, Susanna, but I think somehow I was meant to own this carriage house. Maybe that was what Ike was trying to tell me."

"I doubt it. I think he was just unloading a white elephant."

Tess had meetings from noon until three, which gave her a break from Susanna's skepticism. There were countless people in New England who loved and appreciated historic houses—she just didn't have any in her life. With her satchel slung over one shoulder, she trotted down the three flights of stairs to the lobby of their 1890s building, avoiding the ancient brass elevator, which was too much like climbing into a rat cage for Tess. Susanna loved their office. Why not the idea of an 1868 carriage house?

Tess cut down Park Street across from Boston Common, then up Tremont to Old Granary. She'd picked up a sandwich for lunch—Susanna always bagged it and had another chart to demonstrate her savings—and decided to walk through the centuries-old tombstones while she ate. The shade was lovely, and the city, although just on the other side of the iron fence, seemed very far away.

For no reason she could fathom, Tess found herself looking for the Thorne name. Her own family had come to the shores of Massachusetts in the late nineteenth and early twentieth century, not back with the Pilgrims and the Puritans.

She found one, her heart jumping. Thankful Thorne, born in 1733, died in 1754. Not a long life. Was she an ancestor of the man Tess had met yesterday, of his six-year-old daughter with the Red Sox shirt and crown? Tess suddenly wondered how Andrew Thorne's wife had died. From Dolly's reaction, she suspected it had been a while—but one never knew with children that age. Tess remembered coming to grips with her own mother's death, discovering the reality of it over time, the finality.

She slipped out of the graveyard. The streets were clogged with noontime traffic, one of many daily reminders of how glad she was she didn't commute. So why was she thinking about hanging on to a place an hour up the coast?

Her first meeting went well. They loved her, they had plenty of work for her and were pleasant, intelligent, dedicated people. The second meeting was just the opposite. The clients from hell. They were impossible to please, and they didn't know what they wanted, leaving her on shifting sands. She'd learned early on in her graphic design career that not everyone would love her or her work—and some would be rude about it.

When she returned to her office, she plopped her satchel onto her chair and started loading it up. Susanna, as ever, was at her computer. "I've got an idea," Tess told her. "I'm going to spend the weekend at the carriage house. I'll bring my sleeping bag, pack food. It's the only way I'll know for sure what's the right thing to do, whether to keep it or put it on the market."

Susanna tapped a few keys and looked up, squinting as if part of her was still caught up in whatever it was she'd been doing. She was a financial planner, but also, as she put it, "an investor," which covered a wide territory. She pushed back her black hair with both hands. "Bring your cell phone. You have all my numbers? If some hairy-assed ghost crawls out of the woodwork in the dead of night, you call 911. Then you call me."

"Thanks, Susanna."

"Don't thank me. As soon as you walk out that door, I'm looking up the name and address of every mental hospital on the North Shore. Don't worry. I'll pick out a nice one for you."

Tess ignored her. "The weather's supposed to be great this weekend. I think I'll stop on Charles Street for scones."

"Glorified English muffins," Susanna grumbled. "Three times as expensive."

"And you don't call yourself a Yankee."

They both laughed, and Tess heaved her loaded-up bag onto her shoulder and was on her way.

She walked up Beacon Street and behind the Massachusetts State House to the narrow, hilly streets of residential Beacon Hill, with its prestigious Bulfinch-designed town houses, brick sidewalks, black lanterns and surprisingly eclectic population. She'd moved into her basement apartment eight years ago, over her father's and godfather's objections. She could have gotten more space for the same money—less money—in other neighborhoods, certainly in her home neighborhood. Davey liked to tease her about trying to pass as a Boston Brahmin, never believing she liked the charm and convenience of Beacon Hill, and didn't mind the trade-off of space. With a tiny bedroom, bath and kitchen-living room, she had learned to buy and keep only what she truly needed—which allowed her to pack for her weekend in under forty-five minutes.

She called her father on her cell phone after she'd stopped at a bakery on Charles Street. "I'm on my way to the North Shore for the weekend. I'll give you a call tomorrow."

"You going up there alone?"

She could hear the criticism in his tone. "Yes, why not?"

"Because it's nuts, that's why not. I hate that guy Ike Grantham. Where the hell is he, anyway? What's he been doing all these months?" Her father paused for air. "You don't have a thing for him, do you?"

Tess was irritated with herself for giving her father an opening. She'd asked why not, and now he was telling her. "Ike's a former client. That's *all*. He doesn't have to keep me informed of his whereabouts." She knew that to use the words *missing, disappeared* or even *took off* would be a huge mistake.

"I don't like this," Jim Haviland said.

"You don't have to like it. Love you, Pop. Have a great weekend."

"Wish I had a couple of Little League games to go to," he said, and hung up.

Tess tossed her cell phone back into her satchel. The man never gave up. His ideas about men, women, marriage and family were old-fashioned and completely unreformable. She wondered if her mother had lived, or if he'd remarried, would he still be so stubborn and impossible?

Probably, she decided, and got onto Storrow Drive and headed north.

"Looks as if the Haviland woman's moved in for the weekend," Harl said. "I saw her hauling in groceries and camping gear."

Andrew frowned. "What were you doing, spying on her?"

Harl pinched dead leaves off Andrew's one indoor plant. It was in the kitchen window, and it wasn't in good shape. Harl didn't allow plants in his shop. "I was looking for that goddamn cat."

"You introduced yourself?"

"No. She didn't see me."

Andrew smiled and sat at the table. Harl wouldn't go out of his way to introduce himself to anyone. He'd eaten dinner with them that night and insisted on cleaning up the dishes. Dolly was in the den watching cartoons, mourning over her cat, who, Andrew was becoming convinced, didn't plan on returning.

"Lucky she didn't see you peering through the bushes and call the police."

Harl grunted. "It'd be the first smart thing she did. What kind of woman spends a weekend alone in a haunted carriage house out here on an isolated point?"

"We're not even a mile from the village."

"You don't think she's odd?"

"Harl, *we* live here."

"Well, our great-great-granddaddy didn't off anyone in your living room." He shook his head, his white ponytail trailing several inches down his broad back. He'd let his hair grow since giving up police work. It had turned white a few years after he'd come home from Vietnam, and he'd gotten into bar fights over people saying the wrong thing about his white hair. Andrew had participated in a few of them himself. No point sitting out a bar fight, not in those days.

Harl dumped the dead plant leaves in the trash. "I have to tell you, Thorne, my instincts are all on high alert. You find out how she ended up with that place?"

"Not yet, I haven't asked."

"Ask."

Harl left for his shop, and Andrew went in to shoo Dolly up to bed.

He read her two *Madeleine* books and a few pages of *The Hobbit,* but she was preoccupied with her missing cat. She'd pulled out all her stuffed cats and put them in bed with her, leaving very little room for Andrew to sit next to her for their nightly reading.

"Maybe Tippy Tail's gone on an adventure like Bilbo," Andrew said, referring to *The Hobbit.*

Dolly shook her head, her big eyes brimming with tears. She smelled of a fruity bubble bath that he found particularly nauseating, and she hugged three stuffed cats close to her. "She's dead, Daddy. I know she's dead."

He breathed deeply. A six-year-old shouldn't know so much about death. "Tippy Tail can take care of herself. She's tough. Trust her, okay? Cats like to have their kittens where little girls can't find them."

"Not Tippy Tail."

"Yes, Tippy Tail."

"Harl says we can put up posters. I can draw a picture of her, and—and if somebody sees her, they can call us, and we can go get her!" She sniffled, perking up. "Do you think that would be good, Daddy?"

For someone who hated cats, Harl was going out of his way to find this one. "Sure, Dolly. We can do posters in the morning."

She nodded eagerly, her mood transformed now that she had a plan. This quickly led to indignation. "I don't think Tippy Tail should have runned away. I'm a princess. She's supposed to obey me."

"Cats don't obey anyone, Dolly. That's why they're cats."

She snuggled down into her pillow, a black-and-white stuffed kitten pressed against her rosy cheek, fat tears on her dark eyelashes. She shut her eyes. "Can you read to me some more?"

Andrew read *The Hobbit* until she drifted off. He was aware of his own voice in the silent, still room. It was a kid's room, simply furnished and not overly childish. He wasn't about to redo it every year. There was an oak dresser Harl had refinished, a round mirror, a bulletin board covered with pictures of cats and fairies, crates of toys and stuffed animals, handheld computer games and a long pegboard overloaded with baseball caps, sequined shawls and at least six different crowns.

Above her bed was a framed cross-stitch Beatrix Potter *D* that Joanna had done when she was pregnant, teasing herself even then about "turning domestic." But she'd been happy, excited about their child. Ike Grantham had been off on one of his escapades, not a factor in their lives, although they knew him because they lived in Beacon, where everyone knew the Granthams. Only later, after his sister started dating Joanna's boss, Richard Montague, did Ike mention how he could help her train to climb Mount McKinley. "If you can chase a toddler around the house, you can climb a mountain."

Andrew shut *The Hobbit,* a weighty, oversize edition. He didn't know how much Dolly understood, but he enjoyed reading to her. Harl never did. He could sit still for hours working on a piece of furniture, but not for more than five minutes with a children's book. He was back in his shop now, working. Some nights he'd work until dawn.

What was Tess Haviland, Andrew wondered, doing in her carriage house? It had no furniture, lousy wiring. Was she one of Ike's women? Andrew had been too busy today to ask around town. If anyone would know, it would be Lauren, and Lauren Montague was about the last person he'd want to ask anything. She felt guilty about her brother's role in Joanna's death even though Andrew assured her there was no need. Joanna had wanted to climb Mount McKinley. It wasn't just Ike's doing.

He headed downstairs, picking up Dolly's sneak-ers and the odd toy on the way. He wasn't much of a taskmaster. He settled into a battered, comfortable leather chair in the den and flipped on the ball game. A stiff wind off the water beat against the tall, old windows. A little atmosphere, he thought with amusement, for Tess Haviland's first night on the point.

Six

By ten o'clock, Tess was thinking about calling it quits and heading back to the city. But she'd had two glasses of wine with the Brie-and-cucumber sandwich she'd picked up at the bakery, along with her scones for the morning, and she was too sleepy to drive.

She was tempted to get a hotel room for the night. The wind howled and whistled, rattled doors and windows, and her avocado refrigerator was making strange wheezing noises. And it was dark. She was used to streetlights.

All she needed now were a couple of bats.

Or a ghost.

"Now, stop that," she said aloud, her voice echoing in the big, empty room. She was sitting cross-legged on her sleeping bag. She'd set up camp on the wooden floor just over the kitchen threshold, close to the bathroom and the side door, which would take her straight out to her car.

She had a battery-operated lantern Davey had given her for her birthday one year, a camp mat for padding and her portable white-noise machine with a choice of sounds: ocean, dolphins and whales, a tropical rain forest, a mountain stream. She hadn't bothered turning it on. Nothing would drown out the sound of that wind.

She shifted her position, casting dramatic shadows all around her. She wasn't used to such a huge, dark, cavernous space.

She'd tried leaving the kitchen light on, but it flickered and cast a green glow that made her avocado appliances look sickly. The plan was to have a cup of chamomile tea and read until she felt sufficiently sleepy, then switch off the lantern and not look around, just burrow in her sleeping bag and wait until morning.

She was beginning to regard it as an insult that Ike thought this place suited her. Maybe Susanna had a point. And her father and Davey. How much could she get for it?

She heard a sound, somewhere close. She set her mug of tea on the floor and held her breath, listening. What now?

Barns have snakes...

It was probably just a squirrel or a skunk in the lilacs. She'd picked a big bouquet of them and put them in an old mason jar she'd found in a cabinet, feeling rather warm and fuzzy about her carriage house. That was before the sun went down.

This wasn't the city. She had to expect night sounds she might not recognize. She'd never gone to summer camps in the wilderness. Her father's idea of an excursion was a subway trip to Fenway Park—and the occasional picnic on the beach right across the street from the carriage house.

There it was again. Tess exhaled, relaxing somewhat now that she knew what it was she was hearing.

A meow. It was coming from the cellar, up through the trapdoor.

Dolly Thorne's missing cat, Tippy Tail. It had to be.

Tess debated ignoring the meow, but it came again, loud and whining. The poor cat was obviously in some kind of distress. And even if the animal was just being obnoxious, she could easily go on all night. Tess flipped on the white-noise machine, but it didn't mask the cat's noises, or the wind.

With a put-out groan, she got to her feet and flipped on the kitchen overhead, its greenish light making her feel even more isolated and alone than her lantern. She was wearing warm-up pants and a T-shirt to sleep in, but the cracked linoleum floor was cool on her bare feet.

She walked over to the trapdoor. "Kitty?"

There was no answering meow.

"Kitty, kitty." She knelt on the floor beside the trapdoor, but had no intention of lifting it and peering into her dark pit of a cellar. "Tippy Tail, hey, are you down there?"

A plaintive, utterly miserable yowl came up through the floorboards. Definitely a cat. No self-respecting, murdering Yankee ghost would make that kind of noise.

Tess swore softly. She had no choice. She couldn't leave the poor thing down there to fend for herself. What if she were hurt? How would Tess explain a dead cat to little Princess Dolly?

What kind of coward would leave a distressed cat alone in a dark, dank cellar, anyway?

Tess sat back on her camp bed and put on her sneakers, then grabbed her lantern and headed out the kitchen door. The trapdoor was out of the question. If she fell off the ladder or it came apart under her, she'd die down in the cellar like a rat.

This reminded her to grab her cell phone off the kitchen counter.

The wind was still gusting, and the sky was dark, with no moon. Tess tried not to pay too close attention to the conditions, refused to think about night creatures on the prowl. At ten o'clock at night in the city, there'd be people on the streets. Four in the morning, she might have more misgivings, but not at ten. Up here, she didn't know what to expect.

She debated calling the police or pounding on Andrew Thorne's front door, but decided that would be wimpish. What if it wasn't the missing pregnant cat?

"It damn well better be," she muttered, refusing to consider the alternatives to Tippy Tail.

She flicked on the lantern, its light spreading out across the gravel driveway in front of her.

The smell of lilacs, sweet and homey, helped re-assure her. *Okay, you can do this.*

She ducked onto the narrow strip of yard between her house and the lilac hedge. The shaggy grass was up to her calves, conjuring up more of Davey's warnings about snakes. Tess dismissed them and walked quickly to the bulkhead, its soft, half-rotten wood painted a dull gray. She wondered how the cat could have gotten into the cellar, then spotted a missing pane in a small, two-pane casement window. There you go, she thought. It was just right for a gray cat with a white-tipped tail.

She set her lantern on the ground and pushed at the wooden latch. It broke apart, and she immediately put replacing the bulkhead door on her mental to-do list.

Even if she sold the place, potential buyers would want the bare minimums covered.

She grabbed the edge of the bulkhead and lifted. It was heavy, the old wood sodden with years of rain and snow. She could only imagine what her father, Davey and the rest of the guys at Jim's Place would say if they could see her now.

She propped the bulkhead door open and grabbed her lantern, pointing it down the concrete steps.

Cobwebs. Her stomach muscles tightened. Spiders didn't scare her, but couldn't any part of this adventure be easy?

She wondered what she'd have done when she'd heard the noise if she hadn't known a six-year-old was looking for a missing pregnant cat. Probably gotten a hotel room, she decided, or headed back to Beacon Hill, wine or no wine.

Lantern firmly in hand, Tess made her way down the steep steps, through a gauze of cobwebs. When she came to a six-foot metal door at the bottom, she shone her light on her shirt, pants and arms, just to make sure nothing had crawled off the cobwebs onto her.

Above her, the bulkhead door creaked and moaned in a gust of wind. She had no idea what she'd do if it slammed shut. She didn't want to think about it.

She pushed open the metal door, and her lantern illuminated a small, finished space under a low ceiling. This wasn't so bad. There were proper walls, a concrete floor, shelves, wooden crates and a washer and dryer that predated her kitchen appliances. But who would do laundry down here? She would have to take either the trapdoor or the bulkhead to get here, neither of which she would want to negotiate with a basket of dirty clothes.

There was a light switch by the door. Tess flipped it, and one of three fluorescent tubes overhead flick-ered on. The room, she saw, was dusty and damp, but tidy. She could feel the dust in her throat and wondered about radon. Ike had probably never had the place tested. It could be loaded.

On the other hand, any radon could just seep out the cracks and holes. This was not an airtight modern home. If nothing else, the carriage house "breathed."

Tess cleared her throat. "Kitty, oh, kitty, where are you?"

Nothing.

"Tippy Tail?"

A moan of a meow sounded from deeper within the cellar. Tess walked over to a dark doorway adjoining the laundry room. She held up the lantern, and swore under her breath when she realized it was a dirt cellar. She could see the outlines of heating ducts, pipes, piles of junk.

"Damn. Come on, cat, don't you want to let me take you home?"

It was pitch-dark in the dirt cellar, utterly black, with no windows at all. Tess had newfound respect for Davey Ahearn and the forty years he'd spent going in and out of places like this to fix people's plumbing.

She tilted her lantern, its light striking more cob-webs. "Man, Davey, never mind snakes. I bet you know your spiders."

But thoughts of him and the way he'd doubted her, what she *knew* he'd say if he could see her now, rekin-dled her resolve. She proceeded.

It was a dirt floor, silty, cool and a dull brown. The foundation walls were stone. It was like a cave. As she picked her way deeper into the old dirt cellar, Tess could see the outlines of the trapdoor overhead, light from the kitchen angling through the narrow gaps. She made out the ladder hooked to the ceiling. There was no way. No damn way.

A naked, dusty lightbulb was screwed into a socket in the ceiling, and she had to put her hand through thick cobwebs to reach the string. The bulb gave off a dull, yellowed light. She saw a bunch of dead flies caught in a cobweb.

Pipes and heating ducts hung from the low ceiling, and there was a furnace, a pump, piles of cast-off furniture, buckets, old brooms. Nasty.

The cat meowed again, softly.

"You'd better be a cat." Tess touched the cell phone on her hip, just to reassure herself. "Tippy Tail, don't you want to call it a night and come on out?"

She had three choices. One, call it a night herself and turn up the volume on her white-noise machine. Two, get help from the neighbors. Three, proceed.

At least she wasn't worried about coming upon Jedidiah Thorne. If she were a ghost, she'd find a better place to hang out than down here.

She hit her shin on a rusted bucket. "Ouch—damn it." But she checked herself, keeping her tone cajoling, slightly high-pitched. She didn't want to scare the cat. "Come on, kitty." She felt silly. She'd never had a cat, but one ex-boyfriend had talked to his Siamese this way, so it had to work. "Have you had your babies? Couldn't you find a nice place? I mean, Tippy Tail, this is a dungeon."

Tess coughed, resisted the urge to spit. Dirt and dust seemed to invade her eyes, her nostrils, her throat. She pulled her shirt up over her mouth and pushed farther into the cellar, away from the light-bulb and laundry room.

It was so damn dark, even with her lantern and the lightbulb.

"The hell with it. Tippy Tail, you are on your own."

She pulled on the string, and the lightbulb went off.

The cat meowed again, pitifully, and Tess couldn't abandon her without one more try. The animal was somewhere close, very close. Tess sighed and shone the lantern into a corner piled with old furniture, none of which looked worth saving. There were dining-room chairs, a metal kitchen table, a couple of old nightstands too rickety even for the country look she planned for the carriage house if she kept it. She spotted an iron bed frame that might have possibilities.

Her light hit a pair of golden eyes, and she had to stifle a startled yell. "Well, there you are."

The cat was out of reach, tucked amidst old rags and junk in the absolute farthest corner of the old cellar. Tess couldn't tell if the presumed Tippy Tail had had her kittens. She leaned over a nightstand for a better look, trying not to spook the cat with her lantern.

Suddenly the nightstand gave way. Tess lost her balance, her lantern flying out of her hand, her right arm following the crashing nightstand while the rest of her went sprawling in the opposite direction. She jerked her arm free, but her momentum pitched her backward onto the bed frame.

She landed on her back on the dirt floor.

"Oh, *gross!*"

And *painful*. She hurt just above her hip where the bed frame had dug in. She pushed it away, scrambling onto her knees and reaching for the lantern. She was disgusted, shuddering at the thought of what she might be kneeling in. Cobwebs, decayed animal droppings.

She got to her feet, ignoring the pain in her hip, and pointed the light back toward the corner. She was breathing hard, beyond repulsed.

The cat was gone. The commotion must have frightened her off.

Tess was in no mood. "Tough, kitty. It didn't do much for me, either." She felt her hip. No blood. Probably just bruised. The pain subsided, slowly. "Tippy Tail?"

Her cell phone was missing, too. It must have gone flying at the same time she had. She brought the lantern around, searching for cat and cell phone.

She spotted the phone in the dirt under the bed frame.

But no cat.

She wasn't about to continue the night without a phone. Ignoring her bruises and scrapes, she lifted the bed frame and reached down into the dirt. "Just don't think," she muttered.

Her light caught something. She wasn't sure what, but her response was visceral, almost primal. Adrenaline pumped into her bloodstream, and her muscles tightened, every fiber of her body and soul urging her to run.

Bones.

Her mind registered what the rest of her already knew she had seen.

Bones.

And not rat bones. Human bones.

No. This was not possible. She was imagining things

because she was totally grossed out from falling onto the dirt floor.

She steadied her lantern for another look. *"Jesus."*

It was a human skeleton. A skull, right there in the dirt under the bed frame. She must have dislodged the shallow grave when she'd taken her spill.

Well, it wasn't a real skeleton. It couldn't be. Some weird doctor or mad scientist must have lived here, had himself a little fun. It *could not* be real.

The skull looked real.

"'Alas, poor Yorick.'" Her voice was a rasping, dust-choked whisper, and she couldn't breathe. She coughed, sick to her stomach. "Holy shit."

She was blinking rapidly, unable to get a decent breath. Her heartbeat was wild. She took a step backward, then another, then turned and ran.

When she reached the laundry room, she screamed. It was a cathartic scream, no holds barred, loud and deep and unrepressed. When she finished, she shuddered. "Damn."

She was shaking now, and she flipped off the light and stumbled up the bulkhead steps, just managing to hold on to her lantern. "Holy shit."

A cat having kittens. Cobwebs. A spooky, dark, old cellar.

And a skeleton.

"My God."

She didn't even sound like herself. She charged out into the cool, clear, clean night air and slammed the bulkhead door shut as fast as she could, as if the skeleton might swoop up out of there.

She breathed deeply. Lilacs tinged with ocean salt. The wind was calmer. She breathed again.

"Ike—Jesus, what the hell was *that?*"

She was drenched in sweat, shaking, coughing dust and God only knew what, and she breathed again, trying to calm herself.

She had no idea what to do. Call the police? Her father? Davey? What did she know about the Beacon-by-the-Sea police? She was alone up here in a strange town, at night. Susanna would come in a flash. Her ex-husband was a Texas Ranger, her parents both in law enforcement.

No. Tess shook her head, breathing more slowly now, more deeply. She must have imagined the skeleton—or, with her vivid imagination, turned something innocent into a skull. This place had been in the Beacon Historic Project's hands for five years before Ike had turned it over to her. Surely they'd have noticed if a damn skeleton was buried in the cellar.

Maybe it was just a dog skeleton, or a raccoon. Not human.

Ike.

That was more than her mind could comprehend. She wouldn't even let the thought form completely. This was an old house. Whatever was down in her dirt cellar could have been there for more than a century.

Maybe it was Ike's idea of a joke.

She brushed herself off, wondering what had happened to the cat. And if her neighbors had heard her scream.

Seven

Harl showed up at Andrew's back door with a baseball bat. It was after ten, dark outside. "You hear that?"

Andrew nodded. "It wasn't the wind."

"Nope." Harl rolled the bat in his big, callused palm. "I know a scream when I hear one. You want to call 911?"

That had been Andrew's first impulse, but he shook his head. "We don't know enough. I'll check next door. You stay here with Dolly. She's asleep."

"Watch yourself."

"Our new neighbor probably just tripped in the dark. Let me see what's up."

The bloody-murder scream had drawn him to the back porch, where he'd already flipped a light. He had his flashlight from the kitchen, debated taking some sort of weapon. He dismissed the idea. That was Harl-thinking.

"I'll stay out here," Harl said. He wasn't giving up his baseball bat. "You need help, yell."

"Under no circumstances are you to leave Dolly here alone."

Harl nodded. "Understood."

Andrew set out across the lawn, the grass soft under his feet. He didn't need his flashlight until he was at the lilac hedge at the far side of the yard. Dolly was small enough to find an opening she could fit through, but he followed his side of the hedge out to the street, then hooked around to the carriage house driveway.

He heard someone breathing, gulping in air in the dark.

"Tess?" He pointed his bright arc of light at her kitchen steps, moved it back toward the lilacs. "Tess, are you out here?"

His light caught her in the face as she stood in the overgrown grass at the other end of the driveway. She blinked rapidly, blinded, and he lowered the flashlight.

"Oh, it's you." She choked a little as she spoke, then rallied. "Thank God. I didn't know who might be sneaking around out here. You heard me yell?"

He nodded, watching her closely. "Are you all right?"

"Yes. Yes, fine."

She walked over to the steps, moving unsteadily, almost drunkenly, and sat, putting a hand on her upper chest, as if trying to still a wild heartbeat. She pushed her other hand through her short curls. She wasn't looking at him, didn't seem to be looking at anything.

Andrew switched off the flashlight, the light from the open kitchen door sufficient. "What's going on?"

"I was startled, and I yelled. Screamed my head off, actually." She cleared her throat and attempted a smile. "I found your cat."

"Tippy Tail?" He took another step toward her, still watching. She had strong, attractive features, nothing delicate or tentative about her. But she'd had a scare. He could see that. "Dolly will be pleased."

Tess nodded. "I hope my scream didn't wake her up."

He saw she was more pale than he'd thought, and her clothes were streaked with dirt and cobwebs. He noticed a scrape on her left wrist, another on her jawline. And more cobwebs in her hair.

He stood at the bottom of the steps and touched her jaw next to the scrape. She had soft, smooth skin. "The cat do this?"

She shook her head. "No, no," she said, her voice hoarse. Whatever had happened, she was stemming a shock reaction. Chattering teeth, trembling, rapid heartbeat. She looked as if she had every muscle in her body tensed to keep herself from jumping out of her skin. "I just fell. It was stupid. I heard the cat down in the cellar and went to investigate."

"At night? You're braver than I am. Old Tippy Tail would have been on her own if I'd heard her."

"I was afraid she was having her kittens, and I could hear her through the floorboards. She sounded awful." Tess pushed her hand through her short curls again, and for no reason he could think of, Andrew noticed her long, slender fingers. An artist's hands. "It's an old house. I can hear everything."

"I understand."

Her eyes lifted, focusing on him for the first time. Her smile, although still tentative, seemed genuine, her nerves less rattled. "I know about the house's history. I refuse to be scared, let myself get creeped out. When I heard the cat, I went around to the bulkhead." She pointed to the back of the house, as if to remind herself what she'd done, how it had made sense at the time. "There's a trapdoor inside, but I'm not sure it's safe."

"I've seen that trapdoor. I wouldn't want to go that way, either." Andrew sat on the step next to her; she smelled as if she'd been rolling around in a hundred-year-old dirt cellar. "I don't imagine the bulkhead's much better."

She almost managed a laugh. "So I discovered. Tippy Tail had lodged herself way back in the old dirt cellar. I tripped over some junk and fell."

"That's when you yelled?"

She averted her eyes, and they took on a faraway look, as if she were back down in the cellar, falling in the dark. She blinked a couple of times, focused again on him and forced a smile. "Yes. I kept thinking about snakes. It was ridiculous."

Not so ridiculous in an old dirt cellar, but Andrew decided Tess didn't need him to confirm her worst suspicions. "Hurt yourself?"

"Not really. I'm afraid I scared off your cat, though. I have no idea where she is."

"She hadn't had her kittens?"

Tess shook her head. "No. Just as well. Next time I'll leave her alone."

"Tippy Tail's a survivor. She'll be fine."

"I hope so."

She started to her feet, calmer now, but there was little improvement in her color. She was still pale, shaken from her encounter with Tippy Tail. Andrew followed her up. As she started to turn to go inside, she winced suddenly and grabbed his arm, steadying herself.

"Sorry." She still held on tight. Andrew didn't move, let her gain her balance. "I forgot—I took a pretty good hit on my side." Her grip relaxed slightly, but she didn't let go. "I'm okay."

"Maybe you should come back to my house." Andrew's voice was quiet, and he tried to sound sensible, not dictatorial. Tess Haviland didn't seem the type to want anyone to swoop in to the rescue. "I can make you a cup of tea, and you can see if you discover any more aches and pains."

"I really did take a tumble." She smiled, but he could see the pain in her eyes. But she shook her head. "Thanks, but I've got chamomile tea inside. I'll make myself a cup."

"Okay, but I wouldn't be much of a neighbor if I left you before you're steady on your feet. Come on, I'll fix you that chamomile tea."

She released her grip on his arm, managed a quick nod. She seemed appreciative, not as if she'd given in. "That'd be nice."

They went into the kitchen, and when the light hit her full in the face, Andrew saw just how pale and shaken she was. A spill in an old, dark cellar would throw anyone off, but he suspected there was more. A ghost, perhaps. Tess Haviland didn't strike him as someone who'd want to admit she'd turned shadows into a ghost and screamed bloody murder. She'd probably rather there was a real ghost instead of something she'd conjured up.

She withdrew a cell phone from the pocket of her warm-up pants and placed it on the counter, her hand shaking visibly, even if at this point just from adrenaline. She limped silently into the bathroom. She left the door open, and Andrew heard water running and a string of muttered curses. Whatever else, she had guts. Damned if he'd go into that cellar in the dark after a cat.

He used her shiny camp pot and put water on for her tea. "Mind if I use your phone? I should call Harl, tell him what's going on before he calls in the troops."

"Of course. Please."

She emerged from the bathroom. Her face was scrubbed, her hair pushed back and wet. Some color had returned to her cheeks. And her eyes, Andrew saw, seemed even a bit brighter.

"I imagine your fantasies of owning a nineteenth-century carriage house didn't include washing cobwebs off your face."

"I'm not sure I had any fantasies about this place. I guess Ike thought he was doing me a favor. Go ahead, call Harl."

But Andrew was staring at her. "Ike?"

She sighed. "I assumed you knew—because you live next door, I suppose. I did some work for the Beacon Historic Project early last year and the year before. Ike hired me. I'm a graphic designer in Boston. He transferred the carriage house to me as payment. Maybe it was a whim, I don't know. He took off right afterward, and I haven't heard from him." She leaned against a counter, as if to steady herself. "But go ahead and call Harl, if he'll be worried."

Andrew dialed his number. Harl didn't wait for him to speak. "All clear?"

"Yeah. She fell in the cellar chasing Tippy Tail."

"Damn cat," Harl said, and hung up.

"That was quick," Tess said.

"Harl hates phones."

The water came to a boil, and Andrew poured it into a mug, dangled in a strong-smelling chamomile tea bag and handed the tea to Tess. "You sure you're okay?"

"Yes." She smiled over the rim of the steaming mug, the heat adding color to her cheeks. "Thanks."

He glanced at the camp she'd set up. Even with her lilacs in a mason jar, it looked rough. "Look, I've got a couple of spare bedrooms at the house. If you're injured, you don't want to spend the night on the cold floor."

"Thanks, but I'll manage. To be honest, I haven't decided if I'm going to keep this place. That's why I'm up here for the weekend, seeing if being here will help me make up my mind."

"Sorry it's meant chasing after a cat. Tippy Tail's a stray we took in—she's temperamental. If she comes home tonight, I'll try to lock her inside."

Tess rallied, managing a quick smile. "It's okay. I live in a basement apartment in the city. You should see what walks past my windows."

She sipped her tea, looking calmer, but tired. Andrew decided the scrape on her jaw was superficial, and if the hit she took to her side wasn't, she hadn't asked him to do anything about it.

"I'll leave you to your tea." He went over to her sleeping bag, picked up a book she was reading and a pen next to it. He noticed the portable white-noise machine and smiled; maybe Tess Haviland was more worried about ghosts in the night than she was willing to admit. "If you need anything, give me a call."

He jotted down his phone number and placed the book and pen back on the floor.

Tess hadn't moved from her position against the counter. "Okay. Great." She sipped her tea, watching him as he headed for the kitchen door. He noticed she was no longer shaking. "I suppose if I do end up keeping this place, I'll have my hands full. Dirt cellars, spiders, mice. Who knows what else."

Andrew smiled. "I'd say spiders and mice are the least of your problems. The offer of a guest room stands."

"She's lying."

Harl had opened them each a beer. They were in the kitchen, at the table. Andrew had checked on Dolly, just to make sure she wasn't cowering under the covers the way she did in a thunderstorm, but she was fine, fast asleep. Harl had listened without interrupting as Andrew had related Tess's story about finding the cat in the cellar. He'd known what his cousin would say. Harl didn't believe anyone.

"How do you know she's lying?"

"That wasn't a falling-on-my-ass scream. That was a scared-shitless scream. I know the difference."

"She says she was worried about snakes."

Harl shook his head knowingly. "Nah. Doesn't wash."

Andrew agreed. "What would wash?"

His cousin took a long drink of his beer, an expensive local brew he'd never touch if it weren't in Andrew's refrigerator. He set the dark bottle on the kitchen table. "Ghosts."

"I suppose she could have imagined—"

"Nope. Not imagined. Saw."

"Oh, come on." Andrew wanted to laugh, but he could see Harl was serious. "I don't believe in ghosts. Neither do you."

"Doesn't mean she didn't see one."

"Then it *was* her imagination."

"No."

Andrew frowned at his cousin's logic. "You think she saw a real ghost in the cellar?"

Harl shrugged. "Why not?"

Andrew thought of her pale face, the way she shook, the faraway expression in her eyes. He'd have looked pretty much like that if he'd encountered a ghost. Then again, she could simply have had her first adventure in an old New England dirt cellar and let her imagination get away from her. But he knew there was no arguing with Harl.

"There's something else," Andrew said, and repeated what Tess had told him about her relationship with Ike Grantham.

"Shit," Harl said. "Doesn't that beat all?"

"Ike's eccentric and impulsive, but practically giving away the carriage house—" Andrew shook his head, not able to make sense of it. "I know Tess worked for him, but it must have been a good deal for him or he wouldn't have done it."

"She one of his women?"

"I didn't ask."

"Ike wouldn't have gone down in the cellar after Tippy Tail, that's for damn sure. I'd feel better about this if we knew where the hell that slippery bastard's got himself off to."

Harl was more inclined to blame Ike for Joanna's death than Andrew was, believing the man had slipped through a troubled woman's defenses, into her psyche, and used her for his own ego.

"It's getting late," Andrew said.

Harl didn't move. He took a sip of beer. "Don't you wonder why Haviland didn't just tell you the truth?"

"Harl, if I saw a ghost—whether I thought I saw one or actually knew I saw one—I don't know if I'd go out of my way to tell anyone."

"Ah." Harl settled back in his chair, in no apparent hurry to return to his quarters across the yard. "A sin of omission isn't the same as a sin of commission."

Andrew sighed. One beer, and Harl was in the mood to give him a headache. "It's none of our business."

"She lied. If we hadn't heard her scream, or if you ran into her over the lilacs tomorrow and she didn't mention falling, that'd be a sin of omission. Telling you it was the thought of snakes that made her scream is a sin of commission. A flat-out lie."

"Well, Harl, guess what? I don't care. If she saw a ghost, she saw a ghost. Doesn't have anything to do with me."

"What if it's Jedidiah?"

"Jedidiah has nothing to do with me. Or you." He rinsed out his beer bottle in the sink. "I just want to find Tippy Tail, for Dolly's sake. The rest I don't care about."

"Not me." Harl pushed back his chair and got to his feet, his white ponytail hanging down his back. "I want to know about the ghost."

He left without another word, taking his baseball bat with him. In the ensuing silence, Andrew refused to think about what Tess had actually seen in her cellar. Instead he thought about what he'd have done if she'd taken him up on his offer to spend the night. The guest-room beds weren't made up.

Dangerous thinking.

He thought of her tucked on her camp mat for the night with her lantern, her book, her white-noise machine. Would she sleep in her dusty, cobweb-covered clothes? Would she sleep at all?

More dangerous thinking.

He jumped up, and when he walked down the hall, he could feel how big and empty his house was. He'd renovated a few of the rooms, had more to go.

He headed up to Dolly's room. She was curled up with her stuffed kittens and wore a glittery star crown half off her coppery hair. His sweet, stubborn, imaginative daughter. Whatever else he did wrong in his life, he needed to do right by her.

Tess Haviland had done right by her six-year-old neighbor and her expectant cat, never mind what she was willing to admit about why she'd screamed.

And yet, Harl's reaction had done the trick. She was hiding something. Andrew had sensed it, and now he wondered what it was, and why she hadn't just told him the truth.

Eight

Tess didn't sleep, at least not enough to amount to much. Awake or asleep, her mind kept conjuring ghosts and skeletons, yowling cats, strange men materializing out of the dark. She could have taken up Andrew Thorne's invitation to sleep at his house, but what did she know about him and this Harl character?

At 5:00 a.m., she grabbed her cell phone to call the police—but stopped after punching the nine and first one. She needed to go back down into the cellar first, herself, and make sure of what she saw. *Then* call the police if necessary. This was a small town. Word would get out if it was simply a Halloween skeleton or her imagination.

"The hell with it," she muttered. "Let the police check the damn cellar."

She wasn't going back down there.

But she didn't call.

At seven, she decided to put the carriage house on the market. She wouldn't mention the skeleton. Had *Ike* mentioned the skeleton? She'd never be able to sell the place if she made a big stink and got the police in here, forensics, historians, exorcists, God knew who else.

If it *was* human remains she'd seen, they had to be of a nineteenth-century horse thief, some anonymous person, not Jedidiah Thorne.

Not Ike.

At eight, Tess crawled stiffly out of her sleeping bag into the glorious May sunlight streaming through the kitchen window. How could she possibly have seen a human skull in the cellar? Ridiculous. At worst, she'd come upon the resident ghost and his tricks. At best, nothing at all, just the workings of her creative mind.

Andrew Thorne hadn't believed she'd screamed at the thought of snakes. She was sure of that. She should have said she'd seen an actual snake. Two feet long, with spots. Slithering among the heating ducts. *That* would have wiped the skepticism out of those incisive, very blue eyes.

She took a long, very hot shower in her gold-fixtured bathroom. The heat helped her bruises and eased her tension, but provided no clear-cut answers about what she should do. She changed into her favorite jeans, a denim work shirt and cross-trainers, then made Earl Grey tea and warmed up her apricot scone.

She had breakfast on the kitchen steps, feeling a twinge where she'd banged her hip last night. It was a warm, breezy morning, something in the air suggesting the ocean was just across the main road.

After breakfast, she walked out to the water, over rocks and down to the sand, where the tide was rolling out. The ocean smells were strong here, pungent and salty, yet pleasant. A strand of wet, slimy seaweed curled around the bottom of her sneaker, water easing under her feet. The sun sparkled on the horizon. Boats were out.

When she returned to the carriage house, Tess knew she'd have to work herself up to going back down in the cellar. It was just a matter of timing. She'd planned on walking to the village, perhaps having lunch on the pier. Should she check and see if she'd seen a skull in the cellar last night before or after her jaunt to the village?

After. If she did it before, and discovered she'd seen exactly what she thought she'd seen, there'd be no wandering in shops, no chowder in a cute restaurant with red-and-white-checked tablecloths. She'd have to call the police, probably Lauren Montague. The neighbors.

"Hi, Tess, can I come over?"

Tess almost let out another yell, but gulped it back when she spotted Dolly Thorne's little face peering through the lilacs.

"Is it okay with your father and Harl?"

"They won't mind."

After last night, Tess would doubt that. "You'd better go ask."

The girl rolled her eyes. "Really, they won't mind."

Tess went over to the lilacs. Technically, Dolly was still in her own yard. She had on a crown of glittery red hearts today, which matched the hearts on her shirt.

"Did Tippy Tail come home last night?" Tess asked.

Dolly shook her head, sighing dramatically. "She's lost. I don't know why she keeps running away."

"I don't, either. I guess some cats are like that. Did your dad tell you I saw her last night? I'm afraid we startled each other, and she ran off. I'm sure she didn't go far."

"That happens," the girl said sagely.

"Maybe she's hiding here somewhere. Do you want to call her?"

Dolly crouched amidst the lilacs, calling in a patient whisper, "Kitty, kitty."

A cat meowed from inside the carriage house, and not from the cellar. The plaintive cry was coming, distinctly, from the kitchen.

Tess couldn't believe it.

Dolly jumped up and squealed. "Oh my God!"

"Come on, we'll go ask your dad and Harl if you can go inside with me and check if that's Tippy Tail."

"It is! I know it is! She'll run away—"

Tess stood firm. "She won't run away. But let's hurry, okay?"

She didn't want the girl throwing a tantrum in her driveway, but there was no way Tess was taking her inside without permission from the adults in the girl's life, especially after last night. With slumped shoulders, Dolly slipped back through to her side of the lilacs. Tess followed, squeezing through branches, twigs, drooping blossoms, fat leaves and protruding roots, all of which slapped, poked or tripped her.

When she was finally clear of the lilacs, she landed in an oasis, at least compared to her own yard. The Thorne lawn was lush and green, with a half-dozen rhododendrons just coming into blossom and huge, graceful shade trees strategically placed. Tess couldn't imagine what had motivated Jedidiah Thorne to throw away this life in a duel.

Dolly ran over to a white-haired man near a cottage-like outbuilding. He had a small chest of drawers set up on a drop cloth, paint supplies neatly laid out. Dolly,

Tess realized, couldn't have been out of his sight, even in the lilacs.

"Harl," the girl called, breathless, "Harl, I found Tippy Tail! I found her!"

"No kidding, baby. Where is she?"

"At Tess's house."

Tess smiled, hoping she didn't look too rattled after last night's surprise. In her work, she was often called upon to fake good cheer and a calm disposition under pressure.

Harl moved to meet her halfway. When he got closer, Tess noticed the scars on his face and a tattoo on his arm. He wore a POW-MIA shirt and was missing the tips of at least two fingers. "I'm Harl Beckett, Andrew's cousin."

"Tess Haviland. It's nice to meet you. I think Tippy Tail's in my house. We heard her meow."

He adjusted Dolly's crown, and Tess could see he had a curious calming effect on the girl. Probably this wasn't the effect Harl Beckett had on most people in his life. He said, "Sorry you got mixed up with this cat of hers."

"It's okay," Tess said. "I don't mind."

"I understand last night was a little rough."

His tone was even, his expression unreadable, but she knew he didn't believe her story any more than his cousin. She resisted the urge to turn away, and even managed a smile. "Yes, I had quite the adventure. That'll teach me. I suspect Tippy Tail would have done just fine without me."

"How'd she get in?"

"Broken window. I should repair it this weekend while I'm up here. Did you hear me yell? I tripped over some old furniture and landed on the dirt floor. I kept thinking about snakes."

Harl Beckett studied her a moment, his expression unchanged. "Sticking to your story, are you?"

"I beg your pardon?"

He turned to Dolly, who was obviously losing patience with the chitchat. "Run tell your dad where we're going." Obviously he didn't trust Tess enough to let Dolly go over with her alone. "Hurry up."

Dolly didn't argue, just charged across the yard calling for her father.

Tess hesitated. "Mr. Beckett—"

"Harl."

"I don't know what you meant just now."

"Didn't mean anything."

"You don't believe me," she said.

"Nope. That going to keep you up nights?"

She smiled suddenly, although she had no idea why. "I did think about snakes."

He cocked an eyebrow at her. "And what else?"

She shrugged. "Ghosts."

"Now we're talking."

Dolly raced back across the lawn, breathing hard, cheeks red. "Daddy says to go on, he'll be along in a minute. Come *on,* let's go, let's go!"

"You go on with Tess," Harl said, "I'm right behind you."

But Dolly was already climbing through the lilacs, and by the time Tess made it back through, the little girl was bounding up the kitchen steps.

Tess ran to catch up with her. "Take it easy, Princess Dolly. If Tippy Tail's having her kittens, we don't want to scare her."

Dolly was barely able to contain her excitement, but she nodded gravely and pressed a finger to her lips. "Shh."

Tess pushed open the screen door and glanced back at the driveway. Harl was there, motioning for her to go on in. Dolly slipped past her inside, running quietly into the kitchen. She gasped in delight, covering her mouth with both hands as if to hold back a squeal. Tess stood next to her, following the girl's wide-eyed look.

There, in the middle of Tess's camp bed, was the missing cat, with a litter of tiny, squirming newborn kittens. Four of them. Little bits of matted gray, white and black fur.

How? Tess wondered. How had this happened? Either Tippy Tail had snuck past her in the dark last night and lurked in the house all night, or she'd seized her opening when Tess had gone out to enjoy her tea and scone, then for a walk on the beach.

If nothing else, the cat was an opportunist. This was the only relatively soft, warm spot in the entire house. It certainly beat a dark, junky corner of the dirt cellar.

It wasn't Harl who came into the kitchen, but Andrew, his eyes connecting with Tess. Before either of them could say anything, Dolly waved them into silence. Tess pointed to the cat.

He had the gall to grin, amused.

"It's not funny," she whispered.

"No, Tess, it's very funny."

She wanted to be magnanimous, but a mother cat and four kittens had taken up residence on her only furniture, on her *bed*.

Andrew stood close to her. He smelled of fresh soap, and she could see a small scar on his jaw, almost into his dark hair, and wondered how he'd gotten it. He smiled. "I can see I owe you for all the trouble this cat's caused you."

"Big time."

But he wasn't doing a good job of pretending to be chagrined at the situation. Dolly tiptoed to the foot of the sleeping bag and knelt down, instinctively quiet. Her cat was half-asleep, dazed almost, curled up with her kittens amidst Tess's pillows and the T-shirt she'd slept in. The tiny kittens were suckling, barely moving.

Andrew bent over his daughter. "Just look," he whispered. "Don't touch."

She angled her face up at him, her eyes bright. "When can I pick them up?"

"In a few days. If we bother them now, Tippy Tail might get upset and move them." He glanced back at Tess. "A few days? You can manage?"

As if she had a choice. She couldn't evict a mother cat and newborn kittens. "Sure."

"The offer of a guest room stands."

The cat fixed her golden eyes on Tess, as if she knew exactly how she'd complicated her life. Pay-back, no doubt, for Tess scaring her last night. She'd probably been all set to have her kittens down in the cellar, and then Tess had come whomping in there to the rescue.

Andrew touched his daughter's shoulder, and she grabbed his hand. They moved back through the kitchen and outside without a word. Tess joined them, because there wasn't much else she could do except scare off poor Tippy Tail again.

Once she was safe on the driveway, Dolly jumped up and down and clapped her hands, spun herself around in a circle. "Oh, they're so cute! Oh, Daddy, did you see them? I want to name them." Harl was there, hovering close to the lilacs. "Harl, Harl, you *have* to see them! Oh my God!"

Andrew grimaced. "Dolly, you have to stop saying 'oh my God' like that."

She nodded, obviously not really hearing him. "Can I show Harl?"

"Yes, you can show Harl."

Harl didn't seem eager to see the kittens, but Dolly had him by the hand, dragging him. If his appearance and demeanor were intimidating to others, they had no effect whatsoever on his cousin's six-year-old daughter.

Andrew shifted to look at Tess, the morning sun bringing out the flecks of gray in his dark hair, the angles of his face. As gentle as he was with his irrepressible daughter, Tess suspected he wasn't a man given to easy expression of emotion. "I see you got through the night all right."

He was only slightly better at hiding his skepticism over her snake story than his cousin was. Tess shrugged. "Fine, thanks."

"I'm sorry about Tippy Tail."

"Not your fault."

She glanced back at her house, so far nothing about this weekend was going according to plan or fancy. To add to her uneasiness, she realized she was attracted to Andrew Thorne. Just her luck. She wondered if he'd noticed the shade of blue of her eyes—the way she had his—or if he'd reacted to their physical contact last night. It wasn't expecting he had that got to her but rather the wondering. This, she thought, was what was so impossible about men. If only she could fast-forward into a relationship, check if it was worth being attracted to a man before she committed herself to expending all that energy.

Not that she was contemplating any kind of relationship with Andrew Thorne that didn't involve the word *neighbor* in it. Lusting after him—there was no other word for it—was just a way to get her mind off the skeleton in her cellar.

"Tess?"

She turned, noticed the muscles in his arms and shoulders, his lean, sexy build. Whoa, she thought, and gave him a quick smile. "Sorry. I was just thinking I should find a hardware store. I need to fix the cellar window. I guess I should add a litter box to my list."

He acknowledged her words with a thoughtful nod. "Good. I'll go with you."

"You don't have to. I can manage."

"I didn't say you couldn't manage, I said I'd go with you." He eyed her, and she thought she saw a glimmer of humor. "You'll never find the hardware store on your own."

"This town is about three streets big. I'll find it."

He'd already started down her driveway. "Give me ten minutes. I'll pick you up."

"I'll drive," Tess called.

He glanced back at her, as if he could sense her panic, knew she was having wild thoughts about him and that insisting she'd drive was a way of retaining a measure of control. He smiled. "Okay. You drive."

Nine

❧❧❧

"Lauren, please understand." Richard grabbed a cup of coffee in the kitchen on his way out to the back porch with the newspaper. "I only have a few minutes. When this appointment's nailed down, I'll walk with you to Cape Cod and back if you want."

She tried to smile. "We used to walk all the time, remember?"

"I *do* remember. Of course I do. You sound as if it's been a lifetime. We've probably taken more walks in the eighteen months we've been together than most people have in years."

Lauren sat at the table, watching him, trying not to think how much she loved him. Not today. She wanted to stay aggrieved awhile. "Just a quick walk on the rocks would suit me. You can't spare thirty minutes?"

"I can't, really. Sweetheart, it's not you—it's me. I know that. I'm just swamped, I can hardly form a coherent thought. Let me drink my coffee and read my paper, okay?" He walked over to her, kissed her on the forehead. She could smell his coffee, see the lines in his face. "It'll be all right."

"Did Jeremy Carver say something last night?"

"No, everything's looking good. It would help if we'd hear from Ike."

She waved a hand. "Oh, pooh. This isn't unusual for him. Tell Carver to talk to me, and I'll ease his mind."

"I already did. They can investigate further if they have any doubts. I've already passed the institute's security checks—the Department of Defense and Senator Bowler's office shouldn't be a problem."

"Of course not." Lauren fingered her coffee cup, wishing she could drum up more interest in her husband's impending appointment to Washington. What would she do? Stay here? Go? Throw parties for him? She shuddered inwardly.

"It's important work," Richard said, as if guessing what she was thinking.

"I know it is, Richard. I'll do anything I can."

He nodded. "I've never doubted I can count on you."

"Go on. Enjoy your paper. The dogs and I will go for a walk."

He was out the door before she'd finished her sentence. Lauren dumped her coffee in the sink. The cavernous kitchen, with its tall ceilings and white cabinets, needed renovating, but she had no appetite for it. Lately, her house seemed more like a sprawling, empty inn. Maybe a new kitchen would perk her up. She could talk to Andrew about it.

Her spirits sank, and she moved into the front hall, ignoring the poodles scampering at her feet. She ran outside into a stiff, steady breeze off the water. The house stood on a cliff above Cape Ann, with dramatic views of the shoreline, rocks, the glistening horizon.

The tide and waves, the brutal winter storms, were slowly eroding the sandy cliff, until, eventually, the house would either have to be moved or would be lost to the sea.

Lauren blinked back tears, blaming them on the wind. She didn't care what happened to the house. Let the Atlantic take it. Let its loss be her penance for not doing more to rein in her brother's excesses.

She shook off any thought of him, descended the porch steps so quickly she almost tripped.

She ran down a narrow dirt path, moving automatically, having gone this way so many times in her forty years. A gust of wind nearly knocked her over, and her breath came in gasps. She realized she'd been running, and slowed her pace. If only Richard had come with her. If only they'd held hands, laughed, talked. She wanted to confide in him. She wanted him to tell her everything would be all right.

When she got back to the house, Richard had left a note for her on the counter:

Muriel called. Tess Haviland is staying at the carriage house. ????

The question marks meant he didn't know about Tess.

Lauren felt sick to her stomach.

She walked out through the back door, down the porch steps to her gardens. The house blocked the wind. She ran her fingertips over a deep orange daylily, just in bloom. Then she started picking flowers, one after another, at random, without thinking, without feeling.

* * *

Tess would never have found the hardware store on her own. It was tucked behind a diner on a dead-end side street a block from the village center, a mom-and-pop operation stacked from floor to ceiling with every imaginable item a woman with an 1868 carriage house could need. She bought glass and putty for her cellar window and took a look at starter tool kits. If she kept the carriage house and intended to do any of the work herself, she'd need her own tools. She'd worked as a carpenter's helper through college with a string of her father's pals, but she had no illusions about her capabilities. She was a designer, not a carpenter. She'd need tools, books, advice, borrowed brawn. And luck. Certainly better luck than she'd had so far.

This was all provided she didn't call Beacon-by-the-Sea quits the first chance she got.

Her gaze drifted to a row of gleaming garden spades. She could rebury the skeleton and pretend she'd never found it. It was tempting. But wrong. She needed to verify what she'd found, then call in the proper authorities to have the remains identified and suitably buried…and determine how they'd ended up in Jedidiah Thorne's carriage house.

Maybe the skeleton *was* properly buried. Maybe whoever it belonged to had wanted the cellar to be his final resting place. Or hers.

Tess shuddered, turning her attention back to tool kits.

Andrew joined her in the narrow aisle. He was relaxed, at home amidst tools, nails, cans of turpentine, fifty different kinds of nuts and bolts. The service people all knew him and called him by his first name.

She regarded him with sudden suspicion. "You aren't a plumber or something, are you?"

"Architect." He had a five-pound bag of kitty litter comfortably under one arm. "More or less. You look relieved. Why? Do you have something against plumbers?"

"No. It's nothing. Never mind." But she was smiling, because Jim Haviland, Davey Ahearn and their pals in construction had no use for architects. "I suppose we should get Tippy Tail an extra cat dish. One for your house, one for mine."

Andrew shrugged. "I just use an old margarine tub."

Dolly darted up the aisle. Not one to be left out, she'd hopped in Tess's backseat, her father up front. She was just as at home in the hardware store as he was. She tugged on Tess's sleeve. "I know the dish Tippy Tail wants!"

"I guarantee," her father said wryly, "it will be fit for a princess's cat."

Tess laughed. "Anything's a step up from a margarine tub."

Dolly lobbied for engraving and heavy porcelain, but Tess prevailed when she found a heart-shaped red plastic dish and suggested it matched the sparkly red hearts in Dolly's crown.

"You're quick, Tess."

Andrew had slipped in behind them, not making a sound. His voice was low, resonating in places she didn't want to think about while picking out cat dishes. She'd needed more sleep. A *lot* more sleep. She turned, her arm brushing his, sending a current right through her. "I have clients. I've learned the art of negotiation."

"I think you and Dolly are kindred souls." He smiled,

but didn't move back out of her space. "You both like to have your way."

They dumped everything in her car, and Dolly jumped up and down, wanting chowder on the pier. "I like that idea myself," Tess said. "It's a beautiful day. We can walk." She glanced at Andrew, who hadn't said a word. "Unless you have something else you need to do."

"No." His daughter slipped her hand into his, and Tess couldn't tell what he was thinking, something she found unsettling as she was usually good at reading people. He was especially difficult because he was so self-contained. "Nothing important."

Dolly giggled, slipping her free hand into Tess's. "I like you, Tess."

"I like you, too, Princess Dolly."

They walked over to the pier, lined with cedar-shingled buildings that had been converted into upscale shops. With the beautiful May weather, tourists and locals were out in droves, fishing boats, sailboats and yachts setting out across the picturesque harbor. Dolly wasn't here to sightsee. She wanted chowder and dragged Tess and her father to a cozy, cheerful restaurant. They got a small table overlooking the water. Father and daughter sat on one side of a booth, Tess on the other.

The sun sparkled on the water, bright-colored buoys bobbing in the light surf. Tess smiled at the view. "It must have been wonderful growing up here."

"Dolly seems to like it," Andrew said.

"What about you? Did you grow up in Beacon?"

"Gloucester."

He wasn't the most talkative man she'd ever met. "Your family's been in this area for generations—"

"The Thornes have. They settled on the East Coast in the 1600s."

"Tell me about them," Tess said, eager for a distraction.

"What's to tell? Jedidiah's the only one in the history books. You know what happened. The rest of the lot were the usual mix of bums and heroes. Sea captains, revolutionaries, privateers, fishermen, a few solid citizens." He broke open a crusty roll. "The old cemeteries around here all have a Thorne or two in them."

"What happened to Jedidiah after he killed Benjamin Morse?"

"Prison."

Tess sighed. "I meant after prison. I know he headed west."

"He made it out to San Francisco. As the story goes, though, he couldn't stay away. He came home, called by the ocean, supposedly broke. He worked in the shipyards, got married, had a couple of kids. People had mostly forgotten about the duel. Benjamin Morse, they'd decided, was a man who'd needed killing."

"What a cold thought. We leave those decisions to a jury, not mobs or popular opinion." Tess stopped herself, since Andrew Thorne didn't need a lecture from her. "What happened to the wife?"

"Adelaide Morse." He set his roll on his bread plate. "She became a rich widow."

Tess looked out at the harbor, tried to imagine it in the mid-nineteenth century. "How did Jedidiah die?"

"He was lost at sea."

She almost choked, tried not to overreact. "When?"

"I don't know the exact date. Around the turn of the century, I believe."

"Then he's not buried here in Beacon?"

"No."

"But there's a record of what happened to him—"

"Not really. He went out in a fishing boat by himself and never returned." Andrew shrugged, matter-of-fact. "I figure that was his way of letting go."

Lost at sea. Alone. With no witnesses, no record. No body. Tess noticed Andrew watching her through narrowed eyes. She suddenly wondered if he and Harl knew there was a body in her cellar, suspected she'd seen it—suspected it was their unfortunate ancestor and wondered if she planned to stir up trouble.

She focused on Dolly and the harbor, counted buoys and seagulls. When their bowls of chowder arrived, Dolly immediately decided she needed to go to the bathroom. Tess offered to accompany her. The little girl shook her head. "I can go by myself." She jumped off the bench, then turned back to her father as she adjusted her crown. "Don't put crackers in my chowder. I *hate* crackers in my chowder."

She pranced off to the bathroom. "Well," Tess said, "she does have a mind of her own, doesn't she? And obviously a great imagination."

Andrew gazed out the window, a breeze churning up the surf. "Independence and imagination aren't necessarily a safe combination. Her life might be less complicated if she were one or the other, not both."

"Think of her as a 'creative risk-taker.'"

"Is that what you are?"

"I suppose. I used to work in the design department of a major corporation, but I went on my own almost two years ago. It's been fun, unnerving at times, I admit. But, I haven't gone broke." She grinned at him. "Not yet, anyway."

"If you're trying to make me think you're sensible, you're already off on the wrong foot."

"I'm not trying to make you think anything."

"Aren't you?"

He was naturally taciturn, she decided, which made him seem gruff, even unfriendly, but he smiled at her, sending her insides humming.

He went on. "You let Ike Grantham pay you with a haunted carriage house that probably should have been bulldozed fifty years ago."

Undeterred, Tess ground fresh pepper onto her chowder. It smelled almost as good as her father's, although there were no pats of butter melting into the thick, creamy base. "I don't care if it's haunted. I don't believe in ghosts."

"Even after last night?"

She smacked the pepper grinder back down on the table. "I did *not* see a ghost last night."

"You thought you did."

"No, I didn't, and saying so isn't going to make me change my mind." He was direct, not a man to beat around the point he was trying to make, a characteristic Tess ordinarily would find appealing. Not, however, at the moment. "I grew up with know-it-all men. You can't intimidate me."

"I'm not trying to intimidate you. I'm just stating the facts. I know you saw something, Tess. I could see it in your eyes."

She snorted. "What do you know about my eyes?"

His went distant, and he said, "Not enough, no doubt."

Her throat went dry. "Then you can't—"

"Tess, you weren't just afraid of what you might have seen in that cellar. You were afraid of what you *did* see."

"I was, was I?"

Her hot look and sarcasm seemed to have no effect on him. "Yes."

"It doesn't matter what you believe. *I* know what I saw, and it wasn't a ghost."

It was a skeleton, and she almost told him about it. Only the thought of what she'd do if it turned out to be an obvious plastic skeleton left over from Halloween, a prank, stopped her. The teasing would be unending. She'd never live it down, and somehow, some way, Davey and her father and the rest of the guys at the pub would find out. She'd be getting skeletons for her birthday, Christmas, Valentine's Day for years to come.

"Go ahead. Think whatever you want to think." She decided to redirect the subject. "Do you want me to check on Dolly?"

"No, she'll be back any second. She likes to wash her hands about six times. When she was three and four, the bathroom runs could get awkward, but she manages well now."

"Her mother…" Tess spooned up some of her chowder, which was hot and generous on the clams. "I don't mean to pry."

"Joanna died three years ago. She was caught in an avalanche on Mount McKinley." Andrew tore open a packet of oyster crackers, focused on them as he spoke. "It was several weeks before a rescue team could bring down her body."

"That must have been awful." But at least, Tess thought grimly, there was no possibility it was Joanna Thorne's remains she'd seen last night.

Dolly returned, and they talked about the boats in the harbor, the different kinds of seagulls. Not about her mother, dead in an avalanche the past three years.

They paid for lunch and started back to Tess's car, with Dolly, well fed and reenergized, skipping ahead. "It's a gorgeous day," Tess said.

"Have you made up your mind about the carriage house?"

She smiled. "Not yet."

But as she drove back to the point, her good mood dissipated and she knew she'd have to confront whatever was in the dirt cellar. Alone. And soon.

She dropped off father and daughter at their front door. Andrew was studying her suspiciously, and a quick peek in the rearview mirror suggested she was noticeably pale. It would be another rotten night. Too much thinking, especially about Andrew Thorne and his wife lost in an avalanche, his ancestor lost at sea, his neighbor with a dead body in the cellar. The Thornes had crummy luck.

"If you need help with your window," Andrew said evenly, "give Harl or me a yell. We'd be glad to lend you a hand."

But there was something in his tone she wasn't sure she liked. She pretended not to notice as she turned cheerfully to his daughter. "I'll keep an eye on Tippy Tail and her kittens, okay, Princess Dolly?"

The girl nodded, solemn. "They're just babies. They need peace and quiet."

She climbed out of the car, and Tess could see Andrew biting back a smile as he shut the door. He leaned into her open window. His eyes were that amazing blue again, a mix of sea and sky, warm, mesmerizing. "Let me know if you'd like the guest room."

Definitely, she thought, her life would be easier if her neighbor were a nasty troll, an s.o.b. But she smiled, gripped the steering wheel. "Thanks. I'll let you know."

Ten

```
─────ᗡᗞᗡᗞ─────
```

The woman with Andrew Thorne and his daughter had to be Tess Haviland. Richard thought she looked familiar and supposed he must have seen her in town before. She, Andrew and Dolly had gotten in an ancient Honda together, and Richard fought an urge to follow them. He had to maintain control. He couldn't indulge his emotions.

He returned home, hoping to sit in the sun with a glass of scotch. But Jeremy Carver was there in the driveway, leaning against a gleaming black car. "Mind if we have a word?"

"Of course not."

Lauren was out. Since they didn't employ full-time help, Richard poured two glasses of iced tea, cut a lemon, got out spoons and refilled the sugar bowl, all with his wife's damn poodles scurrying around at his feet. He put everything on a tray and carried it out to the back porch, shutting the door in the poodles' faces. One yelped. "Oh, sorry," he said without remorse.

"Your wife's dogs?" Jeremy Carver said.

"Yes, they're sweet little things, just always under your feet."

Richard set the tray on a side table, something Harley Beckett had restored and painted for Lauren. When they moved to Washington, Richard would insist on full-time help. Lauren could do whatever she wanted with this place, but he wasn't about to serve people when he was at the Pentagon. This was his first marriage, his life before Lauren dedicated exclusively to his education and his work, his experience with women limited to short-term relationships. He'd thought he loved her. Now he wasn't sure if he had the capacity to feel love, simply because it wasn't vital to him.

The afternoon sun was strong on the wide stretch of green lawn and its "rooms" of flower beds, which Lauren did see were properly tended to. But it was cool on the porch, out of the sun. Jeremy Carver had installed himself on the antique wicker settee. Again, the power position.

He reached over and chose a glass of tea, dropped in a slice of lemon. He didn't bother with sugar. "Excellent, Dr. Montague. Thanks."

"Please, call me Richard." He stirred two spoonfuls of sugar into his tea, sat with it on a wicker rocker with a flowery cushion. "I hope you've had a chance to enjoy our little village while you're here."

"Beacon? Yeah, it's a cute place. I headed back down to Boston last night. I have a sister who's about to become a grandmother. She's driving everyone nuts." He laughed, his ruddy face reddening. "And I thought she was bad when she had her first kid."

"I'm sure it must be an exciting time for everyone," Richard said neutrally.

"No kids for you, huh?"

"My wife has a seventeen-year-old daughter."

"Shellie Ann." Carver sipped his iced tea, no indication he was trying to communicate anything with his comment except that he knew the name of Lauren's daughter. "I've got three boys myself."

"Mr. Carver—"

He grinned. "Jeremy."

"I'm sure you want to get back to your family. What can I do for you?"

Carver set his glass on a coaster and rubbed his chin. "I've done a little checking of my own into your brother-in-law. Do you mind if I speak frankly?"

"No, of course not."

"He's an asshole. My opinion."

Richard smiled. "You're not alone in that opinion."

"You were right, the police have no interest in his whereabouts. They say your wife's never asked them to look into it."

"I'm sure she hasn't."

"Why not?"

"You'd have to ask her, but I'd say it's because she's not concerned."

"It's not because she's heard from him and just wants to keep it mum?"

"Not that I know of, no."

"Weird." Carver picked up his tea, took a big gulp and stared out at the lawn. "Pretty flowers. I can't get anything to grow in Washington after the middle of June. Too damn hot."

Richard reined in his impatience. "My wife has an incredible green thumb."

"Yeah, so I see. Look," he went on, "the police might

not have any interest in Ike Grantham, but I can't say the same for the senator. He'll feel a lot better if we can talk to the guy."

"I told you, Ike Grantham has nothing to do with me. I've been married to Lauren for less than a year, and Ike's her brother. We hardly know each other." Richard's tone was controlled, calm, neutral. Defensiveness would only raise Carver's suspicions. "I've always felt he'd come to a bad end, sooner rather than later."

"Because of his personality."

"Yes. He's reckless and inconsiderate. You've learned that yourself in your investigation."

"But people like him," Carver added. "Why is that?"

"His charisma."

Carver waved a hand in abrupt dismissal. "In Washington, you get your fill of charisma." He squinted, radiating a sharpness and ruthlessness that Richard knew he would be unwise to underestimate. "You think he's dead?"

"Personally? Yes, I do."

"What do you think happened?"

"I have no idea. Knowing Ike, I suppose he mooched a boat off a friend and went overboard in a storm because he didn't check the weather reports."

"Why wouldn't the friend report it?"

Richard shrugged. "Maybe he borrowed the boat without asking, or the friend didn't think anything of it when Ike didn't return it. Who knows? This is just one theory. He could have fallen in a remote area, and some hiker will find his remains twenty years from now."

Carver drank more tea, draining his glass. "But you don't suspect foul play?"

This wasn't a conversation, Richard knew. It was

part of Jeremy Carver's investigation into a man his boss would go to bat for. Senator Bowler's judgment and reputation were on the line. Richard sipped his tea, wishing he could add a third spoonful of sugar; but he didn't want to come across as a man who needed excessive amounts of sugar to get down a glass of iced tea. It was the little things that counted.

"Of course not," he said, smooth and unconcerned.

"Well, I suppose you wouldn't, or you'd have been hounding the police, trying to find the bastard."

"That's exactly right."

Jeremy Carver rose. "Thanks for the tea. Do you mind if I walk through the gardens on my way out?"

"Please do. If my wife were here, she could show you around. I can try—"

"That's okay. I've taken up enough of your time. You want me to help with the cleanup?"

Bile rose up in Richard's throat. "No, thanks. I'll handle it."

After Jeremy Carver finished his tour of the gardens, and his car finally pulled out of the driveway, Richard's guts clamped down on him, fiercely, painfully. He knew he wouldn't make it inside. He ran out into the yard, plunged into the herb garden and fell on his knees, puking up everything in his stomach. Then came the dry heaves. One after another. Thank God Lauren wasn't there.

Finally, reeling, spent, he stumbled back to the porch. He dumped the last of the ice cubes from his tea down the front of his shirt, rubbed one over his face and tongue.

"I swear to God, I'll kill you before I let my sister marry you."

Ike's words. He'd had his chance. And failed.

Richard had to keep his focus. He couldn't think about the past, what was done. Who was the Haviland woman? What did she want? And why now?

He had to know. The stakes were too high to leave anything to chance.

The afternoon turned warm, almost summerlike. Andrew gave up on getting anything done and sat on the front porch with a glass of lemonade he and Dolly had made together. She dragged out an army of dolls and stuffed animals. She wanted him to play with her. He could be the daddy.

If only the guys he'd beat up in a string of Gloucester bars could see him now, he thought as Dolly ran up to her room for one last, totally necessary stuffed animal. The rest of the gang were heaped on a blanket in a corner of the porch.

Tess Haviland had not asked for help repairing her cellar window. He'd decided it was best if he didn't think too much about her and her blue eyes, her artistic hands, why she kept lying about what she'd seen last night.

Across the street, over the rocks and across the narrow, sandy beach, the ocean beckoned. He was already teaching Dolly how to sail, and he wondered if a love of the sea was in Thorne blood. He doubted it. They'd been a pragmatic lot. To most of them, the sea was probably just where they'd made their living. It was what they knew.

Except, perhaps, for Jedidiah. He'd been a romantic, a man who'd accused a prominent local citizen of beating his wife, of cowardice and a lack of honor. He'd been an outsider in Beacon-by-the-Sea, the upstart who'd just finished building his small estate on a point near the village. Whatever else he was, Jedidiah had loved the sea. Andrew was sure of it.

Lauren Montague's cream-colored Mercedes pulled alongside the road in front of his house. The Mercedes was an older model, no doubt because Lauren wouldn't want to look ostentatious. She climbed out of the driver's seat and waved at him over the hood, the sunlight catching the highlights of her hair.

Andrew got to his feet and walked over to the porch steps, wanting to avoid having to ask her to have a seat. It wasn't gracious of him, but Lauren wasn't high on his list of people he wanted popping over for a visit.

She tucked strands of her straight, windblown hair behind her ears as she came up the walk, skirting Dolly's bicycle. "I hope I'm not interrupting—I'll only be a minute."

"Not a problem. What's up?"

She smiled. "It's a gorgeous day, isn't it?"

"I suppose."

"Oh, Andrew. You're such a Puritan."

Not bloody likely, he thought.

"I brought a present for Dolly," she said.

She stood at the bottom of the steps, as if not sure she should proceed further. She was always self-consciously cheerful and energetic around him, worse since Ike's abrupt departure last year. Although they'd never discussed it, Andrew knew she felt guilty over her brother's role in Joanna's decision to climb Mount McKinley, blaming herself in part for not reining him in. Periodically, she'd show up with gifts for Dolly, as if they could provide absolution for herself.

Andrew walked down and joined her on the walk. He could hear the tide going out, seagulls crying as they hunted for easy food. "She's upstairs looking for a stuffed animal."

"I can just leave it with you." She opened her expensive leather tote and withdrew a clear plastic bag. Through it, Andrew could see purple-and-red flowers, frothy white flowers, a bit of pink ribbon. Lauren handled it gently. "It's a garland. I was in a crafty mood and made it myself, with flowers from my garden. Dolly can wear it as a crown. I know she loves her crowns."

She thrust the garland at Andrew and stepped back quickly, as if she didn't dare get too close. He eyed the flowers. "I'll give it to her when she comes downstairs."

"Don't make her write a thank-you note like last time. It was adorable, but, Andrew, she's only six. She can't be expected to write thank-you notes."

After Lauren's last gift, Dolly had scrawled "Thank you" in milky pink gel ink and had drawn a picture of a cat. She'd spent a lot of time on the cat. Andrew shrugged. "Okay. No thank-you note."

A knowing smile lifted the corners of Lauren's mouth. She was an odd mix of contrasts. Elegant, breezy, gracious, often tactless. Andrew hoped her need to give Dolly little gifts would run its course.

She shifted, glancing out at the street. She could hold her own with high-powered executives, at fund-raisers and cocktail parties, with her husband's brainy friends, but Andrew and his six-year-old daughter put her at a loss. "I suppose I should be running along."

"Thanks for stopping by."

She gave him a chiding smile. "Always so polite."

"Not always."

She left, and Andrew gave Dolly the garland when she burst back onto the porch with a stuffed whale he'd forgotten she had. Of course, she loved the garland. She gasped in delight, and after he helped her open the bag, she put the flower crown on her head.

"Oh, Daddy, I *am* a princess!"

He laughed, and they set about pouring more lemonade and playing stuffed animals. Dolly tried to boss him around, wanting him to do precisely what she wanted him to do when she wanted him to do it, but he held his own.

When she got home, Lauren grabbed the poodles and let them chase her around the yard until she was panting and sweating. The dogs collapsed in the shade, their little chests heaving. She wished she could lie there with them in the grass, knowing nothing more than they did.

She didn't know where Richard was. She didn't care. This was her problem, and hers alone.

She sank onto a teak bench, surrounded by rhododendrons and white lilacs. She could hear the trickle and gurgle of the nearby waterfall fountain, a new addition to her gardens, carefully constructed of stone and water plants. Ordinarily she would have found its sounds soothing, but today they were irritating, everything setting her on edge.

After leaving Andrew's house, she'd turned around on the dead-end side street where Jedidiah Thorne had built his carriage house. Tess Haviland's car was parked in the driveway. She was out of sight, probably calculating whether she'd do better selling the place as is or fixing it up first. As is wouldn't cause Lauren a problem: she could snap it up herself. But if Tess decided to fix it up, or if she took an interest in the carriage house and kept it for herself, that could be a disaster.

Lauren brushed away tears that were hotter even than her flushed skin. If only she could go back a year, arrive at the carriage house sooner…and stop Andrew Thorne from killing her brother.

It must have been an accident, an act of passion and pent-up rage. Oh, God, she thought, who could blame him? He was raising his and Joanna's little girl alone. Ike had infected his wife like a virus, insidiously eroding all her defenses.

What must Andrew think now, with Tess next door?

He hadn't looked concerned when Lauren had brought him the garland. Despite his rough upbringing, he was nothing if not stoic, losing control only that one time in the carriage house, with tragic results.

The thought of him propelled Lauren to her feet. All her life, she'd been the one in the background doing what needed to be done to protect her brother, cleaning up after he'd been rude, impulsive, reckless or otherwise impossible.

She'd always made sure his excesses didn't hurt anyone else. She would do so again, no matter how unappealing her options, how much she still loved her brother and always would, and missed him—no matter how much she hated what she'd known for a year.

Her beautiful, outrageous brother was dead.

She had to concern herself with the living, with what was right.

Marcy, her favorite of the three poodles, rolled onto her back, and Lauren laughed, sinking onto the grass and rubbing the animal's stomach. "You know just what I need, don't you?" She felt the dog's quick heartbeat, let it strengthen her resolve. Marcy had been hit by a car two years ago, and yet, as tiny and broken as she was, she'd pulled through. "Let a little of your luck rub off on me, sweetheart, okay? Don't be stingy, because I'll need it."

Eleven

Tess sat out on her kitchen steps, feeling the strain in her neck and back from crouching to fix the cellar window. She'd managed the repair job without actually going into the cellar. She had a new plan—she'd go back to Boston tonight and get Susanna to come up with her in the morning. They'd search the cellar together. Susanna could handle a skeleton. If it turned out to be a figment of Tess's imagination, she could count on Susanna not to tell the whole world. She kept people's finances to herself, after all.

It was a good plan. Sensible.

Tess didn't consider herself a coward for not wanting to investigate the dirt cellar on her own. She'd gone down there by herself in the first place, hadn't she? She had nothing to prove, and if a crime had been committed—at whatever point in the past hundred thirty years—it might be smart to have a witness.

She spotted Dolly slipping through the lilacs and eased off the steps, down to the driveway.

"Is it okay if I come over?" Dolly asked, still technically in the lilacs and thus her own yard. "Harl says I'm not supposed to be a pest. Am I a pest?"

Tess smiled. "Mosquitoes are pests. A princess can never be a pest."

The little girl giggled as if Tess had said the funniest thing she'd ever heard. She looked behind her, on the Thorne side of the lilacs, and yelled, "Daddy, she says it's okay!" She turned to Tess and jumped out into the tall grass. "He'll be right over."

Tess had the feeling Andrew and Harl weren't about to let Dolly come over unchaperoned until they were satisfied about what had happened last night. Under the circumstances, she could hardly take offense.

"I brought Tippy Tail some food." Dolly reached into her pocket and withdrew a crumpled, squished individual packet of cat food. She showed it to Tess. "It's her favorite."

"Do you want to put it in her dish?"

Her eyes widened with excitement at such a prospect. "Could I?"

"Sure. Just tiptoe so you don't disturb her and the kittens. We should probably wait for your dad."

She rolled her eyes. "He won't go through the bushes. He says he's too big. Do you think he's too big?"

Tess laughed. "No, Dolly, I don't think he's too big."

He materialized behind her. "Too big for what?"

It was a question to which there was no good answer, and Tess saw the glint in his eyes. She said, "Dolly wants to feed Tippy Tail. I said it's okay, but probably just two of us should go inside. Your cat's on the skittish side."

"You two go ahead."

That was all the encouragement Dolly needed. She

bounded over to the steps, stopped herself, then did an exaggerated but very quiet tiptoe. She turned her face up to Tess and whispered, "I have a loose tooth. See?" It was the sort of non sequitur Tess was coming to expect from the six-year-old. "Harl says he can pull it out with his pliers."

"You don't believe him, do you?"

She nodded. "Uh-huh!"

"Dolly," Andrew said. "You know Harl's just teasing you."

She giggled again, and Tess realized that Dolly Thorne had her rather unusual babysitter all figured out. And her taciturn father, too, no doubt. She was no more worried about Harl really pulling her tooth with a pair of pliers than he intended to do so.

She tore open the crumpled packet and dumped the food into the cat's new dish. Tippy Tail, stretching, still scraggly-looking, emerged from Tess's camp bed and padded over to the little girl. Dolly ran her hand over the cat's back. Tess thought the old cat looked as if she'd just delivered four kittens and could use a nice, long rest.

"Are you okay, Tippy Tail?" Dolly cooed. "You have cute babies. You be good to them, okay? I know you will." She looked back at Tess, her eyes bright with affection. "Tippy Tail is a good mommy cat, isn't she?"

Considering the animal had intended to have her kittens in a dirt cellar, Tess wasn't so sure. But what did she know about cats? "She seems to have good maternal instincts."

"What's instincts?"

"An instinct is knowing in your heart what's the right thing to do."

"Oh." Dolly stood up and watched Tippy Tail eat,

then, dutifully keeping her distance, peeked at the kittens, who were all asleep on the sleeping bag. She whispered, as if Tess didn't know any better, "We should leave them alone."

She ran out the side door and plopped down on the steps as if she was in for an extended visit. Andrew motioned to her with one finger. "Got to go, kiddo."

"Can Tess come over for supper?"

Tess winced, standing at the bottom of the steps. "Actually, Dolly, I'm thinking about heading back to Boston tonight. That's where I live—"

"Please!"

Andrew leaned against her car, arms folded across his chest, looking relaxed and sexy, slightly less suspicious than last night and at lunch. "You're welcome to join us for dinner before you head back."

"Thanks, but—"

"Why're you going back to Boston?" Dolly asked. "Why can't you stay?"

Andrew gave the barest hint of a smile. "That's a good question, Dolly."

"Well, because I have a lot of work to do, and I'm not getting any of it done here." But the lie was transparent, even Dolly Thorne looked dubious. Tess sighed. "And my Tippy Tail adventures last night have me a little off center. The thought of staying here alone doesn't exactly thrill me."

Dolly's forehead creased. Then her eyes brightened, and she clapped her hands together. "Silly! Who wants to stay in this old place? It's got *mice*. Harl says so." She jumped up, yanked on her father's hand with excitement. "Tess can sleep over at our house, right, Daddy?"

He tugged gently on one of Dolly's braids. "I've already made the offer, sport."

The little girl swung around to Tess, who could feel her stomach muscles tightening. When a six-year-old was involved, she had to be careful, whether in being attracted to her father or lying to him. She said, "I don't know. Why don't we wait and see?"

Then, as if to deliberately exacerbate her situation, a familiar brown pickup rolled into the driveway.

Tess swore under her breath. "Oh, no."

"What is it?" Andrew asked.

"My father and one of his buddies."

Dolly frowned. "Where's your mom?"

"What? My mom?" She felt as if she'd been hit in the gut, but managed a smile at the little girl. "My mom's in heaven, too."

"She is? She died?"

Tess remembered being perfunctory about such things at six one minute, weaving fantasies and dreams the next. She nodded, trying to match Dolly's mood. "Yes. She died when I was a little girl."

"Like my mommy."

"My mother had a very bad disease, cancer."

"Ick."

Andrew said softly, "Dolly, we should go. Tess has company."

She jumped up, skipping across the driveway as if she and Tess had just been discussing picking flowers.

Davey Ahearn got out of the driver's side of his heap of a truck, his best friend of many years climbing out of the passenger side. Davey had a fresh cigarette lit.

Tess shook her head. "No way. You're not smoking in my house."

"Not even a hello first, just put your butt out? You and your old man. He wouldn't let me smoke all the way up here. Couple of pains in the ass." He tossed his cigarette onto the gravel and ground it out under his steel-toed boot. Then he noticed Dolly. "Geez, I didn't see the kid."

She gave a regal toss of her head, the sunlight catching the flowers in her crown. "I'm Princess Dolly."

"Yeah? No kidding. I'm Davey Ahearn, the hired help."

"If you'll excuse us," Andrew said to Tess. "Dinner's at six. Come whenever."

That was all Davey needed. Tess could see him go on high alert. She ignored him. "Can I bring anything?"

He shook his head.

She knew she had to introduce them. If she didn't, it would make things worse. Her father came around the truck, and she said, "Pop, Davey, this is Andrew Thorne and his daughter, Dolly. They live next door. Andrew, my father, Jim Haviland, and my godfather, Davey Ahearn."

"You the architect?" Davey asked.

Andrew nodded. "More of a contractor these days."

"Yeah, you're not as big a jackass as most architects I've had to work with." He glanced at Dolly again and reddened. "Sorry."

Jim Haviland was more pensive, taking in Andrew with a tough-minded scrutiny Tess had come to expect whenever her introductions involved a man, no matter who it was. But he said, "Pleased to meet you," and let it go at that.

Dolly disappeared through the lilacs, calling for

Harl, on some other tangent, and Andrew seized his opening.

Tess ticked off the seconds until he was reliably out of earshot. Only then, she knew, would her father and Davey speak.

"So," Davey said, easing in beside her, "you take this barn instead of cold hard cash before or after you checked out who lived next door?"

"Davey, I swear to you, if you don't wipe that smirk off your face—"

"I hear his wife died a few years ago."

"Davey."

Her father crossed his arms, rubbed a toe over a small, protruding rock in the driveway. "Dinner, huh?"

"It's a courtesy. His daughter's cat had kittens—" She groaned, throwing up her hands. "Come on, I'll explain while I give you the grand tour. What are you two doing up here, anyway? And don't you have my cell phone number? You could have called."

But the idea that these two men needed to call before seeing her didn't even register with them. She saw her father giving her house a critical once-over from the edge of the driveway. He was trying to look neutral. When he had to try, it meant he wasn't, and usually not because he approved.

Davey picked up his ground-out cigarette butt and set it inside his truck, turning back to Tess. "Business was lousy at the pub. Too nice a day. So, your old man and I decided to take a drive up here, see what's what." He gave the kitchen steps a test kick. "Good, at least I can get inside without falling on my ass."

"This place has character, though, doesn't it?" Tess tried not to think about last night but she didn't want to tell her father and Davey what she'd seen, not until she was sure herself what it was. She'd have to keep them out of the cellar. "Isn't the location just gorgeous? You can smell the ocean."

"Smells like dead fish," Davey said.

She ignored him. "Come on. But you have to be quiet, I don't want to scare Tippy Tail. That's Dolly's cat. She had kittens in my bed early this morning."

Her father exhaled in a loud whoosh. "Jesus H. Christ," he breathed, and followed his daughter and best friend into the carriage house kitchen.

Davey grinned at the sleeping kittens and mother cat in her camp bed. "Did I tell you this place was a god-damn barn? These guys are cute now, but wait'll you get little kitty turds all over your kitchen floor. They won't be so cute then."

"They don't look so cute now," her father said. "I don't get what people see in cats."

"I set up a box with a towel in a corner in the bathroom," Tess said. "It's a lot cozier than out here in the open. I'm hoping Tippy Tail'll move the kittens there, free up my bed."

She showed them around the kitchen, and as they moved through the house, the two men checked out the wiring, the plumbing, deciding which were the load-carrying beams and what problems and possibilities they presented—focusing, of course, on the problems. Tess didn't point out the stain in the living room, but Davey shot her a look that said he'd seen it and had drawn the same conclusion she had. Ghosts, nineteenth-century murderers.

"How'd you sleep last night?" her father asked.

"Fine."

"Yeah?"

"Yes, fine."

"Bullshit. You were worried about ghosts."

"You knew?"

"That this place is haunted? Of course I knew. Your mother loved telling me about the crazy, murdering ghost. I guess he killed some wife-beating bastard way back when." He looked around the big, empty room, shaking his head. "But I figured, you in a haunted house, that's your business, I wasn't getting into it. Besides, you didn't give me a chance."

"I don't believe in ghosts," Tess said.

Davey laughed. "Ha, I bet you did last night." But then his gaze fell on the trapdoor, and he shook his head. "Oh, man. I hate trapdoors."

"There's a bulkhead."

He sighed without enthusiasm. "Come on. Let's go. Show me the cellar, let me check out the pipes."

Tess led her father and Davey around back to the bulkhead, telling herself if they found the skeleton, there'd be hell to pay, but at least she would know it was real and she would have to deal with it.

"Davey, you've been crawling around in people's basements for forty years." She pushed open the six-foot door at the bottom of the bulkhead and let them go past her. Both men had to duck. "What's the strangest thing you've found?"

"I make it a policy not to look. I focus on the pipes." He made a beeline through the finished laundry room and stood in the dirt cellar's open doorway. "Ah, hell. I hate dirt cellars."

"It's a nineteenth-century carriage house," Tess said, "so it shouldn't be a surprise."

He scowled at her. "It's not."

"You know," her father said, "you give a cat a dirt cellar, you've got a hell of a big catbox."

"Gee, Pop, I'm so glad you came up here. What took you so long? I mean, I've been here, what, twenty-four hours?"

He ignored her, and she walked across the cool concrete floor and stood next to Davey. With the late-afternoon light angling through her repaired window, the cellar seemed almost ordinary. "People ever bury things in their dirt cellars?"

"You mean like pets? They'd stink."

She felt her stomach fold in on itself, but tried not to react visibly. Decaying corpses weren't one of her areas of expertise and not something she wanted to think about. Still, it was a point to consider. If the skeleton had been buried as an intact corpse, and not just bones, surely it couldn't have been recent, or it would have called attention to itself during the natural process of decomposition.

Her father was scrutinizing her. "Tess?"

"My mind's wandering. Sorry. There's a light under the trapdoor. But don't feel as if you have to go in there. I mean, you can see the pipes from here, can't you?"

Davey grinned at her. "What, it gives you the creeps?" He made a phony, B-movie ghost sound and laughed, amused with himself. "Relax. I've seen worse than this. Let me take a look."

Tess lingered in the doorway while he and her father went into the older part of the cellar, their attention clearly on the pipes and heating ducts, not on what was underfoot. She bit down on her lower lip, waiting, feeling only a slight twinge of guilt that she hadn't warned them what could be in store. If there was no skeleton, there was no skeleton. Simple.

"Actually," Davey said, "these pipes aren't bad. Cellar's dry, too, which is a good sign."

Her throat was suddenly so constricted she couldn't answer. She kept feeling herself falling last night, spotting the skull in the dirt, letting out that blood-curdling scream.

Finally, she couldn't stand it anymore, muttered something about getting some air and fled up the bulkhead steps.

She ran headlong into the rock-solid body of Andrew Thorne. He caught her around the middle and held firm. "Easy, there, where are you going?"

Tess choked back a yell, tried to control a wild impulse to break free and run out to the ocean, charge into the waves. She felt as if she were covered in cobwebs, unable to breathe. But she made herself stand still, realized she had a death grip on his upper arms. She eased off. "I couldn't breathe down there. It must be the dust. Allergies." She coughed, suddenly very aware of the feel of his hands on her waist. "I'm okay now."

She could hear her father and Davey in the laundry-room door and backed up a step, releasing her grip on Andrew. He lowered his arms and rolled back on his heels, his eyes half-closed. She met his suspicious gaze straight-on, but had the uncomfortable feeling he could see right into her brain and pull out the image stored there of the yellowed skull lying in the silty dirt of her cellar.

"I came by to remind you to bring a key to the carriage house." His voice was quiet, dead calm, his eyes still half-closed, still appraising her. "We'll need to look after the kittens while you're in Boston."

"Yes. Of course." Not that he couldn't get in, easily, without a key.

"You sure you're okay?"

"I think so." She sniffled, wrinkling up her nose to prove it was the dust. "I must be allergic to something down there."

Andrew said nothing, but his expression was serious, even humorless. He knew she was hiding something. She could feel it. And here she'd just presented him with another lie he could chalk up against her. But what did she really know about *him?* If there was a dead body in the cellar, wasn't it possible he knew about it? Or Harl did? She *had* to be careful.

Davey and her father lumbered up out of the cellar, and Tess could feel the blood rush to her face when they saw Andrew back in her yard. They'd jump to conclusions. They always did.

But Andrew retreated quickly, though not quite rudely.

Tess turned to her father. Obviously he and Davey hadn't stumbled onto any skeleton. If they had, they'd have said something by now. She took this as a positive development. "Pop, why don't I get you and Davey something cold to drink?"

She brought out cold sodas, and they walked out to the main road and across to the water, down to the wet, packed sand. It was low tide, the surf gentle, quiet in the late-day sun. Tess regarded the two men at her side with affection. They were the most prominent men in her life, constant, uncompromisingly honest. Her father was a longtime widower, Davey twice married, two old friends who worked hard and asked so little of her. She knew her father just wanted grandchildren and Little League games, and that Davey, who had grown kids of his own, would get in the dirt with them, show them how to hold the bat, the way he had shown Tess as a kid.

The problem was, she didn't have a man in her life. The men she met either didn't understand her father and Davey and the rest of the guys at Jim's Place, or they understood them too well. She didn't mind saying she wanted a relationship, but she wasn't going to settle for the wrong man just to have one. She knew she could be happy on her own. That had never been a question.

As for children—that was something else altogether. She was so young when her mother died, and there'd never been another maternal figure in her life. She didn't have a natural trust of her maternal instincts, didn't even know if she had any.

"You should have told me about this place," her father said. Davey had gone up ahead, his hands shoved in his pockets as he walked within inches of the water.

Tess nodded. "I know." She glanced over at him, this man who'd been by her side for so long. "You won't think I'm giving up on men if I decide to keep it?"

She was quoting his own words back to him, one of his most stubborn, most old-fashioned convictions that if a woman bought property, it meant she was giving up on having a man in her life. It was one thing to buy a house if she were widowed or divorced—but single? Never married? It was tossing in the towel, he'd told her at least a hundred times.

"Giving up? Nah. Not after meeting that Thorne guy."

Tess groaned. "Pop, if I decide to keep the carriage house, it won't be because of who lives next door."

He sighed, watching two gulls careen toward the shallow water before he replied. "Listen to me, Tess. You don't want to end up like me, all alone, or like Davey, with a couple of ex-wives hounding him for money all the time. Getting a place of your own—yeah, it's like saying you give up, you don't care if you find someone." He added frankly, "Men can sense that, you know."

"They cannot."

"Mark my words." He grabbed up a clamshell and flung it into the surf. "It's that last little prick you went out with. He threw you off."

"He didn't throw me off. He was a jerk. He'd check the stock market when we had lunch. No more investment bankers for me."

She smiled, well aware she wouldn't change how her father thought about relationships, or about her. But there was more to his concern than an old-fashioned outlook on women and marriage, only they'd always avoided going that deep. It was too painful, not just for her, but for him, too. She was terrified of motherhood, terrified of dying too soon, leaving behind children who loved and needed her. Not because they couldn't go on, but because they did.

She pushed away the thought, as she always did.

Davey swung back to them, obviously sensing what she and her father had been talking about. "One day, Tess, you won't have to worry about your old man getting in your business. The two of us'll be on our walkers in the home."

"Davey Ahearn in a home?" Tess laughed. "You tell

me one home in metropolitan Boston that would have you. No way. You're not moving from the neighborhood until you go to the great big plunger in the sky."

As she turned to head back, she saw Andrew out on the beach with his daughter. They were throwing a Frisbee, and Tess could hear Dolly's squeals of laughter above the surf and gulls, the hum of the wind. She imagined them thirty years from now, Dolly as a grown woman out on the beach with her father, who was still alone, who'd sacrificed so much for his daughter.

Twelve

❧❧❧

Dinner was on the back porch. Hamburgers off the grill, salad, watermelon and chocolate chip cookies from a local bakery. Tess drove over, having decided she'd head straight back to Boston after dinner. A night in familiar surroundings would clear her head. She felt less of a sense of urgency now that her father and Davey hadn't found anything in the cellar, more convinced she really had conjured up a skull last night. Or a ghost.

Harl didn't stay for dinner, instead taking his plate back to his shop, muttering that he had work to do. Dolly tugged on Tess's hand and whispered, "Harl *always* has work to do."

Tess laughed, knowing the feeling. "That's good, isn't it? You wouldn't want him to be bored."

"Chew-bee thinks he's a *bank robber*."

"Who?"

Andrew set a plate of grilled hamburgers on the table. Function beat out charm on the back porch, but the setting on the warm May evening, the scent of lilac, grass and sea, was all the atmosphere Tess needed. He said, "Chew-bee is one of Dolly's pretend friends. She sometimes says things Dolly knows she shouldn't say."

"Harl used to be a policeman," Dolly explained to her company. "I *told* Chew-bee, but she doesn't listen."

Tess understood pretend friends. As father and daughter argued back and forth, she noted that Andrew never made Dolly say that Chew-bee wasn't real. He never imposed his own concrete way of thinking on her, which was one reason, Tess thought, Dolly exercised her creative imagination so freely, something first-grade teachers wouldn't necessarily appreciate. Tess liked the open way the two talked to each other. She'd never gotten along well with controlling, dictatorial men. Being opinionated was something else altogether. She knew the difference between a man with strong opinions and one who wanted to control everyone in his life.

But she didn't just notice Andrew's manner with his daughter, she also noticed how he moved, the way his eyes changed with the light, the play of muscles in his arms, every tiny scar. Part of her wanted to blame lack of sleep and the strangeness of her first weekend in Beacon-by-the-Sea for making her hyperaware of her surroundings. But another part of her knew it was more than that, wanted it to be.

They talked about renovations, winter storms, what shrubs and trees tended to do best this close to the ocean, window boxes and snakes. It was a free-ranging conversation, peppered by commentary from Dolly, who, when she was finished after dinner, insisted on dragging Tess off to see her tree house.

"It's all right," Andrew said. "I'll clean up."

It was dusk when they crossed the lawn, Dolly scooting up the rungs on the oak tree, Tess going at a more cautious pace. The tree house was made of scrap lumber, with the kind of precise construction that indicated either—or both—an architect and a furniture restorer had been involved. The ceiling height was perfect for Dolly. Tess had to duck.

Dolly showed her a Winnie-the-Pooh tea set, her cache of animal books and stuffed animals and a hand-held video game that she'd left out in the rain. She also had a bright red firefighter's hat.

"This is an excellent tree house," Tess said.

She shrugged, sighing. "It needs windows."

Tess couldn't hold back a laugh. The critic. "Are you going to be an architect like your father?"

"Nope. I'm a princess."

"But princesses have to have something to do."

"Oh, I'm going to be a princess astronaut."

With that, it was back down out of the tree house and off across the lawn to show Tess her bedroom. They passed Andrew in the kitchen. "She's exhausting," he warned.

"I'm having fun," Tess said, and realized happily that she was.

Dolly skipped through a gleaming wood-floored hall and up a beautiful, carved dark wood staircase. The house was simply decorated, the den obviously recently renovated, a room across the hall, which was covered in drop cloths, clearly still in the works. Dolly's room was at the top of the stairs, and she immediately pulled down all her various crowns. Then it was her multitude of dolls and stuffed animals, and finally up onto her bed to point to a picture. "That's my mom."

Tess looked at the smiling woman in the picture,

taken on a rock by the ocean. Dolly had her coppery hair, maybe the shape of her eyes. "She looks like quite a mom," Tess said.

"I dreamed about her last night."

"Did you?"

The girl nodded. "Yep," she said, matter-of-fact, and jumped down off the bed. "Do you have a daughter?"

"No, I don't have any children, but I'm not married."

"Are you going to live in the carriage house?"

"Eventually, maybe. It needs a lot of work. Right now, I live in a small apartment in Boston."

"Can I come see it?"

"Oh, I don't know. Sometime, maybe," Tess stammered, at a loss. She didn't want to give the girl false encouragement, nor insult her. This was what unnerved her about kids—she never knew what they were going to say, always had to be on her toes. But it was nice, too, stimulating in an odd way. And the *idea* of a six-year-old intimidated her more than the reality, at least in the form of Dolly Thorne. She quickly diverted the conversation. "I can walk to work. I like that a lot."

"I walk to school."

Dolly chatted on, zigzagging from subject to subject according to a logic all her own, until something drew her to the window. She covered her mouth and gasped dramatically, her entire body getting into the spirit. "Harl's making my window!"

She was off, and when Tess turned from the window herself, she saw that Andrew was leaning in the doorway. She felt an unexpected rush of heat. Dolly bulldozed right past him.

"Have you been there long?" Tess asked, suddenly self-conscious.

"Long enough to know she was about to talk your ear off."

"I held my own. Seeing Dolly makes me realize just how young I was when my mother died. She had leukemia." Tess gathered up several stuffed animals Dolly had dumped on the floor and set them back on the bed. "Anyway, that's neither here nor there. It's got nothing to do with you and your daughter."

He walked into the room, glanced out the window as he spoke. It was dark now, but he didn't seem concerned about Harl and Dolly working on a window for her tree house. "Joanna died doing something she loved to do. I don't know if I could have watched her waste away."

"Sudden death isn't easy."

"There's no easy way to die young. I hope Dolly will make some sense out of it when she's older."

"She's making sense of it now," Tess said, then gave him a quick smile. "Chew-bee probably helps."

He laughed. "If Chew-bee weren't thin air, I'd send her to her room."

Tess picked up a rag doll and put her back on the shelf. "Very clever. I think I'll make up a pretend friend. She can write letters to deadbeat clients demanding they pay up, and she can say all the things I'd get into trouble for saying."

"Be careful what you wish for."

"Yes. I wished for a cottage by the ocean, and look what I got."

He remained in the doorway, watching her as she moved around the small, girlish room. "Ike can be very persuasive."

"You're not kidding. I drove past the carriage house

a couple of times, but basically I took it sight unseen. I never even stepped foot in it."

He smiled. "Is that an example of creative risk-taking?"

"It's probably just nuts."

She stopped in the middle of the room, unable to think of any more busywork to do. She'd have to walk past him in the doorway. "You and Ike weren't friends?"

"No."

"He grew up in Beacon—"

"And I'm from a rough section of Gloucester. Two different worlds."

She found herself wanting to know more about his life, what made this man so self-contained. "Harl's from Gloucester as well?"

"Down the street from my folks. They're hardworking people, not real complicated. The world got complicated on them, neighborhood went to hell. They did their best."

"Do they still live in Gloucester?"

"Yep. In a better neighborhood."

"And Harl—he was a policeman?"

"Detective." Andrew drew away from the door frame, straightening, suddenly seeming even taller. "One day, between police work and Vietnam, he'd seen enough. He walked out, grew his hair, grew a beard, turned a hobby into a business. After Joanna died and I moved in here, he fixed up the shed out back."

"If he's your cousin, does that mean you don't have any brothers and sisters?"

He smiled almost imperceptibly. "Not a chance. Three brothers, one sister, all in Gloucester. Bunch of nieces and nephews."

"And are they all pure granite like you?"

"Worse."

She laughed, but saw he was watching her, attuned to even her smallest reaction. It was unsettling, a kind of single-minded attention she'd never experienced turned on her. She focused on one of Dolly's crowns, a fixed spot, to keep her balance.

"Come on," he said quietly. "Let's take some cookies and milk out to Dolly and Harl, see if they're ready to come in out of the dark."

But he stayed in the doorway, and when she started past him, he caught her gently around the waist, as if he'd been waiting just for this moment. Without thinking, she placed a hand on his chest, saw a flash of heat in his eyes. She felt her mouth go dry, a sudden urge to stay right where she was all night, in this half embrace overpowering her senses, unable to think of skulls in the dirt, of Ike or lies.

"You okay?" Andrew asked softly.

"Just fine."

His mouth found hers, the kiss so natural, so perfect, it seemed to have been destined. She shut her eyes, savored the play of his lips on hers, the taste of them. Both his arms went around her, drawing her closer, until she was against him, sighing at the feel of his hard, lean body. Her lips parted, and his hands tensed on her sides as he reacted, their kiss deepening. Liquid heat spilled through her, fired every fiber of her.

She ran her hands down his sides, held him as he half lifted her onto him, wanting to melt into him, become one with him, her body burning for that release. He cupped her hips, drawing her hard against his arousal.

The feel of him, the heat of him, brought a gasp of

awareness, reality. She opened her eyes, and he lowered her, pushed her gently back against the door frame. His eyes were as dark as midnight, telling her that she shouldn't mistake his stoic nature for control. He was on the precipice, sweeping his gaze over her, taking in just how aroused she was.

He skimmed his fingertips over her breasts, ignoring her quick breath, and touched her mouth. His was set in a hard line, as if he'd done something he regretted, knew was wrong. "You're a dangerous woman to have next door."

"That took both of us."

He nodded.

"It doesn't have to happen again," she added quickly.

"That's where you're wrong." He kissed her again, lightly, his eyes sparkling with sudden humor. "Cookies?"

"Yes," she said with a grin. "Cookies would be wonderful."

She stopped back at the carriage house to lock up. Distracted over going to dinner next door and her father and Davey not finding the skull, she'd forgotten. It wasn't as if it'd make much difference. Anyone who wanted to get into the place could with little imagination or effort. But there was no point in inviting trouble.

While she was here, she decided to check on Tippy Tail and the kittens, especially with the mother cat being so skittish. Tess slipped into the kitchen, turning on just the outdoor light over the side steps. It provided enough light for her to make out the tiny kittens and their very awake mother. Tippy Tail stared at her with half-closed eyes in that haughty cat-way, but didn't move. Tess shuddered, remembering the gleam of golden eyes last night in the dark cellar.

The carriage house was quiet, and she cast eerie shadows as she moved to the sink. Going back to Boston tonight was the right thing to do, she told herself. She probably hadn't seen a damn thing last night, and she'd kissed Andrew Thorne. She needed to get her bearings. Maybe she wasn't cut out for owning a country house.

She turned on the balky faucet and splashed water on her face. She breathed, leaning over the sink, water still dripping from her face. She could use the warm spring evening, wine and chocolate chip cookies as an excuse for what had happened between them. Take Andrew off the hook, as well. The conditions were ripe for a kiss.

But talk about precipitous, she thought with a long, cathartic sigh. She liked to trust her instincts in her work, but they weren't necessarily reliable when it came to men. With her design work, she would always go with her instincts, see where they led her, because they were grounded in her experience and education, her success. Not so with her relationships. She'd had some good relationships, even if they hadn't lasted, but some notoriously rotten ones, too, especially in the past few years. Now she was more carefree—or supposed to be. Her father and Davey said she'd gone from being too impulsive to too picky. But what did they know?

She dried her face with a paper towel and touched her fingers to her mouth. And smiled. It had been a hell of a kiss.

She glanced back at the cat. "Couldn't you at least give the box in the bathroom a try?"

Maybe the night on her own would inspire Tippy Tail to depart from Tess's camp bed. Tess would be back in the morning. She'd search the cellar and identify what she'd seen that had transformed itself, at least in her mind, into a skeleton. She wasn't cutting and running.

She switched off the lights and went outside, thought about knocking on Andrew's door and taking up his offer of a guest room. But that would be a mistake. She needed to get herself back to familiar territory and process the past twenty-four hours, not set herself up for even more to sort out.

The wind gusted, whistling in the trees. Even in the dark, she could see the white-and-pale-lavender blossoms on the lilac hedge whipping around in the stiff breeze. She shivered and jumped off the steps. Time to clear out.

There was a loud creak and a *whomp*.

Her heart raced. She stopped, not moving. What the hell was that?

The bulkhead door. She relaxed slightly. Davey must not have secured it properly and the wind had blown it up and back down again. The latch, she recalled, was in rough shape. The thing probably hadn't been used in years.

But what if she was wrong?

She doubled back and unlocked the kitchen door, ran inside and dumped her mason jar of lilacs into the sink. She took the jar with her back outside, slowing her pace. Her eyes were reasonably adjusted to the darkness.

It couldn't be a ghost. Ghosts didn't use the damn bulkhead. They could go through the cracks in the walls. They were *ghosts*.

She opened her car door, figuring that whatever she did, it would be with a gas pedal under her foot. She set her mason jar on the passenger seat and snatched up her

cell phone. Maybe she should just call it a day and get
the damn police over here. Tell them she thought she'd
seen a skeleton last night, heard something tonight, and
let them have a look.

Harley Beckett came through the lilacs, and Tess
dropped the cell phone and grabbed her mason jar. "Was
that you I heard?" She slid out from behind the wheel,
back onto her gravel driveway with both her jar and her
cell phone. "You're lucky I didn't throw my jar at you."

"Back inside." His expression was dead serious, his
tone uncompromising. He pointed to the kitchen door.
"Go."

Tess didn't move. "Why? What's going on?"

"I heard something. Back inside. I'm not arguing
with you."

"It was the bulkhead door. The wooden latch is rotted."

She could see him gritting his teeth. "At least wait
in your damn car."

"No. I'm going with you." She proceeded past him
into the grass, then stopped, handing him her mason
jar. "Here, you're the ex-cop. You'll know how to use
this better than I will."

"I'd rather have a .38."

But he took the jar and apparently gave up on con-
vincing her to do what he said, because he pushed ahead
of her without a word. They walked through the tall
grass between her yard and the lilacs, their fragrant
scent overpowering now, strangely disquieting.

As Tess had anticipated, the bulkhead door was unlatched, and another strong gust lifted it an inch or two,
then banged it back down again.

"My father and Davey must have left it like this," she said.

Harl eyed her, his expression intense as he apparently considered the situation and her role. He wouldn't necessarily top her list of people she'd want looking after one of her kids. He pointed to her. "Hand me your cell phone."

"Why? You're not calling the police, are you?"

"Haviland, you're a pain in the ass. I don't know what Andrew sees in you. Give me the phone."

She handed it over. "What did you hear? Do you think someone was back here, sneaking around in my cellar?" She took a breath, the taciturn nature of Jedidiah Thorne's descendants enough to unravel anyone. "I'm beginning to think this place *is* haunted."

"I'm calling Andrew." Using what he had left of his right thumb, he banged out a number. "Thorne? Harl. She's fine. We'll be right over." He clicked off the phone and handed it back to her. "Let's go."

"No way. I'm going back to Boston. It was the *wind*. I see now where Dolly gets her active imagination, from you and her father."

Harl snatched the cell phone out of her hand, hit redial. "She's arguing. I'll come stay with Dolly. You come here and haul her ass over. My woman-hauling days are long gone."

Tess set her jaw. "I'll be gone before he gets here."

She had him, and he knew it. Unless he used physical force, he couldn't stop her. "All right. Good. Go."

"You can't expect me to stick around out here with two strange men—"

"Nope. You're being smart. Get in your car and go."

She eyed him suspiciously. He didn't have the subtlety or patience to try persuasion, but this was giving up too easily. "What are you going to do?"

"I've got a chest of drawers I need to finish painting."

A flat-out lie, and they both knew it. There was nothing she could do. She wasn't telling him about the skeleton, not now, not here. What if it had been him she'd heard, trying to sneak into the bulkhead? He wouldn't have known she'd doubled back to lock her door. After all, what did she know about Harley Beckett? Or Andrew Thorne, for that matter.

She had no good options.

These two men had no more reason to trust her than she did them. Less. She'd lied to them. What would they think if she drove out of here and Harl went down to her cellar and found the skeleton?

At least she was well aware that kissing Andrew had no bearing on anything.

"Call me if it turns out there was someone out here," Tess said, and gave Harl her cell phone number as she started toward her car. She glanced back at him. "But it was the wind."

He said, "Tess, I have your cell phone."

"Well, damn it, give it to me."

He tossed it to her, studying her closely. "You want your mason jar back, too?"

"No, you can keep it."

Her cell phone rang in her hand. She clicked it on, and Andrew said, "Drive carefully."

She almost caved—but she couldn't tell him about the skeleton. Not here in the dark, with Harley Beckett watching her every move, suspicious, not after the scare she'd just had. She couldn't rely on instincts, not this time. She had to *think*.

"I will."

"I can't leave Dolly here alone, not if there's even a chance there was someone out there. Harl doesn't want to call the police?"

She lowered the phone and asked him. "Harl, do you want to call the police?"

"To do what, fix the latch on your bulkhead?"

She returned to Andrew, edging her way to the car. "He says no."

"Tess," he said softly, "what happened last night?"

"Snakes." She cleared her throat, sticking to her story even if she knew he didn't believe it, never had. She'd tell him the truth when she could, not now. "I was worried about snakes."

She climbed in behind the wheel, got out her keys, tried two before she got the right one into the ignition. Andrew hadn't yet hung up. Neither had she.

"Tess."

She licked her lips, her throat burning. "I'll be back in the morning."

Silence.

"Tell Dolly that Tippy Tail ate all the food she brought her."

She clicked off and backed out of the driveway, wondering how long it would take before he and his cousin, both or one at a time, searched her cellar. Would they wait until daylight?

What if they already knew a skeleton was there and decided to move it? What if they'd put it there? What if one had and the other didn't know about it?

She was getting carried away. They wouldn't be making such a big deal about why she'd screamed last night if they had any responsibility for the skeleton. They'd get her out of town as fast and quietly as possible, then make their move. They wouldn't invite her to dinner. Andrew wouldn't have kissed her.

What if they were suspicious of *her?*

Her mind was racing. She couldn't think coherently.

She pulled in to a well-lit gas station on a busy main road and called Susanna Galway.

"Susanna? Good, you're home."

"Where else would I be on a Saturday night? What's up? How's the haunted carriage house?"

Tess couldn't get a word out. Her throat was so constricted, and suddenly she couldn't seem to get any air. She made a choking, gurgling sound.

"Tess?"

"I found a skeleton in my cellar."

The words came in a rush, and Susanna sighed. "Well, damn. Human?"

"I think so."

"You *think* so? What do the police say?"

"I don't know, I haven't called them."

"Their number is 911. Easy to remember."

"Susanna…"

"I'm hanging up. You call me after you've talked to them."

"There are complications—"

"Ghosts, I know. And you're not sure what the hell you saw. You don't want people thinking you're a weenie or the sort of woman who conjures skeletons out of thin air. Yeah, I know all the complications. You've also got a rich eccentric who's been missing for a year. *Call the police.*"

She hung up.

Tess stared at her dead cell phone. Then she dialed the police.

Thirteen

❧❧❧

"A skeleton? Hell, I was hoping for buried treasure."

No one took well to Harl's dubious sense of humor. Andrew glowered at him, but Harl shrugged, unrepentant. They were all on Andrew's back porch. Harl, Andrew, two cops—and Tess. Andrew didn't think she looked the least bit contrite. She'd cleared out, called the police and met them back here, before he and Harl had had a chance to work out who'd do the first search of her cellar. Harl took no pains to hide his flashlight and the pick and shovel he'd collected from the toolshed.

"You go on," he told Andrew now. "I'll stay here with Dolly. I've already done the dead-body-in-the-basement thing in my day."

The officers, two regular patrolmen on the small Beacon-by-the-Sea force, had already questioned them about the flapping bulkhead. Harl stuck to a recitation of the facts, without editorializing or speculating. He'd heard something earlier in the evening and investigated, discovering Tess and the unlatched bulkhead catching in the wind. Nothing else.

Andrew had nothing to report. Given the position of

his house, he hadn't heard the bulkhead, or whatever it was, but had spotted Harl out back. They'd conferred briefly, and Andrew waited on the back porch with the phone in case the police were needed.

"I couldn't leave my daughter here alone," he'd said without looking at Tess.

Neither he nor Harl mentioned last night's bloody-murder scream, snakes or ghosts.

Tess led the police across his yard, taking the long way around the lilacs. Andrew followed at several paces. A skeleton. For the love of God.

"How did you manage to sleep last night after finding human remains?" the older of the two officers asked. His name was Paul Alvarez, and he had a good reputation, even by Harl's standards.

"I didn't," Tess answered.

"You'd convinced yourself it was a ghost?"

"I didn't know what I saw. I still don't. Maybe it was nothing. I *hope* it was nothing."

Even now, Andrew thought, she wasn't ready to commit. He could understand. The eye might see a human skeleton in the dark while the mind refused to accept it, especially in a haunted house once owned by an eccentric heir no one had heard from in a year.

"Well, let's take a look."

Paul Alvarez led the way down the bulkhead. The younger cop, Mike O'Toole, was on the pale side, looking as if he very much believed in ghosts as he and Alvarez made their way into the dirt cellar. Andrew stood in the doorway to the dirt cellar, Tess a few steps inside. She was agitated, arms crossed on her chest as if to keep herself from shaking, but spoke calmly, with determination. She pointed deep into the cellar. "It was back there, by that old bed frame."

Andrew glanced around at the cellar with its low ceilings, dirt floor, water pipes, heating ducts, old furnace, junk. Jed's carriage house had potential, but it was a money pit. What had Ike been thinking when he gave this place to Tess? Despite his many flaws, Ike wasn't the sort Andrew would expect to bury someone in a dirt cellar—or end up buried in a cellar himself like a dead skunk. That he didn't deserve.

But if it was Ike, he hadn't buried himself down here.

Andrew shook off the thought and all its implications. First things first. Maybe Tess's imagination had gotten the better of her. He wanted to be in there with shovel and pick himself, poking around in the dirt.

O'Toole grabbed an old rake handle and ran it around over the dirt floor. Tess glanced back at Andrew, her eyes as pale a blue as he'd ever seen. "It's not there." She sounded tense, not relieved. "I was so sure…"

She pushed deeper into the cellar, pointing, squatting herself and searching. Andrew watched her, not the police. She was in control of herself, surprised and tense at finding nothing. Alvarez and O'Toole expanded their search, scanning the rest of the cellar with their high-powered flashlights.

There was no skeleton. No skulls, no bones. Nothing.

"Maybe someone snatched it," Tess said. "Maybe that was what the noise was."

The two cops weren't going there. "It's an empty, run-down, old house with a bad reputation. It was your first night here, you were down here alone under difficult circumstances…" Alvarez shrugged. "Are you sure it was a human skull you saw?"

She sighed. "Yes."

"But that doesn't mean that's what it was," he said.

"No, you're right, it doesn't, especially under the circumstances. That's why I didn't say anything right from the start—I wasn't sure myself."

They came out into the laundry room. O'Toole's color was better. Alvarez said, "There's not much more we can do at this point. I'm sorry. If anything changes, let us know."

"Fair enough. Thanks."

When they got back to Andrew's house, Harl was still on the porch with his pick and shovel. Andrew figured his cousin wouldn't rely on a police search of the cellar. He'd have to take a look himself before he'd be satisfied.

Tess, still pale and edgy, finished up with the police. After they left, she said without looking at Andrew, "I should get along back to Boston."

"Not so fast." He pulled out a chair at the table on the porch. Harl had put out two beers. Andrew opened one and set it on the table in front of the chair. "Sit."

Harl tilted back in his chair and eyed Tess, who looked ready to bolt. "I wouldn't argue. I've seen that look in his eyes before, about two seconds before he hit a guy over the head with a beer bottle. Five stitches."

Andrew gritted his teeth. "Harl."

"It's true."

"It's not true. He didn't need five stitches, and it was self-defense."

Harl shrugged. "So's this."

With a groan of frustration or confusion, or both, Tess swooped down onto the chair. Her body was rigid. She crossed her arms on her chest and sat at the very end of the chair, as if she'd spring up and out of there any second. She leveled her pale blue eyes on Andrew. "I know I should have mentioned the skeleton sooner."

"Yeah, no shit," Harl said.

Andrew stayed focused on Tess. "Why didn't you?"

"Because I'd intended to check the cellar myself to make sure before I told anyone. I didn't want to upset people or end up looking like an idiot if it was nothing. When Davey and my father showed up and didn't find anything, I decided to wait until morning and bring a friend." She didn't flinch at his hard gaze. "I procrastinated."

"Now what?"

She lifted her shoulders and let them fall, exhaling, suddenly looking tired. "Now? I don't know. I guess it's more likely I didn't see anything than someone slipped into my cellar while I was at dinner and stole human remains. It's easier, and more logical, to believe what we heard was just the bulkhead catching in the wind."

Harl snorted. "If you'd said something sooner—"

"But I didn't."

Andrew stayed on his feet, angry with himself, with her. But he shoved his anger down deep, concentrated on the problem at hand. "Did you think Harl or I might have something to do with it?"

"I had a million reasons, all of which seemed to make good sense at the time. Look, I can't undo what I did. In hindsight, maybe I should have taken you down into the cellar last night and had you verify what I saw, or at least called the police."

Harl suddenly rose, grabbed his shovel and pick and tore open the screen door. "The hell with it. What's done is done. Come daylight, I'll have a look down there my-self. Andrew?"

"Dolly's going to a friend's house in the morning. I'll be over."

"Tess?"

She swallowed and licked her lips, outwardly com-posed, but Andrew could only guess what was going on inside her. "I can be back here early—"

"You're in no condition to drive," Harl said quietly. "Stay in the guest room. Trust me, Andrew doesn't have a bunch of bones stuck in the closets around here." He grinned, winked. "I've checked."

"That's not it—"

"It doesn't matter. Stay."

He left, the door banging shut after him. Tess jumped, startled, on edge. Andrew could see how tough the past twenty-four hours had been on her, trying to sort out what to do about what she'd seen—or thought she'd seen. He tried to soften, but found he couldn't. He was pissed as hell. But badgering her over what she now knew she should have done wouldn't get them anywhere, and it wouldn't make him feel any better to make her feel worse.

"I convinced myself it was a nineteenth-century horse thief," she said, not looking at him now. "Then when you mentioned at lunch that Jedidiah was lost at sea, I seized on the idea that maybe he didn't die at sea. Maybe the bones were his."

"You're sure they were human?"

She nodded. "I took anatomy in art school."

"Did you think this was all the work of a ghost?"

Her chin tilted up, catching the light, and he could see her color had improved. "It still could be. Maybe whoever's haunting the carriage house makes people see bones in the dirt, skulls, dead people."

"But you don't believe in ghosts," Andrew said.

"I believe in what I saw. It doesn't matter if it was a ghost, some kind of hallucination or real human remains. Well, it does matter, but that's not my point. I saw what I saw. Whatever it was."

"What would you have done if the police had found your skeleton?"

She managed a smile. "Fainted."

"Bullshit. You didn't faint when you practically fell on top of it last night when you were alone."

"Let's say this is the scenario that I both wanted and dreaded—that the police didn't find anything. It means I get to look like a nitwit, but it also means whatever I saw last night isn't there anymore." She took a swallow of her beer and got to her feet, steadier if not any less on edge. "I should get going."

"I don't think so." Andrew pointed to her beer. "I'll put a call in and have you picked up for driving under the influence."

"I've had two sips!"

"Take a look."

She held up her bottle and seemed surprised when she saw it was almost empty. Under ordinary circumstances, one beer wouldn't be a problem, but tonight wasn't ordinary—she was beyond the point of no return, and she knew it. "Damn. Your cat's still occupying my bed. I suppose I could borrow a couple of blankets and sleep in my car."

"I told you, I have a guest room."

Her eyes were steady on him, almost cool. "I'm still invited?"

He remembered the feel of her body against his and wondered if that was what she was thinking about, more than her nonexistent—or missing—skeleton. "Yes, but no more lies."

"If you didn't believe my snake story, what makes you think you'd have believed I saw a skull in the dirt?"

"Tess."

She breathed in, no hint she was the slightest bit afraid of him, how he'd react to her—or even particularly wracked with guilt over withholding what she'd seen last night. "I did the best I could under rotten circumstances. Look, I know you're ticked off because of the kiss, because it seems to you I should have come clean before we went that far—well, let's just chalk it up as one of those things. It happened. We don't need to make anything of it."

That was not the right response. She saw her mistake instantly, but she was too late. He caught an arm around her, pulled her to him. "It wasn't just one of those things, not for me." His voice was low and deadly, barely under control, and his mouth found hers again, a fierceness in him he couldn't explain, couldn't deny. His mouth opened, his tongue sliding between her teeth, his body pulsing, throbbing. He was in a dangerous mood. The taste of her, the feel of her, only inflamed him more. He slipped his hands under her shirt, eased his palms over her hot, smooth skin. "I could take you now. Here. Do you understand?"

She nodded, her eyes gleaming with passion. "Yes."

She put her hands on his forearms at her sides, but instead of pushing him away, she urged them slowly up inside her shirt, until his thumbs were under her breasts. He eased them over her bra, brushing her nipples.

"You don't know what you're doing," he said, his voice raw, his body on fire.

"I do know."

This time, her mouth found his, her lips already parted. He pushed his hands back down her sides, wanted to scoop her up and carry her inside, but fought back the need. He made himself draw away. "I'll make up the guest room."

She tugged her shirt back down and pushed a slender, strong hand through her short curls. "Are you sure that's a good idea?"

He smiled ever so slightly. "I think the guest room's an excellent idea."

For the love of Christ.

Lauren staggered into Richard's study and poured herself a scotch. No water, no ice. She didn't want to bother with a glass, just drink straight from the decanter, but knew her husband could wander in at any moment. He was due back from dinner with friends. She'd left early, pleading a headache. Since they'd arrived in separate cars, it wasn't a problem.

She'd planned everything so carefully, just not Tess returning to the carriage house that way.

The whiskey splashed over her hand. She was shaking uncontrollably. Her teeth chattered against the glass as she gulped, the scotch burning on its way down.

Ike.

She wanted to scream his name. She wanted to sob and beat her fists against the wall, smash glasses, throw over furniture. Her brother was *dead*. She'd hoped, prayed, pleaded with God that she wasn't right.

He was in the trunk of her car in a black plastic trash bag.

Her brother.

Dead.

Just as she'd known he was since that day he'd told her he was off to the carriage house and would see her later.

She sank onto the leather chair, spilling scotch on the arm. It beaded, and she flicked it off with her fingertips then licked them. They still tasted of her surgical gloves.

Her brother, dead in the carriage house cellar.

She hadn't been sure until tonight. She'd guessed... known. But this was different. Now it was real.

"Lauren?"

Richard's voice penetrated her like a hot, sharp knife. She fell back against the chair, wanting to slip down to the floor, through the rug, between the cracks in the cherry floorboards, all the way down to the basement, where she could lie in the dark stillness until death claimed her. Who would know? Who would care?

"Lauren, are you still up?"

She could hear his footsteps out in the hall. She straightened, wondering if he'd smell the dank carriage house cellar on her, if he'd smell death.

He stood in the doorway. "There you are. Darling, have you heard? I didn't want you to hear it without me here—"

"Hear what?" She rallied, noticed her hands weren't shaking as she drank more scotch.

Richard came toward her, his expression filled with concern and compassion. He took her glass away, as if she might not handle what he had to tell her. "The po-

lice called on my way home. Lauren, they've been out
to the carriage house."

"Wh-what?"

"Tess Haviland's claimed she found a human skeleton buried in the cellar."

Blood pounded in her head. The room spun. Richard, more gentle than she'd ever seen him, took both
her hands. She thought she might vomit. "What are you
talking about?"

"It's ridiculous. Paul Alvarez said so himself. They
didn't find anything, but he wanted you to know, in case
this woman is up to something."

"What could she be up to?"

"Nothing, I'm sure. That's how the police think,
that's all."

"Ike thought the world of her—"

"I know, I know. It all must have been her imagination. Let's go to bed, shall we? Get rid of that headache
of yours, once and for all?"

"Oh, Richard. I love you, do you know that? You're
the best thing that's ever happened to me." Her eyes
filled with tears, and she felt drunk, stupid, even after a
few sips of scotch. "Will you make love to me tonight?"

"Of course, darling."

She giggled. "'Darling.' That's so retro."

But he took her by both hands, lifted her to her feet
and led her upstairs.

After he made love to his wife, Richard put on his
bathrobe and stood in the shaft of moonlight slanting
in the windows overlooking her gardens. The poodles
were asleep on the white chaise longue. He could have

opened a window screen and pitched them out, one by one.

Sex had steadied him. Centered him. He could think now.

Lauren had fallen asleep. She'd clawed at him, almost drawing blood. They'd never had such raw, unrestrained sex. She'd been uninhibited, almost wanton. He'd responded in kind, exulting in the effect he was having on her. Instead of her usual ladylike shudder when she came, she'd screamed and thrashed.

He could handle Lauren.

It was Tess Haviland who worried him.

Fourteen

❧❧❧

Tess sensed someone was watching her. She rolled over in the twin bed in the guest room and came eye-to-eye with a stuffed black-and-white cat in the hands of Dolly Thorne. The little girl giggled. "Her name's Kitty. I've had her since I was three years old." She was wide-awake, still in her pink pajamas with kittens all over them, her coppery hair tangled. No crown. "Daddy said not to wake you up."

"I'm awake," Tess croaked, squinting at the bedside clock. Seven. Not bad, but she was exhausted. Too much tossing and turning, thinking about kisses and skeletons, kittens in her bed, men and intruders. She struggled not to seem grumpy. "Well. Good morning."

"Will you play stuffed animals with me?"

"I need coffee first. Okay? Your dad's up?"

"Uh-huh. He's taking a shower."

Tess didn't even want to think about it, but before that command reached her sluggish brain, the picture formed of Andrew's lean, taut body naked under a stream of hot water. She'd been awake for all of thirty seconds and already was off on the wrong foot. If she didn't get a grip, today would be just as tumultuous as yesterday. It might be, anyway—Susanna Galway was planning to show up first thing. Tess had called her before going to bed.

"Cops hate missing bodies," Susanna had said. "Of course, they want to believe you didn't see anything."

Tess didn't like the idea of a missing body herself. She focused on Dolly. "Let me pull myself together. Then we can see what's what."

Dolly obviously took this as confirmation Tess would play stuffed animals with her. She ran off skipping, her bare feet padding softly on the rug. Tess threw off her blankets and sat up in the Red Sox T-shirt and flannel boxers she'd worn to bed, struggling to wake up. The guest room was cute, its windows overlooking the ocean. From the old-fashioned flowered wallpaper, she guessed Andrew hadn't gotten around to renovating it yet. White curtains billowed in a cool morning breeze. Tess sat a moment, listening to the surf and the gulls, picturing herself hanging wallpaper with Andrew Thorne.

"Damn," she breathed, shaking off the image.

She could hear him speaking to his daughter down the hall, a scene so ordinary it took Tess's breath away. He and Dolly were a family. She needed to keep her wits about her, not barrel in and mess up the life they'd created for themselves. At least, for someone unaccustomed to dealing with six-year-olds, she thought she was handling herself well with Dolly. She was a cheerful kid, not as combative and outspoken as Tess had been at that age with her own mother's death still so fresh.

She used Dolly's bathroom down the hall, grateful she didn't have to share with Andrew, smell his soap, breathe in the steam from his shower. She picked bath toys out of the tub and opted for a shocking-pink towel with a big yellow fish on it. When she climbed into the shower, she imagined Andrew hearing the water running, picturing her the way she had him.

It had to be the skeleton. She trusted her instincts and impulses when it came to her work, but not men— at least not romantically. She could work with men, argue politics and baseball and otherwise hold her own, but romance, intimacy, falling in love… She shuddered just thinking about how many times she'd stopped at the precipice and decided, "No, not him," and refused to jump.

She dressed in a pair of ratty work jeans and a fresh Red Sox shirt. She and Susanna would check the cellar themselves.

She had breakfast on the back porch with Andrew and Dolly, just cereal, toast and juice, but with the sunlight and the sounds of the ocean, it was perfect. Tess had half hoped she'd see Andrew and wonder what had gotten into her yesterday. Instead she had to admit something about the man set her senses on fire. Even when he was pouring a cup of coffee, she noticed the muscles in his forearms, the angles of his face.

Dolly saw Harl working on her tree house, remembered her new window and scooted off. Tess smiled over the rim of her mug, enjoying her last sips of coffee. "I think I'm off the hook for playing stuffed animals."

"Don't count on it." Andrew sat across the table, studying her with the kind of frank intimacy that said he knew exactly how close they'd come to tearing off their clothes and making love last night. That said he remembered every detail of their kisses. "How are you this morning? Did you get any sleep?"

"Some, thanks. I need to get next door. A friend of mine is coming up this morning."

"I'd like to take another look in your cellar," he said.

She nodded. "Maybe we can figure out what it was my mind turned into a skeleton."

Andrew didn't answer. He was, Tess realized, tight-lipped and controlled by nature, but not a man who missed a thing. Something else for her to remember. She set her mug down, part of her wishing she could stay here all day, going from coffee to iced tea to wine, not doing anything more demanding than playing stuffed animals with a six-year-old.

When they set out across the yard, Dolly ran over, torn between helping Harl finish the window in her tree house and checking on the kittens. Finally, she yelled over her shoulder, "Harl, I'm going over to Tess's house! I'll help you later. Don't worry, okay?"

Harl popped his white head out of the tree house door. "Go on. I'll see if I can manage without you."

She giggled and put her warm little hand into Tess's. "Harl's funny."

"You think so?"

"Yep."

Andrew glanced at Tess as if to say Dolly couldn't be expected to know any better.

They took the long way around the lilacs, and when she saw the carriage house in the morning sun, Tess was struck by its graceful lines and picturesque setting. She could almost forget the police crawling around in her cellar last night. Had there been an intruder? Would the police want to talk to her again today, or anyone else?

Ike Grantham was the previous owner, his sister the director of the Beacon Historic Project and the one who'd given Tess the key. Wouldn't they want to talk to Lauren Montague and at least try to get in touch with Ike?

Only if they believed there might have been a skeleton in her cellar, Tess thought. And they didn't.

She wondered if word of her call to the police had gotten around Beacon-by-the-Sea, if people would understand how she could have at least *thought* she'd stumbled onto human remains in the old Jedidiah Thorne carriage house.

Dolly skipped up the kitchen steps, but Andrew quietly moved in front of her, going in first.

"Oh my God," Dolly screamed, panicked. "They're gone! *Daddy!*"

But he touched her shoulder and pointed into the bathroom. "No, they're not, Dolly. Look. Tippy Tail's moved them into the box."

She placed a palm over her heart dramatically. "Oh my God, they're so cute!"

"Dolly."

She glanced up at him. "I know, I shouldn't say 'Oh my God.'"

"You really shouldn't."

Tess smiled at the father-daughter exchange. She was relieved to have her bed, such as it was, free of Tippy Tail and family. While Andrew and Dolly checked on them, she scooped up the lilacs she'd dumped out in the sink last night in her haste for a weapon, and tossed them into the trash. She glanced around the kitchen. The carriage house needed so much. She liked the idea of a country house, a weekend project, the physical work that would be involved. If the skeleton proved to her satisfaction to be nothing but a figment of her imagination, she could see herself keeping the place.

Then Andrew came out of the bathroom, his sleeves rolled up to his elbows, and she thought, *Maybe not.* Her neighbor could prove to be a bigger complication than whatever it was she'd seen in her cellar.

"Can I name the kittens?" Dolly asked her father in an excited whisper.

"Just for now. The people who adopt them will want to give them their own names."

"I'm naming the black one Midnight," she said.

"Okay, but we're not keeping him."

"What if it's a girl?"

"Then we're not keeping *her.*"

They went back outside, and Dolly got a stick from the lilacs and decided to draw pictures on Tess's driveway while she and Andrew checked out back. In daylight, there was still no clear indication of an intruder. But no forced entry was necessary since the bulkhead only had a broken, rotted wooden latch, no proper lock.

Andrew tested the soft wood with his toe. "Harl's never heard anything back here before last night. Neither have I."

"It wasn't me. I wasn't about to go back down there in the dark."

His gaze settled on her. "What was your relationship with Ike Grantham?"

"He was a client. We were never friends, if that's what you mean. He's so charismatic and intense, it's not that easy to establish firm boundaries with him, but I'd say we did."

"He gave you a historic oceanfront property."

"As payment for work I'd done, and 'oceanfront property' is a stretch. You know Ike. He's eccentric and impulsive. That's why it took me a year to get up here—I never really believed this place was mine. For all I knew he'd show up on my doorstep and demand my firstborn child or something."

Andrew nodded, removing his foot from the bulkhead. "Ike's not easy to understand."

"What do you think's happened to him?"

"It makes no difference to me. I haven't seen much of him since Joanna's death."

"Then you weren't friends before—"

"No."

He started back toward the driveway, and Tess exhaled, realizing suddenly that she'd been holding her breath. Joanna Thorne had died a terrible death, and Andrew wouldn't be normal if he didn't to some degree blame Ike Grantham for encouraging her. He didn't cause the avalanche, and he didn't make Joanna's decision for her. But Tess remembered how adept Ike was, how incredibly persuasive, at making people work outside their comfort zone. Maybe he'd led Joanna Thorne to believe she was ready for Mount McKinley when she wasn't.

Tess's cell phone rang in her jeans pocket, startling her but mercifully interrupting her train of thought.

"I'm in Gloucester," Susanna said. "I'll be there in twenty minutes."

"You don't need directions?"

"Davey drew me a map. He says he knows pipes, I know money, and I should take a look at this place. You've got him worried this time. Ghosts, nineteenth-century duelists, the neighbors."

"You didn't tell him about the skeleton, did you?"

"Hell, no. Twenty minutes, okay?"

"I'll be here."

Andrew glanced back at her. "Didn't tell who?"

"My godfather. You know, it's bad enough if it gets around Beacon that I called the police about a nonexistent skeleton in my cellar. If it gets around the neighborhood, I'll never live it down. Never."

"Your friend's from your neighborhood?"

"Her grandmother is. Susanna and I share office space in Boston. She understands how I grew up, the only child of a widowed father in a tight-knit blue-collar neighborhood."

He smiled almost imperceptibly. "Nothing stops you. Maybe you learned that growing up the way you did."

"I suppose. With my father and Davey in my face all the time, I learned to think for myself. And losing my mother so young—she taught me that we all only have right now, this moment." Tess looked up at the sky, picturing her mother sitting on the rocks by the ocean, just listening to the surf. It was one of the clearest, most reassuring images she had of her. She shifted back to Andrew and grinned suddenly. "On the other hand, it means I'm not very good with five-year plans, much to Susanna's distress."

When they reached the driveway, Harl was thrashing his way through the lilacs. "I'm taking a chainsaw to these things." He picked a leaf off his beard. "You two want me to keep an eye on Dolly while you take another look in the cellar?"

"I have a friend coming," Tess said.

"So? I'll send her down." He went over, plopped down on the steps and took Dolly's stick and drew a tic-tac-toe on the driveway. "I'll be O."

Andrew touched Tess's arm. "Let's go, unless you think he'll scare off your friend."

"Susanna? She's not afraid of anything."

"No, no," Dolly was saying. "You can't do two O's in a row."

Harl frowned at her as if he didn't know any better. "Why not?"

"It's *cheating*."

"Oh." He drew fresh tic-tac-toe lines and handed the stick over to Dolly. "Then you go first."

Taking that as their cue, Tess shot ahead of Andrew and headed back to the bulkhead.

The cellar again produced nothing. No skeleton, no evidence one had been snatched, no sign of an intruder, not even anything to suggest what Tess had actually seen the other night that her mind had transformed into a human skull.

She wasn't surprised. She sat with Susanna out on the kitchen steps, drinking the last of her soda. Susanna had arrived while Harl and Dolly were still playing tic-tac-toe, and he'd sent her down to the cellar with Tess and Andrew. They were all back on the other side of the lilacs now—Andrew, Harl and Dolly. Tippy Tail and kittens were asleep in their box in the bathroom. Tess could almost delude herself into thinking all was well, but her instincts said otherwise.

Susanna took a long drink of her soda and pressed the cold can to her cheek. "The way I see it, you have four scenarios. One, there was no skeleton. That's the option we all like best, no matter how embarrassing to you. It's the one the police will fly with until they have reason not to. Two, there was a skeleton, but it's a ghost. That's probably our second-best option. People'll believe it or they won't. It doesn't matter. It's a ghost, and that's that."

"Why would a ghost turn itself into a skeleton?" Tess asked reflectively, her own soda untouched.

"Why wouldn't it? Ghosts are ghosts. They do their own thing." Susanna leaned back against the step above her and stretched out her long, lean legs. "Third option, there was a skeleton, and it's some poor bastard from a million years ago."

"My nineteenth-century horse thief theory."

"Or Jedidiah Thorne didn't die at sea."

Tess nodded since it was a scenario she'd considered herself. "But who'd care enough to steal his remains?"

"His descendants might. Maybe they know something we don't about how he died and want to keep it their little secret."

"It doesn't wash with what I know about the Thornes. They're not exactly North Shore blue-bloods who want to protect the family name. Jedidiah was already convicted of murder." Tess sighed, hating discussing something so real and potentially tragic as a dead body buried in her cellar in such a clinical fashion. "The important thing isn't what I *want,* it's learning what the truth is."

"You know the fourth scenario," Susanna said.

"Ike."

"Yep. That's the one no one likes. He ends up dead in the carriage house cellar. Whoever buried him there doesn't realize you own the place. You pop up here, push comes to shove, they slip in and dig him up."

Tess didn't want to give this fourth option any credence. She set the soda can on her knee and watched the condensation on the outside drip onto her jeans. "Someone should try to locate him."

"That would be the thing to do, yes."

"One would think his sister—"

"One would."

Tess glanced at her friend. "If there was a skeleton down there and someone stole it last night, I could have put myself in a dangerous position by saying I saw it. I should have pretended I didn't see a thing."

"Too late. You screamed bloody murder. The neighbors knew you'd seen something. It'd be worse if you didn't mention it. Better to have everyone know. Now if someone runs you off the road or something, we'll all think you were right about the skeleton, after all."

"This is supposed to make me feel better?"

Susanna shrugged, pragmatic. "No, but that's not why I'm up here. By the way," she added, easing gracefully to her feet, "why didn't you tell me about the guy next door sooner?"

"What's to tell?"

She raised both eyebrows and shook her head. "No wonder Davey and your dad worry about you. Tess, *I* noticed this guy, and I have made it a policy not to notice men. He's your lean, tight-lipped, rock-ribbed Yankee. I can see him dumping tea in the harbor and hopping a whaling ship with Ahab, killing a wife-beater in a duel." She polished off the last of her soda. "And he spent more time in the cellar watching you than hunting a skeleton."

"Does that mean you don't suspect him of offing Ike and burying him in the cellar?"

"No."

"He has a six-year-old daughter."

Susanna was silent.

"I slept in his guest room last night," Tess added.

"And?"

"There's a certain attraction at work between us."

"No kidding. Davey already told me, you know."

"Davey? He saw us together for maybe three seconds—"

"All it takes."

Tess gave up. Even Susanna's clients knew not to expect false comfort from her, just her bald assessment of the facts. Her reality checks could leave clients teetering, but they knew where they stood, what they had to do. Often, they knew it before they sat down with her, but needed that blunt back-and-forth with her to admit it.

"Tell me what you know about dead bodies," Tess said.

Susanna cast her a calculating look, vivid green eyes narrowed. "What makes you think I know anything about dead bodies? I know money."

"Your ex-husband's a Texas Ranger. You must have picked up a few things."

"My ex-husband's a snake in the grass," she said calmly.

Tess judiciously remained silent.

Susanna groaned. "Okay, okay. I suppose you want to know how long it takes a corpse to turn into a skeleton?"

"Pretty much."

"For this, I deserve a walk on the beach. Shall we?"

Susanna refused to say another word until they'd crossed the main road, climbed over the rocks and were walking along the cold, wet sand in their bare feet. She breathed in the salt air. "Best to talk about dead bodies when the air is good."

"I took anatomy in art school, but we didn't get into this sort of detail."

"Flesh rotting off bones, you mean? It didn't come up in my money classes, either." She stopped a moment, curling up her toes in the sand. "I missed the ocean in San Antonio, I have to say, although there's nothing quite like a Texas sunset. All right. Dead bodies. Conditions make a difference. A body left out in the open in hot, wet conditions would decompose rapidly. Cool, dry conditions delay decomposition. Usually. Take Ben Franklin and company down in Old Granary."

"Ben Franklin's buried in Philadelphia," Tess said. "His parents are buried in Old Granary."

"Whatever. Point is, the ground there was wet and spongy. That would speed things up."

Tess grimaced. "Gross."

"You asked."

"I know. What else?"

"An unclothed body tends to decompose faster than one that's clothed, especially if it's tight clothing."

"The mummy effect."

"Was your body—"

"I didn't see any clothes," Tess said quickly. "That doesn't mean there weren't any."

"If I buried a body in a cellar and wanted to hurry up decomposition, I'd strip it. It'd be a pain in the neck, but you have to figure the whole business wouldn't be much fun. I'd take the time."

And unclothed remains might take longer to identify, buying time for whoever had—what? Tess shuddered at the thought—the real possibility—that she'd stumbled on a murder victim.

"Most of this is common sense," Susanna went on. "We've all seen dead deer and skunks and such on the side of the road. It's a different picture in summer than in winter, in Florida than in Wyoming. You follow?"

"Oh, yes. I follow."

"As I recall, children and diseased bodies tend to decompose faster than healthy adults." She let the tide wash over her ankles, yelped at the cold water and dashed back to the warm, dry sand, then went back for more. "Also, fat people go faster than skinny people."

"I don't even want to think about that one. It's disgusting."

"Think of it as natural. Mutilated bodies also decompose faster. Makes sense, don't you think?"

Tess walked along the sand, the cold water lap-ping at her feet as she thought about the natural process of decomposition occurring on a corpse buried in a shallow grave in the carriage house cellar. What she saw the other night *had* to be her imagi-nation. "What would slow decomposition?" she asked quietly.

"Dry, cool conditions, as I said. And bogs. If you get dumped in a bog, your body can last for ages." She shrugged, matter-of-fact. "Anthropologists love bogs."

Tess breathed out. "Charming."

"A lot of people think lime speeds decomposition, and it can, but only if the body's wet. Otherwise it can slow the process. And arsenic. Arsenic slows decomposition."

"There's lime in the cellar. For the lilacs."

"I noticed."

"Could a body buried in the carriage house cellar

last March, when Ike took off, decompose between then and now?"

"Yes."

Tess couldn't speak, felt her head spinning. She was so cold that the seawater seemed warm under her feet.

"Are you going to barf?" Susanna asked.

"No. I'll be okay."

"You want me to throw water on your face?"

"I'm fine."

"Tess, I want you to listen to me. Whatever you saw the other night is dead or nonexistent. If they're dead, they know how they died, and they know how they ended up in that cellar. *You* don't need to know." Susanna grabbed Tess by the shoulders, her thick, black curls hanging down her shoulders, her eyes bright, intense. "Nobody gets buried in a cellar for a good reason."

Tess nodded grimly. "I know."

"Chances are there's no truth to be found out and justice to be served here. Even if there is, it's not your job."

"That's what I keep telling myself." Her voice was quiet, calmer than she'd anticipated. "Right now, I'm ending up looking like some hysterical nut."

Susanna gave her a pointed look. "Better than ending up buried in someone else's cellar."

Tess managed a smile. "True."

"Now, are you feeling better? You're not going to throw up or faint?"

"I'm *fine*."

"Good, because Ahab's walking across the rocks."

"You're thinking of Ishmael. Ahab's the one with the missing leg."

Susanna grimaced at the approaching figure of Andrew Thorne. "If this guy favors his ancestors, I can see why Moby Dick wanted a piece of Ahab. Talk about your take-no-prisoners type. Can't you see him on deck with a harpoon?"

"The whaling industry did incredible damage—"

"Tess. I'm not talking about endangered species. I'm talking about your neighbor. You've seen him with his daughter. I haven't."

"What are you saying?"

Her expression turned serious, less animated. "I'm saying you should be careful before you end up way over your head in very deep, cold water."

Andrew arrived, squinting at the two women in the bright sun. "Am I interrupting?"

Susanna Galway gave him her brightest, prettiest smile, which Tess had seen melt even Davey Ahearn and Jim Haviland. "We were just discussing nineteenth-century American literature. Doesn't this place make you think of Herman Melville?"

Tess could see Andrew didn't believe Susanna. He knew they'd been talking about him. But he said, "I can see how it would." Then he turned to Tess. "Word's out about last night. Lauren Montague's here."

Susanna dropped her shoes onto the sand and tucked one foot in at a time. "Time I headed back to Boston. Tess?"

"Later," she said, aware, as Susanna would be, of Andrew's eyes on her.

"You'll call me?"

Tess nodded and slipped on her own shoes, remembering running on the beach as a child, flying a kite, listening to her mother tell tales of New England history, her father watching her every move, knowing that their time together was short. She felt as she did then, aware of what was going on, yet determined to pretend as if her life were normal and nothing bad would happen.

Fifteen

In daylight, Lauren was even more impressed with what she'd done last night. It was a miracle she hadn't been caught. She breathed in the scent of lilacs, now, forever, mingled with the stench of death. Of Ike. Her brother. Dear God, if only he'd let Joanna Thorne find her own way out of her restlessness and depression. If only he'd left Beacon-by-the-Sea after her death instead of hanging around, cheerful, dreaming big dreams, on the prowl for someone else to idolize him.

For a while, Lauren had been sure it was Tess Haviland her brother had chosen as his new project. Yet, as the young graphic designer walked up the carriage house driveway, Andrew Thorne beside her, the hem of her jeans damp and sandy, her short blond curls whipped by the wind and her cheeks decidedly pale, Lauren knew it couldn't be so. Ike went for the vulnerable, the depressed, the ones who wouldn't act on their own dreams without him. That wasn't this woman. It might not have been Joanna, if he'd left well enough alone.

Andrew couldn't have meant to kill him.

Lauren smiled at him, but he didn't smile back, not out of rudeness but obliviousness, she decided. If he'd killed Ike in a premeditated fashion, she'd never have tried to protect him. As it was, she wondered what he must be feeling now, knowing the police hadn't found Ike's remains. Fear? Relief? Anger? He was impossible to predict.

"Hello, Tess," she said graciously. "I hope I haven't come at a bad time. I heard about last night. How absolutely horrible for you."

"Well, it looks as if there never was any skeleton. Luckily."

Lauren nodded. "Indeed. Better this turned out to be a false alarm than an actual dead body."

"Have you talked to the police?"

"Paul Alvarez called. My husband had already heard." She moved away from the lilacs, the sun warm on her face. "Paul wants me to get in touch with my brother, but it's not that easy. Seven years ago, Ike took off for nine months without telling me where he was, without even so much as sending me a Christmas card. It's just the way he is."

Andrew leaned against Tess's rusted car, but Lauren wasn't fooled. She knew he was taking in everything, wondered if he'd guessed what she'd done for him. But it wasn't just *for* him. It was the right thing to do. Her brother had taken his wife, left his daughter motherless. If Andrew had lost his temper, reverted to his waterfront brawling days, who could blame him? A jury, perhaps, the way they'd blamed Jedidiah Thorne over a century ago, no matter how much Benjamin Morse had deserved his fate. Truth and justice could be so complicated, she thought.

Tess was frowning. "Are the police going to track him down?"

"Why should they go to such trouble?"

"Ms. Montague—"

"Lauren," she corrected with a smile.

"Lauren, Ike was one of my clients, and *I* want to know he's okay."

"Then find him. Be my guest. I stopped spinning to Ike's tune a long, long time ago." Her tone was cool, but she felt hot inside, out of control, the way she had last night with Richard. She was bruised today, aching, and yet satisfied. "If he wants to come back, he'll come back. If he doesn't, he won't."

"What if he can't?"

"You mean, what if it was Ike's remains you saw? What if someone killed him, buried him in the carriage house cellar and then dug him up when you took an interest in your property?" Lauren smiled again, gentle despite the lava flows burning through her insides. "That's too far-fetched for me, I'm afraid. And the police, too, I might add. If it's something you want to pursue, be my guest."

"Do you have any idea where Ike might be?" Tess asked.

Lauren sighed. "No, I really don't." She softened deliberately, yet could feel things cooling slightly inside her, as if the outward demeanor she'd maintained for the past year was all at once merging with the inner turmoil she'd been feeling, the ambivalence, the desperate uncertainty over what she should do. She plucked a lilac blossom and touched it to her nose. "Look, I don't mean to sound callous. If I, in any way, even for a second, believed you saw my brother's remains, I'd be sitting on the police until they got moving. I'd hire my own detectives."

"I didn't mean to imply—"

"I know," Lauren said, neatly cutting her off. "Please don't apologize. By the way, how do you like the carriage house?"

"Except for seeing things, just fine."

Tess was stiff, unrelenting and, Lauren knew, convinced of what she'd seen, no matter that she couldn't prove it or even tell herself there was no chance she'd made a mistake. "Please," Lauren said, "don't hesitate to use the Beacon Historic Project archives if you wish to research the carriage house. It has an amazing history, as I'm sure you already know. Stop by anytime."

Tess nodded stiffly. "Thanks."

"Andrew," Lauren said, moving toward him. "I've parked my car at your house. I'd like to say hi to Dolly while I'm here. You'll walk with me?"

He acquiesced, but only after a quick, concerned look at Tess. Something was going on there, Lauren decided. Well, what of it? The point of protecting him wasn't romantic. She simply couldn't allow Andrew Thorne to stand trial for killing her brother—even if it was involuntary manslaughter. It just wasn't right. Dolly had already lost her mother because of Ike. She didn't deserve to lose her father, too.

When she was at her car, Lauren finally turned to Andrew. The wind had shifted, coming off the water now, chilly and damp. She pushed back her hair. "This Tess Haviland worries me, Andrew. She's artistic and obviously has a fanciful imagination. I hope she isn't here just to stir up trouble."

His expression was unreadable, controlled as always. "Why would she stir up trouble?"

"Richard's up for a Pentagon appointment, you know. Senator Bowler is supporting him. It's a sensitive time. You know the senator has enemies—all politicians do." She pulled open her car door, the hot lava flowing inside her again. She had to control it, the way Andrew would, and use it to her advantage. And his. She cut him a self-deprecating smile. "I know that must sound ridiculously Machiavellian, but you must remember this sort of thing from Joanna's work with Richard."

He nodded. "One rat maze after another."

"Yes, that's one way of putting it. I'd hate to see Richard get hurt. He wants this appointment very much. He's dreamed of it for years."

"You think Tess made up the skeleton to undermine him?"

Andrew's tone was neutral, but Lauren felt the bite of his doubt, anyway. She slid onto the car seat, looked up at him with what she hoped was strength, conviction and the right measure of graciousness. "I'm keeping an open mind. I hope you will, too."

She left, gripping the wheel too hard, until she had to pry her fingers loose. She stopped at the project offices. Even Muriel Cookson wasn't around on a Sunday. Lauren relaxed at being in the familiar surroundings, the antiques, the flowers, the pictures of herself and Ike in happier times.

She really did have to get him out of her trunk.

"Oh, Ike," she whispered. "Dear God."

Two minutes later, Jeremy Carver walked into her office and sat on the wingback chair in front of her desk. He propped one foot up on the opposite knee. "I thought that was your car out front."

"I often come in on the weekend."

"Dedicated."

"Yes."

He nodded. "I know what that's like. Mind if I smoke?"

"Yes, Mr. Carver, I do."

"No problem." He leaned back, a man aware of his unprepossessing appearance yet also the extent—and the limits—of his power. "So, why don't you tell me about your visit with Tess Haviland?"

Harl, Dolly and Tess decided to plant catnip for Tippy Tail and the kittens. Andrew pointed out that the kittens would be in new homes before they were big enough to appreciate catnip. It was Tess's idea. She'd ventured off in her little tank of a car and returned with a trunkful of herbs. Rosemary, sage, thyme, oregano, chives and catnip. "Even if I don't keep the carriage house," she'd said, "herbs will help sell it."

Andrew didn't know anyone who'd bought a house because of herbs in the garden. She'd suggested planting the catnip in his yard—she didn't want to encourage Tippy Tail to think of the carriage house as home. A nice gesture, but probably too late, seeing how she and her kittens were in a box in the bathroom.

Harl didn't approve. He was supervising. He'd produced garden tools and picked out a spot at the far end of the yard, where Dolly and Tess set to work. "Catnip doesn't spread, does it?" he asked. Tess shrugged. "I don't know. I'm learning as I go along."

"Well, if it does, there's always weed killer."

He finally returned to his shop, back to working on the chest of drawers he was painting. Andrew had finished up his yard work and sat on one of the Adirondack chairs under the shagbark hickory. "I guess planting herbs keeps her mind off skeletons," he said, watching Tess and Dolly bring the watering can over to the catnip. Dolly insisted on helping carry it, which meant she kept banging into it and water splashed out over both of them. Tess didn't seem to mind.

Harl was meticulously applying paint to a drawer. "I think she's got one of those minds that jumps around a lot. Artist. Always thinking."

"Doesn't your mind wander while you're painting?"

"No."

Andrew drank some of the ice water he'd poured for himself. He hadn't offered Tess or Dolly any. They were too busy. And he wanted a minute here in the shade, before Tess left for Boston, to think.

"She saw a skeleton," he said finally.

Harl didn't look up from his painting. "I know it."

"Jedidiah died at sea. There's no grave for him."

"What are you saying? That he was murdered, buried in the carriage house cellar and the lost at sea story is a cover up?" Harl asked. "I don't buy it. And he died in, what, the 1890s? A skeleton that old, someone would have uncovered it years ago putting in the plumbing or installing a new furnace. Doesn't wash."

Andrew agreed. He'd thought through all the possible scenarios last night, then again while he worked in the yard. "It'd have to be a hell of a coincidence."

"She's not even sure what she saw. If the police had more to go on, they'd act. Otherwise, they're not rocking the boat." Harl dipped his brush into the paint can, then thought better of continuing. He didn't like to work and talk at the same time. He carefully wiped the brush. "Lauren doesn't want to pursue the possibility it might have been Ike down there. The police don't have any reason not to defer to her wishes."

"You and I could push for an investigation," Andrew said. "As the neighbors."

"We could do it ourselves."

"That's ex-cop thinking."

"It's caught-between-a-rock-and-a-hard-place thinking. Police aren't going to investigate on our say-so, not with Lauren Grantham Montague wanting to drop this thing."

"She thinks Tess could be stirring the pot," Andrew said, watching Tess across the lawn with his daughter. They'd poured so much water onto the catnip, it'd made mud, spattering their legs. They both were laughing, delighted with their mess.

Harl was silent.

"That's what you mean if we investigate this ourselves," Andrew said. "We'd start with Tess."

"Makes sense. She knew Ike, he gave her the carriage house, she saw a skeleton her first night there. For all we know, she made up the damn thing just to see how people'd react." Harl straightened stiffly, one hand on his lower back as he yawned. Today was one of those days he looked as if he'd been shot in the line of duty, first in Vietnam, then as a cop. "Maybe she's decided something's not right with Ike's whereabouts, and this is her way of rocking the boat, smoking out what's going on. Something."

"The longer Ike stays away, the more it looks as if

something's happened to him—after he took off. Or before."

"It's easy to speculate, but we have to go where the facts lead us. Have to keep an open mind, stay objective. He could have gone out for an innocent boat ride, fallen overboard and gotten eaten by sharks. Maybe he borrowed the boat from a friend without asking, the friend reports it stolen, never thinking of Ike." Harl laid his brush on top of the paint can, came over and sat on an Adirondack chair. "I can think of a million ways Ike could have taken off, gotten himself killed and we're none the wiser."

"Or ways he's taken off and just hasn't reported back to anyone in Beacon-by-the-Sea."

"Yeah. Maybe he and sister Lauren had a fallingout that she doesn't want the rest of us to know about. Or maybe," he added, staring across the lawn at Tess and Dolly, "our pretty Tess killed him herself."

"Harl."

"Oh, I've got more far-fetched scenarios than that. One involves Mars. I've been brainstorming this thing."

"I thought you didn't think while you were painting."

"I don't," he said. "This was when I wasn't working."

And it meant Harl probably hadn't slept any last night. Andrew got to his feet, could feel the air shifting, the clouds moving in from the southwest along with rain. He didn't mind. They could use the rain. He heard birds singing in the shrubs and trees, felt the ground soft under his feet, stepping in places where Tess and Dolly had splashed water.

"You let them *crawl* on you?" Tess groaned. "That's totally gross."

Dolly giggled. "It is not. They're only worms. I think they're cute."

"Worms are not cute, Princess Dolly. Kittens are cute."

"When can I pick them up?"

"In a few days. Your dad will let you know." Tess noticed him, smiled as she stood up, mudsplattered, hands caked with dirt. "They say you get more in touch with the earth if you don't use gardening gloves."

"What do you think?" he asked.

She laughed, her eyes crinkling at the corners, shining. "I think I need a good manicure."

Dolly jumped up, an even bigger mess than Tess. She spread out her dirty hands and came after Andrew, but he finally scooped her up and dangled her upside down by her ankles. She laughed and screeched and still managed to smear him with mud. He plopped her back down, and she immediately charged off. "I'm going to get Harl!"

Harl headed her off before she got too close to his paint job.

"You two must be doing something right," Tess said. "She's a great kid."

"She came that way. She was a happy baby, too."

"Did it scare you—the idea of raising her on your own?"

The serious question caught him off guard, but he shrugged, pushing back the rush of emotion. Dolly. He'd do anything for her. It had been that way from the beginning. "You do what you have to do."

She seemed to understand, and he remembered that she'd lost her own mother at a young age and must have watched her father sort out his life after her death, carry on. She brushed some of the drying mud off her hands. "I should go clean up." But her light, lively eyes turned up to him, and she added, "Six-year-olds scare the hell out of me, more so maybe than missing skeletons and strange noises in the dark."

"I don't think so. I just think you're out of your comfort zone with kids. You can't let them scare you."

"I'm not afraid of *them*. It's myself. Saying the wrong thing that ends up sending them into therapy or an opium den—or worse."

"That's the trick, isn't it? To teach them that they are responsible for their choices, not their parents, not their teachers, their friends."

"Yes, but there are things we adults can do to totally screw up a kid's life. Like beat them to a bloody pulp, come home in a drunken stupor—"

"Die on them?"

His voice was soft, as soft as he could make it, but her mouth snapped shut. She took in a quick breath. "I can remember my mother sitting on the rocks not far from here, wrapped in a blanket while she watched me play. I think, somehow, I knew it wasn't her fault she was abandoning me. Kids can figure that out."

"Hang around Dolly awhile. You'll see that kids can figure out most things. They know the difference between someone who genuinely cares and is doing their best, and someone who's pretending, going through the motions."

She sighed. "I'm not good at faking it."

He smiled, flicking a hunk of dried mud off her long, slender fingers. "I know."

"Andrew, yesterday—it was just a weird set of circumstances. We were operating outside our comfort zones." She spoke in a low voice, serious, but trying to apologize, he felt, for something she didn't regret. "I'm sorry I didn't tell you about what I saw."

"Do you want to go on as if we didn't—"

"Yes."

"Okay. Go ahead."

She frowned. "Not just *me*. You, too. It won't do any good if I'm the only one who pretends it didn't happen."

He'd started off toward the house, knowing he hadn't responded the way she'd expected. He'd never been one to operate off someone else's script. He was the antithesis of the Granthams' graciousness and easy charisma. No good at it. Felt phony. He was almost as bad as Harl at cocktail parties, remembering one at the Grantham house when Joanna was alive. She could do small talk, said it was a skill he could learn, like fishing or building a house. She'd wandered through the spacious rooms, smiling, playing her role as Richard Montague's trusted assistant. He was going to the Pentagon now, married to Lauren Grantham. Her brother was off somewhere. And Joanna was dead.

"Andrew?"

He was ten paces away from her, but turned, saw her expression. She wasn't panicked. She was—intrigued, he thought. He moved closer. "I look life square in the eye," he said. "It's the only way I can operate. I have no regrets about yesterday." Then he added, "Except one."

"And that would be?"

Her eyes were gleaming, excited, no sign she'd ever had any intention of pretending nothing had happened between them. Repressing it, maybe. Or trying to. He noticed the shape of her mouth, its slight tilt at the corners. He smiled. "I shouldn't have made up the guest-room bed."

Sixteen

⟡

His Pentagon appointment was on hold.

Richard poured himself a scotch as he absorbed the news. Jeremy Carver had delivered it personally, calmly. He was in Richard's chair in the study now, watching his reaction. "Once we have a definitive answer on your brother-in-law's whereabouts, we can move forward," Carver said. "The senator believes it's in everyone's best interest to wait."

"The senator? Or you?"

"I speak for the senator."

"Yes, of course."

Richard tried to keep the contempt out of his tone. He was smarter and more educated, did more important work than almost anyone else he knew, yet he always had to go through the mind-boggling boredom of pretending he was just a regular guy who didn't think himself above anyone else. Anti-intellectualism reigned. He had no doubt if he weren't married to a Grantham, he wouldn't be on his way to Washington.

He sipped his scotch, felt it burn all the way down, waited a moment for the burning to subside. It was late evening. Lauren was with her book club. He'd hardly seen her at all today and wondered if she regretted last night. Maybe she was embarrassed. He smiled a little, thinking of it. To have sexual as well as intellectual power over her was something to relish.

But he had no power over Jeremy Carver. None at all. Carver would bail without hesitation. It wouldn't matter that Richard was the best mind for the job, that his experience and knowledge were without parallel. Carver only cared about what was good for his boss. Nothing else mattered. Richard admired that level of clarity. He seldom operated in such a simple, black-and-white world.

Someone had Ike's body.

Someone.

"Would you care for anything to drink? There's iced tea, sparkling water, springwater. Lemonade, too, I believe."

Carver shook his head. "No, I need to get back to Boston. I have a plane to catch."

"To Washington?"

He nodded. "I'll keep in touch. Listen, the minute we hear from Ike, or your wife tells us how we can get in touch with him, we're back in business."

"Lauren doesn't know where her brother is."

"No? Well, I think that's weird."

"You never met Ike," Richard said simply.

"We all have our family problems. The senator won't hold a difficult brother-in-law against you. But a scandal? A goddamn missing dead body? That's something else."

"I can't control Ike Grantham. That's putting an unfair burden on me."

"Yeah? Welcome to the big leagues, Dr. Montague."

Richard took another swallow of scotch, didn't even feel the burn. The light was dim in the study, producing no shadows whatsoever, the air outside still, gray with impending rain. "And Tess Haviland likely saw nothing in that cellar."

"Maybe, maybe not. Either way, I can't help but question her timing. You're up for a Pentagon appointment, and she's finding dead bodies in the cellar." Carver got to his feet, pointing at Richard. "She could be a problem for you."

"You mean that she's making trouble for me deliberately," Richard said quietly. "That assumes I have enemies."

Carver grinned and started for the door. "We all have enemies, Doctor, even a bright, important guy like you." He patted the door frame, turned and winked. "Produce Ike. Let me check out this Haviland woman, see if someone's paying her to make your life miserable. It could be one of the senator's enemies, you know."

"I'm an expert on terrorism, Mr. Carver, not politics."

"I know. Why do you think I'm here?"

Tess awoke in a panic. She was in her own bed in her own apartment, fighting a terrible sense of urgency, a crawling anxiety that defied rationality. She tried to focus on the familiar shifting shadows in her half-dark bedroom, the sounds in the courtyard outside her window. But her mind charged ahead, her heart racing. She couldn't breathe.

She was stuck with a run-down nineteenth-century carriage house. She owed taxes on it. It was haunted. Its previous owner hadn't been heard from in over a year. The taciturn descendant of the convicted murderer who was haunting it lived next door.

He had a daughter who thought she was a princess and a white-haired cousin who probably had post-traumatic stress disorder.

A stray cat had delivered kittens in her makeshift bed.

She'd kissed Andrew Thorne and talked to him as if she could fall in love with him with no effort at all.

Under the circumstances, she could hardly blame herself for making up a dead body in the cellar.

Except she hadn't.

Tess could feel the panic welling up in her, the urge to hyperventilate, run. She kicked off her blankets to ease the sense of suffocating.

She'd seen bones. A skull. Human remains. *A dead person.*

She rolled over onto her stomach and switched on the bedside lamp. Her first panic attack in months. They'd come often when she was just starting up her business, going out on her own. She'd told Ike about them. "Normal," he'd told her in that confident way of his. "Get yourself some kava. You'll be fine."

She didn't want to think about Ike.

Her digital clock switched from 4:59 to 5:00 a.m. Close enough to morning, she decided, and flopped over onto her back, staring at the ceiling, concentrating on her breathing. In for eight counts, hold for eight, out for eight. Her heartbeat slowed. Rationality returned. She flipped on her white-noise machine, her small bedroom filling with the sounds of the ocean. Not a good choice. She switched to a tropical rain forest. But it was too late, her mind already filled with images of kissing Andrew in the doorway of his daughter's bedroom, on the porch in the dark.

She hadn't conjured up the skeleton.

That was the problem. She wasn't that imaginative, or that crazy, and it wasn't a trick of the light or a damn ghost. It was a *skeleton.*

And now it was gone. The police had looked, she and Susanna had looked, Andrew had looked.

Davey and her father could have missed it. They'd been interested in pipes and heating ducts, not what was under their feet.

She wondered how close she'd come to catching someone charging out of the cellar Saturday night with a bag of bones.

She took herself back to that night after dinner, when she'd returned unexpectedly to lock the door. She'd meant to head straight back to Boston. Who had she told? Andrew. Harl. Dolly. But her car hadn't been in the carriage house driveway, so someone could have reasonably thought she'd cleared out.

"I'm a graphic designer," Tess muttered at the ceiling, "not a damn detective."

She rolled out of bed and pulled on running clothes, then gulped down a glass of orange juice in the kitchen and headed out into the cool, rainy Boston morning. The narrow streets of Beacon Hill were quiet at this early hour, slick with the overnight rain. It had tapered off to a chilly, steady drizzle. She jumped off the curb and ran on the street, the brick sidewalks too treacherous when wet. She went at a slow, steady pace to warm up, stopping on Beacon Street to do some stretches before crossing over to Boston Common, where she mingled with a few other early-morning joggers, working up a sweat, fighting off her demons.

When she returned to her apartment, she showered and stumbled into the kitchen in her bathrobe. She poured herself a bowl of corn flakes, cut up a banana and sat at the table below her street-level window. If she'd stayed at her corporate job, she could be above ground by now, in a bigger apartment. But Susanna had warned her about cash flow, maintaining a larger cash reserve now that she was a "sole proprietor."

She thought about lilacs and the smell of the ocean. Except for the complications, the carriage house was just what she wanted.

She finished her cereal, got dressed and headed over to Beacon Street. She loved being able to walk to work, not having to depend on a car. People were out walking their dogs now, but it was still only seven-thirty when she greeted the doorman at her building.

Susanna Galway was already at her computer. "God, you look awful," she said.

"Good morning to you, too."

"Tell me you saw a skeleton in your apartment last night. That'd be great. We could take you to a shrink and forget the police."

"No such luck."

Tess set her satchel on the floor by her chair. She could barely remember what she had to do today. Any client meetings? Something with her printer, she recalled vaguely. Normally she kept everything clear in her head and didn't have to consult her calendar.

"I've been roaming around on the internet for info on your buddy Ike and those two next door," Susanna said.

That sparked Tess's curiosity. "And?"

"Nothing new on Ike. The *Globe* ran a picture of him and Joanna Thorne after her death. He was a good-looking son of a bitch, wasn't he?"

"Don't use the past tense."

Susanna ignored her. "Were you attracted to him?"

"No, I never had any romantic interest in him. I don't think he had any in me, either." Tess sank onto her chair, her thighs sore from running, or from planting catnip with Dolly Thorne yesterday. Dolly didn't do anything by half measures. "Ike's always struck me as a rather sad character, if you want to know the truth."

"Heir to a fortune, handsome, physical, sails, plays tennis, climbs mountains, has women falling all over him—except Tess Haviland of Somerville, Massachusetts. Sure, your basic sad character." Susanna tapped a few keys on her computer. "I can see how he could end up buried in an old dirt cellar."

"Susanna."

"Sorry. I keep forgetting you like the guy. You want me to pour you a cup of coffee?"

Tess shook her head. "No, I'll get it. What did you find out about Harley Beckett and Andrew Thorne?"

"Andrew's in demand as an architect and contractor. Good reputation, at least nowadays. Quite the brawler in the past, if a profile of him in the Gloucester paper's to be believed." She rose, graceful as ever, even before eight in the morning, and crossed to the coffeepot. Tess hadn't moved fast enough. Susanna filled a mug with her super-strong brew and delivered it to Tess's desk. "Harley Beckett's another story."

Tess gratefully wrapped both hands around the hot coffee mug. "He's older than Andrew."

"And he volunteered for Vietnam."

"Volunteered? He wasn't drafted?"

"Nope. Signed up. He was shot late in his tour of duty. Had a rough time for a few years after he came home, then managed to get himself on the Gloucester police force. He stabilized, worked his way up to detective. Shot again a few years ago. Bank robbery. He ended up killing the guy who shot him." Susanna pushed back her dark hair with one hand, her expression serious, her skin so pale it was almost translucent. "It was some guy he grew up with."

"That must have been awful," Tess said inadequately.

"He quit and turned to furniture restoration a short time later."

"Ike Grantham had nothing to do with the bank robbery, I hope."

"No, but Beckett's done a lot of furniture restoration work for the Beacon Historic Project. He's mentioned on their website."

"I hate this," Tess whispered.

"Good. You should. Tess, not one thing about this mess sits right with me. You want my advice? Keep an open mind. Stay objective. Don't be a participant."

She thought of kissing Andrew and thinking of kitten names with his daughter, planting catnip with her. "Too late."

Susanna sighed heavily. "I know."

Andrew returned from a project site in Newbury-port in time to meet Dolly on her way home from school. He was wet and muddy. Fog had settled in on the coast, and it had rained steadily since noon, a cold, miserable rain that felt more like early April than late May. On the whole, it fit his mood. He'd punished himself most of the day for letting himself get caught up in Tess Haviland's dramas. No woman he knew would have ventured into that cellar Friday night in the first place, cat or no cat. It was an indication, and not a good one, of the kind of personality with which he was dealing. In one weekend, she'd turned his calm corner by the sea upside down, with kittens and a skeleton and long, deep kisses.

He shook off the memory of the feel of her. That had been his doing, too, not just hers. He had misgivings, but he couldn't manage to summon up any regrets. If Tess marched into his office at the moment, damned if he wouldn't kiss her again.

He occupied the front and back rooms left of the center hall of a 1797 clapboard building in the village. It was not owned by the Beacon Historic Project, and thus he did not have to answer to Ike Grantham or Lauren Grantham Montague, just an ordinary landlord. He checked his messages, hearing Dolly calling hello to the real estate people on the other side of the building. She often stopped by on her way home from school. Harl, who accompanied her, would avoid coming inside if he possibly could, even in a nor'easter. He did so today, standing out in the rain. Just as well. Before heading to Newbury-port, Andrew had been to see Dolly's teacher.

His daughter burst into his office, a ray of sunlight, and jumped onto his lap. She was, at least, without a crown. She beamed at him. "Daddy, I went down the big slide today at recess!"

"That's what I hear."

"You *know?*"

She was indignant, even at six not one who appreciated anyone stealing her thunder. Andrew decided to get straight to the point. "I had a talk with your teacher today during lunch. Dolly, Miss Perez says you've been telling other children tall tales about Harl."

She frowned. "What's a tall tale?"

She knew what a tall tale was. They'd had a version of this conversation several times in her short six years. This was a stalling tactic, and Andrew didn't plan to let her get away with it. "You told the kids at school Harl's a bank robber."

Dolly hunched her shoulders and giggled, obviously pleased with herself, yet aware the adults in her life might not feel similarly.

Harl must have sensed they were talking about him. He showed up in the doorway, but didn't say a word.

"Dolly," Andrew said, "Harl's not a bank robber."

She uncovered her mouth and leaned in close to her father. She spoke in a conspiratorial whisper. "It was Chew-bee. She says he's a bank robber. She told the kids he got shot. Daddy, did Harl get shot?"

"That was a long time ago." Dolly had given up most of her make-believe friends in kindergarten, but not Chew-bee, most likely because she was handy to have around. Blaming Chew-bee was a sure sign that Dolly knew she'd stretched the truth beyond acceptable limits. "You need to stick to the truth, Dolly, okay? If you want to make up stories, that's fine, but you need to let your friends and teacher know they're made up."

"I don't make up stories. Chew-bee does." She looked next to her, as if someone was standing there, and frowned deeply, her brow furrowing. She pointed a finger. "Now, Chew-bee, don't make up stories!"

Andrew set her down, and she ran past Harl, off down the hall to visit everyone else in the building.

She was a great favorite, and her people skills, Andrew hoped, would make up for her propensity for crowns and tall tales.

Harl slouched in the doorway, arms folded on his chest, tattoos showing. "Bank robber, huh? I bet Miss Perez loved that."

"Oh, yes. She did say she managed to nip the bowing and curtsying in the bud, and she appreciated not seeing Dolly in a crown today."

"Yeah, I had to peel it off her head. She was major-league pissed. I don't know what the hell's wrong with wearing a crown to school. Rita Perez is an ex-nun, you know. No sense of humor."

"She was very diplomatic."

"I'm serious. An ex-nun."

"Did you ask her if she's a former nun?"

"No, but I can tell."

"Harl, Dolly can't tell her friends you're a bank robber. She can't wear crowns to school. She can't make her friends bow and curtsy. That's got nothing to do with whether or not Rita Perez was ever a nun."

"She was," Harl said.

Andrew said nothing.

His cousin grinned. "Did she really think I was a bank robber?"

"I don't know. Maybe."

"You tell her I'm an ex-cop?"

Andrew got to his feet. Some days, he wondered at the twists and turns his life had taken. How the hell did he get here, in picturesque Beacon-by-the-Sea with a six-year-old and his white-bearded, white-ponytailed, reclusive cousin? And no woman in his life?

He thought of Tess, and sighed.

"I told Miss Perez you'd been in Vietnam. She thinks you should explain war to Dolly."

Harl snorted. "Forget that. That's chucklehead thinking, telling a six-year-old about war. Dolly's fine."

"Miss Perez thinks so, too. So do I."

"Then do we have a problem?"

Always cut-to-the-chase Harl. Andrew grinned at him. "Only if the cops come after you for robbing banks. God knows what Dolly's classmates are going to go home and tell their parents."

"Ha, ha, ha," Harl said, and left.

Andrew went out into the center hall to say goodbye to his daughter. She was bounding down the stairs from the lawyers' offices on the second floor, snacks she'd bummed clenched in both hands. "I'm going to Boston this afternoon," he told her. "Harl will give you dinner tonight."

"Can he make macaroni and cheese?"

"Sure."

She ran outside, and Harl, hovering at the entrance, said, "Boston?"

"Yes. Tess Haviland lives on Beacon Hill and works on Beacon Street, and her father owns a bar in Somerville. Every carpenter, plumber and electrician in metropolitan Boston knows Jim's Place."

"She'll be pissed, you spying on her."

But Harl approved, and Andrew shrugged. "I'm investigating."

"You want me to go, and you stay here and make the macaroni and cheese?"

"No, I'll go."

Harl grinned. "Yeah, I figured." He started down the

street, tugged Dolly's single braid. "What's this about me being a bank robber?"

"That was Chew-bee."

"Chew-bee? That little rat. Tell her I'm going to throw her in the harbor."

"It won't matter," Dolly said dramatically. "Chew-bee will swim right out of there."

"Chew-bee's a pain in the neck."

"I know, Harl. She just doesn't listen."

Harl glanced back at Andrew, knowing he was listening, and winked. Dolly might be imaginative and motherless, but two cousins from a rough section of Gloucester weren't doing such a bad job of raising her. If her first-grade teacher thought otherwise, that was her problem.

Right now, Andrew had more to worry about than Dolly's tall tales. He shut down his office, got in his truck and spread out his map of Boston on the passenger seat. He might have been to Jim's Place years ago, maybe even broken a few beer bottles and chairs there.

But maybe not. Somehow, he was sure if he'd ever met Tess Haviland before, he'd have remembered.

Seventeen

❧❦❧

The early news was on the television above the bar at Jim's Place, and Davey Ahearn had just slid onto his stool. Tess had hoped she'd beat him into the pub. She tried to ignore him. Her father was taking an order at several tables pushed together, crowded with university students. She had no doubt he'd spotted her. He always knew who came in and out of his place.

She tried not to look furious, out of control and just plain frazzled. She was getting behind in her work, and it had been one of those days she was bombarded by calls, faxes and emails. Even her regular mail was more than usual.

But that wasn't it. What had tipped the scales was seeing Andrew Thorne down in Old Granary Burial Ground, walking among the tombstones and glancing up at her window.

Spying on her.

By the time she'd charged down her four flights of stairs, around Beacon to Park and down Tremont, into the centuries-old cemetery, he was gone.

She'd packed it in for the day and headed to Jim's Place.

"You're in deep shit," Davey said, never mind that she was pretending she hadn't seen him. "A skeleton. Jesus H. Christ, Tess."

"Davey, I'm not in the mood."

"Jimmy heard last night. He's been waiting all day for you to show up and ask his advice. Me, I had an emergency kept me busy. Flooded basement. No skeletons."

She cast him a foul look. "You're making me sorry I came here."

"You're not sorry," Davey said. "You're never sorry. You take life one bite at a time, no worrying, no regrets."

"I have regrets."

"Name one."

"That you're my godfather."

"Ha."

Her father eased back behind the bar. Without a word, he spooned up a bowl of thick beef stew and set it in front of her. He buttered two slices of white bread, cut them in triangles, put them on a plate and also set that in front of her.

Tess said, "Pop, I've stirred up a hornets' nest."

"Hornets? Hell, I'd take hornets any day over a goddamn dead body."

"It wasn't a body. It was bones. There's a difference."

He stared at her. "There's no difference."

"There is. A body is—" She stared at her bubbling beef stew, fighting for the right words. "Fresher."

"Oh, shit," Davey said. "There goes my appetite."

Tess was focused on her father. "How did you find out?"

"I have my sources. You know that."

Susanna wouldn't have squealed, not about a skeleton. "I could have moved to California. You don't know a soul in California."

"Why do me that favor?" He snatched the towel off his shoulder, started cleaning the wooden bar furiously. "No, stay here instead, step on dead bodies right under my nose and don't tell me. I love it that you didn't move away."

Tess was silent. It had never once occurred to her to move away. She had friends in San Francisco she liked to visit, but Boston was home.

"Eat your stew," her father snapped. "You look as if you haven't slept in days."

Davey went around behind the bar and helped himself to another bowl of stew. He was immaculate, his big mustache perfectly groomed. If he'd been wading in a flooded basement all day, he didn't look it. Probably had a date later on, Tess thought. A widowed bar-owner father, a twice-divorced plumber godfather. No wonder she had her issues with men.

And Thorne. What a sneaky bastard.

Davey returned to his stool, dipped a hunk of bread into the steaming brown gravy. "Worst I figured was snakes."

"What did the police say?" her father asked.

"They don't believe I saw anything."

"You want me to talk to them?"

"No!" She almost choked on her stew, which she'd mindlessly started to eat. She wasn't hungry. "No, Pop, that's okay. There's not much they can do, even if they did believe me."

Davey made ghost sounds at the other end of the bar.

"Pop," Tess said, staring at the hunks of meat in her stew, the fat carrots and potatoes. Her life didn't have to be this complicated. "Pop, why didn't you remarry?"

"What?"

"Never mind. It was a stray thought. You're right. I haven't slept well." She smiled at him. "The stew's just what I need."

He shook his head as if there was no understanding her and returned to his work, fixing drinks for the university students. Beers, mostly. He placed the frosted glasses on a scarred tray that he carried to their tables. When a guy complained about the delay, Jim Haviland pointed a finger at the door and offered him subway fare home. He was in no mood. Usually he'd just hand complainers a towel and offer to pay minimum wage if they thought he needed more help.

When he returned to the bar, Tess told him about no one having heard a peep out of Ike Grantham in a year, and Joanna Thorne dying in an avalanche, and Jedidiah Thorne dying at sea. He listened to every word as he continued to work. Then he said, "You mean even the sister hasn't heard from this rich flake?"

"That's right."

Davey, who'd managed to listen without interrupting, sighed. "A year's long enough for what's crawling in that cellar to have turned him into bones. Jesus, Tess. You couldn't have given me a heads up before I went in there?"

"I was thinking I'd imagined it. When you didn't see anything, I hoped that was the all-clear."

"Oh, thanks. Set me up for a goddamn heart attack. *Plumber drops dead on top of skeleton.* Real nice. You should have said, 'Davey, Pop, you mind looking over in that corner there, make sure I didn't see a skeleton last night, after all?'"

Tess ate more of her stew. He had a point. "You're right. I'm sorry."

"I know I'm right, and the hell you're sorry."

"It was an awkward moment."

"Tess, getting a piece of meat stuck in your teeth is an awkward moment."

"Davey, okay, I get your point."

She frowned. Something had caught her eye at the back of the pub. A movement, a reflection. She spun around on her stool.

"Damn."

Andrew Thorne was at a table at the far end of the bar. He had his back to the wall, in the shadows.

Tess stiffened and glared at her father. "Why didn't you tell me he was here?"

"Who?"

"Who, my foot. Andrew Thorne. My neighbor."

"He's here? Oh, yeah. I didn't recognize him."

Tess breathed in through her nostrils. It was a bald-faced, unabashed, deliberate lie, and he didn't care if she knew it.

He scooped ice into a glass. "You don't tell me things, don't be surprised I don't tell you things."

"This is *not* a time for fair play's turnabout, Pop. I trusted you!"

He leveled a fatherly gaze on her and didn't say a word.

"Got what you deserved," Davey muttered, sipping his beer.

Tess jumped off her stool, heat rushing to her face. She pushed past the students and kicked an out-of-place chair on her way to the back of the bar. She pushed up her sleeves. She was still in her work clothes, hot, her skin suddenly hypersensitive.

Andrew had an empty beer glass and bowl of stew in front of him. He looked up at her, his eyes very blue, steady. He leaned back in his chair with a confidence she wouldn't have expected from him being so deep into her own turf.

She wanted to throw something. "What do you think you're doing?"

He kept his eyes on her. "Having a beer and a bowl of stew. I hear the clam chowder's excellent, too."

"Earlier." She'd barely stopped for air, could feel her hand touch the corner of the table, uncontrollable energy surging through her. "At Old Granary outside my office. What were you doing there?"

He stretched out his long legs, eyes, that amazing blue color, still pinned on her. She wasn't sure he'd even blinked. "Checking out John Hancock's grave."

"Bullshit, you were spying on me. Why?"

He shrugged. "Because Ike Grantham gave you the carriage house next door."

"He didn't *give* it to me. I *earned* it."

"And because you say you found human remains in the cellar."

Her breathing was shallow, rapid. She could taste the dirt and the dust from that night, see the skull, its yellowed teeth.

She spun around and yelled to her father, "Pop, throw him out."

"You don't like him, you throw him out."

Davey had turned around in his stool, his back against the bar, a smirk on his face as he watched the show—which only further infuriated Tess.

She flew back around at Andrew, her hand still on the corner of his table. "Get up, Thorne. You have no business being here. If you wanted to check me out, you should have come up to my office and knocked on my door. You should have *asked* me to take you here."

His eyes narrowed, fine lines at their corners, a muscle working in his jaw. "I have a six-year-old daughter, Tess. I'll do what I have to do to make sure you're not a threat to her."

"Get *out*."

He folded his hands on his flat middle and didn't move.

Tess knew she was out of control, didn't care. This was her father's pub, *her* space. Andrew was insinuating himself into her life, deliberately trying to throw her off balance because he didn't trust her. Or because he had something to hide? Possibilities came at her. Damn, she'd stepped on a hornets' nest all right, and now they were mad and swarming.

She lifted the table with one hand and pulled it away from him. He remained in his chair, but his eyes had darkened noticeably. Tess didn't care. She picked up an empty chair and flung it. It toppled over, and one of the university students said, "Hey, what's going on?"

"A brawl," Davey said. "Stay out of it."

Andrew didn't say anything. He unclasped his hands and calmly scratched the side of his mouth.

Tess kicked over the second unoccupied chair at his table, then picked it up and slammed it back down on the floor. Days of frustration, tension and lack of sleep were taking their toll, and she wanted release. She'd seen a brawl or two. She wanted to bust up the place, get some kind of reaction out of Andrew Thorne.

She grabbed his stew bowl and threw it against the wall. The pottery was so thick, it broke only into two pieces.

"Jimmy," Davey said, "you keeping track of the damage? It's going to add up."

Andrew kept his gaze pinned on Tess. It was kissing him, too, she realized, that had her out of control. Her reaction to him. Physically, emotionally. She'd tried to pass it off on the odd weekend in Beacon-by-the-Sea. She'd told herself when she saw him again, it wouldn't be there, this over-the-top reaction to him.

But it was. Even staring down at him from her fourth-floor window, she'd felt it.

"We need to talk," he said calmly.

She took a swing at him, figuring he was inert, but one hand shot up with lightning speed and caught her by the wrist before her fist could connect with his jaw.

He moved easily to his feet. "Calm down."

"There is nothing a woman hates more than being told to calm down."

"Tess."

The feel of his hand on hers was like a hot brand. She couldn't breathe. "Let go of me."

"Not until you promise not to punch me."

He'd done this before. Bar brawls. He wasn't just a North Shore architect.

"Hey, Tess," Davey said. "You've got to learn to pick your fights. The guy's got height, weight and experience on you."

Fury boiled up inside her, and she leveled her foot

at Andrew's shin and let loose, catching him off balance. He swore. She slipped out of his grip and spun off toward the door.

He grabbed her by the elbow just as she was stepping over Davey's feet. "Tess, I said, we need to talk."

"No, we don't."

She snatched up Davey's fresh beer with her free hand and let it fly, its contents catching Andrew in the face and spewing over three dusty construction workers who'd just walked in. "Hey! What the hell?"

The place erupted. It was as if her temper and bad mood were contagious. Andrew was forced to drop her wrist in order to defend himself against a beefy man who thought the beer was his doing.

Seizing her opening, Tess jumped on Andrew's back with the blind hope of summarily tossing him out of her father's bar. She could have left. She could have gone on her way and let Jimmy Haviland and Davey Ahearn deal with Andrew Thorne. But the chance to throw him out herself was too good to pass up. This was her place. This was where she was safe. This was sacred ground. He had no business spying on her anywhere, but especially not here. She felt violated, invaded.

He didn't budge, instead reaching one arm around in back of him and sinking his grip into her thigh. "Tess, damn it!"

When she reached for Davey's stew bowl, her godfather rolled off his stool and peeled her off Thorne. "Take a swing at me, Tess, and I'll pop you in the chops."

Jim Haviland came around in front of the bar. "Okay, if I were Ben Cartwright, I'd fire my shotgun in the air, but I'm not. So, everyone, shut the hell up and sit down."

They complied, and he handed out brooms, dustpans, dampened bar towels and a round of beers, on his daughter.

She was unchagrined, but refused to look in Andrew's direction. He was standing behind her, breathing fire now. That was something. At least she'd penetrated that cool Yankee control.

She glared at her father. "If you'd thrown Thorne out like I said—"

"You know, Tess," Davey interrupted, still between her and Andrew, "I've always thought you were the head-over-heels type. You never were going to go quietly or slowly. I figure, you throw a table and a couple of chairs at a man, it means—"

"Suppose I throw a chair at *you,* Davey?"

He grinned, unrepentant.

"I'll get the mop," Tess said. "Help clean up." Her father shook his head. "No way. You've done enough damage. Go home and cool off." He handed her a cup of ice. "Pour that down your back. Get a good night's sleep. In the morning, you go back to those detectives, tell them you saw a goddamn skeleton and someone stole it out of your cellar. Make them look into it."

But she was in no mood for anyone to give her advice. "I'll do what I have to do." She was surly now, her head spinning, and she could feel Thorne's eyes boring into her. "Send me my bill."

Her father was losing patience, too. "I will, you can count on that."

"Come on," Andrew said, his tone quiet but uncompromising, "I'll give you a ride home."

Tess bristled. "I'll take the subway."

"Fine. I'll give you a ride to the subway station." She relented, only because her father's likely next move was a call to the police, and she'd be spending the night in a holding cell. She shot him a knowing look. "We're even. I didn't tell you about the skeleton. You didn't tell me about Thorne."

"No way we're even." He grinned at her suddenly and leaned against the smooth, scarred wood of his bar. "I figure this time, for a change, you got the short end of the stick."

Eighteen

❧❧❧

Andrew ended up with a small cut on his arm from fending off one of the construction workers and a bruise where Tess had kicked him. She didn't have a scratch on her. It was as if she'd gone through the brawl with a protective force field around her, a perk, he supposed, of being Jim Haviland's daughter.

She was wrung-out. He could see it in the stiff way she moved, in her eyes and the determined set of her mouth. She'd fight her fatigue. She was in the mood to fight everything.

"Your father says you're not given to seeing things," Andrew said.

But the idea that he and her father had talked behind her back obviously didn't sit well with her, and she didn't respond. She had her arms crossed on her chest and was staring out the side window. They'd passed the Museum of Science, and he'd fought his way onto Storrow Drive. It was dusk, the city lights glowing against the slowly darkening sky.

"I think your father makes a hell of a beef stew."

"That's what everyone thinks."

So, he wasn't anything special. She wasn't giving an inch. "He never remarried after your mother died?"

"No."

"Girlfriends?"

"Some." Out on the Charles River, a lone sculler dipped his oars rhythmically, Tess watching. "He gave up a lot for me."

"Maybe the right woman never came along."

"My mother was the right woman. After she died, there was no one else for him. That's the way he looked at it."

"He didn't want to be disloyal?"

She shook her head. "No. It's just that falling in love again was impossible for him. Real love is a rarity. He was lucky to have had it at all, never mind twice in one lifetime."

It sounded like an excuse to Andrew, or a fantasy on her part. "That's pessimistic."

"Practical. Realistic." She cut a glance over at him, her body still rigid. "I'm talking about real love, not lust, not friendship."

He smiled. "Lust is important."

She turned back to the window and resumed her silence.

Andrew decided this wasn't the moment to tell her that her father had waxed philosophical on his daughter and men. It wasn't that Andrew had asked. Jim Haviland, bartender supreme, had done the talking. He'd said men were few and far between in Tess's life these days, that she'd gone from being too impulsive to too picky—maybe because she had an idealized view of him and her mother, as she'd been only six when she died. He'd talked while he cleaned glasses and stirred the stew, the bar empty that early.

Moving to the back table was Davey Ahearn's idea. He'd seen Tess walking from the subway. It was a setup, pure and simple.

If she'd thrown a chair at him and kicked him, jumped on him, anywhere but her father's pub, with him and her godfather right there, Andrew didn't know what would have happened.

Well, he did, but there was no point thinking about it with her still spitting fire, even as beat as she was.

He wound his way onto Beacon Hill, downshifting on the steep hills. Tess seemed as comfortable here as she did in her father's blue-collar neighbor-hood. Andrew pulled in front of her building, brick with black shutters, brass fittings on the doors. Her apartment had its own entrance behind a wrought-iron fence next to the front stoop and down several steps.

"I notice you didn't need me to give you directions," Tess said.

"I drove by earlier." He pulled alongside the curb and turned to her. "Harl and I decided we needed to check you out. Mission accomplished. I don't blame you for being upset. Now, go home. Cool off."

She nodded at the cut on his arm. "Did I do that?"

"One of the construction workers."

"Billy. He's a hothead. He loves a good fight."

"Seems he's not the only one."

"You deserved it." She softened slightly, sighing. "But it wasn't just you. It was my father, Davey goading me. I don't know, maybe there was something in the beef stew."

"Is that an apology?"

"No." She grinned at him and slid out of the truck. "Thanks for the ride."

He drove to the end of her street, then glanced in his rearview mirror and saw her with her keys out, standing on the sidewalk. He couldn't stay. He wasn't about to leave Dolly and Harl alone on the point with a possible body snatcher in the area.

But he couldn't go off, not just yet.

He backed into a parking space, pulled on the brake, cut the engine and jumped out. He'd been feeling this way all day, a little crazed, a little off center. Unpredictable. A wonder he hadn't thrown her over his shoulder and carried her out of Jim's Place caveman-style—an impulse the Havilands and Davey Ahearn didn't need to know about.

"We still need to talk." He walked up to her as she stood beside the wrought-iron gate. The gray skies and approaching darkness only made her hair seem blonder, her eyes clearer, but still that very light blue.

She shrugged. "About what? You came to Boston to see if I was a nut, a troublemaker, a stalker, a collaborator with Ike Grantham in some nefarious scheme—to do what, I don't know. What else? A killer. Yes, I suppose you had to be sure *I* wasn't responsible for a body in the carriage house cellar."

"It never occurred to me you'd killed anyone."

"But nut, troublemaker, stalker and collaborator still stand?"

He resisted the urge to smile. "Not stalker."

She singled out a key and walked around the wrought-iron fence to the stairs down to her apartment. "I should have phoned my father first thing this morning and told him not to let you anywhere near his place."

"You have no idea how not welcome I was this afternoon."

"Good. And actually," she added, a glint in her eyes, "I have a fair idea. Do you want to come in?"

"For a minute."

He followed her down the stairs to a heavy door with a lousy lock. It opened into a small entry with two doors, one to her apartment along the street, another to a second apartment in back. They had lousy locks, too. But when she pushed open her door, he noticed a string of chains and dead bolts that worked from the inside. "Davey stopped by one afternoon," she said by way of explanation.

"Normally I probably wouldn't notice your locks."

"And normally I lead a very ordinary life."

Andrew considered all the contradictions that were Tess Haviland. She was a graphic designer who lived in a Beacon Hill basement apartment. Father a widower. Godfather a plumber. No maternal role models in sight. Office above an old cemetery. Owner of a haunted carriage house given to her by a rich eccentric who happened to be missing.

A woman who'd gone looking for a cat in a cellar and stumbled onto a skeleton, then kept her mouth shut about it.

A woman who might have fallen into bed with him this weekend, almost literally within hours of meeting him, if not for Harl and Dolly.

Or Dolly, anyway. Andrew doubted Harl was much of a deterrent in the sleeping-with-strangers department—for him or for Tess.

"Ordinary," he told her, "is in the eye of the beholder."

She grinned at him. "And I behold myself as ordinary."

"Why?"

"Because I was an odd kid, the one with the dead mother. I like being a regular person."

He edged from the hallway into the living room, which was tiny and had a kitchenette on the other end. She'd decorated with an eclectic mix of flea-market charm and artistic, urban sophistication. There was nothing self-conscious or elitist in the way she put things together, a rooster tray on the coffee table, colorful pillows strewn on the neutral-colored couch.

And a stack of laundry. Lingerie. He noticed a lacy little bra, nothing panties.

She followed his eye, and with a rush of color to her cheeks, snatched up the stack and marched past him to her bedroom. She returned a moment later. "I live alone. I don't have to pick up after myself every single second."

"If it'd been a stack of towels, you wouldn't have bothered."

"It *wasn't* a stack of towels." She ran her fingers through her short curls, and he looked again for signs of bruises, scratches, cuts from their brawl. None. "Can I get you something to drink?"

"No, thanks."

"Do you think the police did anything today?" she asked abruptly.

He shook his head. "I doubt it."

"They've decided I'm nuts. It's easier."

"Less complicated," he agreed.

"Who knows, maybe the skeleton was Chew-bee's doing. Or maybe she stole it. I think Chew-bee looks after your stretch of coast. Sort of your guardian angel."

"A pain-in-the-neck guardian angel. Dolly blames everything she can on her."

Tess laughed, and it sounded good. "I like the way that kid thinks."

He spotted a picture of Ike and Tess with design work she'd obviously done for the Beacon Historic Project. It was among a cluster of similar photo-graphs, Ike's smile a hot arrow through Andrew. He wouldn't have expected such a reaction, would have said he was over hating Ike—or had never hated him at all. Seeing him here, in Tess's apartment, was a jolt. An unpleasant one.

"Ike was pretty awful at times," Tess said quietly, coming beside him. "But I never took him seriously. I guess that was easy—he was just a client. He was a slasher. He saw people's weaknesses, zeroed in on them."

Andrew nodded. "And he was dead accurate most of the time. That didn't make him any easier to like."

She took the framed picture into her hands, touched his image with real regret, but no yearning, no hint he'd gotten under her skin. "A friend of mine took this picture. A guy I was dating, actually. Ike didn't like him— he said the guy wouldn't know which end of a plunger to use, and I'd never be happy with a man who didn't know how to unstop a toilet."

"Was he right?"

"About the guy? I don't know, we didn't date long enough for me to do the plunger test."

She was teasing, but Andrew saw it as a defense, a way of avoiding what Ike had seen about her. "I meant was he right about you?"

"I know how to use a plunger. That's what counts." She swung off to the kitchen end of the small, compact room. "Are you sure you don't want anything to drink? Pop puts too much salt in his beef stew, I think. I'm dying of thirst."

She filled a glass with water, and Andrew found himself watching her throat as she drank. This wasn't good. He joined her in front of the sink. There wasn't enough room in the kitchen for two people. "Tess, I don't think you had anything to do with whatever you found in the carriage house cellar." He spoke softly, firmly, his eyes connecting with hers. She set her empty glass on the counter and stood very still as he continued. "I didn't, either."

"You?"

"Hasn't that crossed your mind?"

It had. He could see it had. But she only gave a curt nod.

"I have to go home. I can't leave Dolly—"

"I know."

He touched a moist spot on her lower lip. "Maybe you shouldn't stay here alone."

"No. I'll be fine."

"You can drive up north with me—"

"I have work to do," she said quietly, "and I need to think."

He let his fingers skim up her jaw, into her hair. But he didn't look at her. "Ike was in love with my wife."

"I know."

"I think she might have been a little in love with him. They didn't act on it."

"He was difficult in a lot of ways," Tess said, "but he wasn't a scoundrel."

Andrew bit back a sudden, totally unexpected smile. "Scoundrel? What kind of word is that?"

"It's a perfectly good word! Scoundrel. It sounds like what it means."

"So does kiss," he said, looking at her now, her eyes shining, warm. "Kiss. Say it. It sounds like what it means."

"Kiss."

And his mouth found hers, still cool from the water. She sank against the counter, her hand catching him at the side, her fingers digging in lightly. He could feel her pulse jump. Something about him got to her. He knew it, had sensed it almost from the moment they'd met. And her. He'd thought about kissing her when she'd looked up at him from the lilacs after she'd sent Dolly home. But he didn't believe in destiny, hadn't in a long time.

He threaded his fingers into her hair and eased them down the back of her neck, the skin soft, warm, smooth. If he didn't pull back soon, he didn't know if he'd be able to.

"Next time you're in a barroom brawl," he whispered, "throw the furniture with a purpose. Don't just slam it around. That just inflames the situation."

"Maybe that's what I was trying to do." Her eyes had taken on some of the grayness of dusk, her mouth still very close to his. "Inflame you."

They kissed again, harder, deeper, longer. He pressed her up against the counter, drew her thighs around him. Route One and the trip north seemed a million miles away, and he didn't give a damn about Ike Grantham.

"He wasn't in love with me," Tess said, almost as if she'd reached inside his mind.

He knew she meant Ike. "It doesn't matter."

"He *wasn't.*"

Andrew eased back, taking in the shape of her

mouth, the way her shirt was wrinkled, askew. It would have been so easy to carry her into the bedroom. "We've been talking about him in the past tense."

She nodded, straightening, tucking in her shirt. "I noticed. It's because he's been gone so long."

"Tess."

"I can't think it was him I saw—his remains." She grabbed her glass and refilled it with water from the tap, her back to him. "It's okay. You can go. I'll be fine here."

"You could call your father or Davey—"

"Just what I need." She turned back, leaning against the counter with her glass of water. "There's one thing you should know. About what Davey said."

Andrew smiled. "After he plucked you off of me?"

"It was a mistake, throwing his beer at you. I should have grabbed someone else's. And yes, that bit about me not going quietly or slowly, whatever that was. It's bullshit."

"Ah."

"It is. Davey doesn't know anything about love or women."

"He knows you."

She snorted in half-feigned disgust. "He does not! He and my father are so old-fashioned—they hate it that I live on Beacon Hill. They think I should go back to a corporate job with a steady paycheck and benefits. Graphic design makes no sense at all to them." She drank some of her water, then pressed the glass to her cheek, and he figured she was hot. Liked it that she was. "Pop's worried owning a carriage house is a message to men that I've given up on the idea of marriage."

"Have you?"

"What? Now you sound like them! My point is, Davey doesn't know anything."

Andrew winked at her. "But he knows how to unstop a toilet."

She groaned.

"Call a friend. Call Susanna Galway. Tess, if someone did steal a skeleton out of your cellar—"

"Then you need to be home with Princess Dolly. Go. If I get spooked, I'll call Susanna." She shoved him toward the door. "Six-year-olds come before a woman who barely an hour ago wanted to hit you over the head with a beer bottle."

"And five minutes ago wanted to jump into bed with me?"

Her breath caught, her eyes sparkling. There was no denying what they both knew to be true, and she didn't even try. "All the more reason to hit the road."

Andrew did so two minutes later, merging with Beacon Street traffic, noticing that night had come and the air had turned cooler. He drove back onto Beacon Hill.

The drapes on her windows were pulled, her lights on, no one out on her quiet street. He knew he had to leave her, that whether she called her family or friends, or got in her car and came north, was her choice to make. He thought about going back in there, packing her up and stuffing her in his truck—and when they got to Beacon-by-the-Sea, to hell with his guest room.

But that wasn't his call. Not tonight.

Tonight, his call was to go home to his daughter.

Nineteen

There was something about driving around with her dead brother in her trunk that Lauren rather liked. She glanced back at her car parked in front of Andrew's house and felt a terrible thrill. She knew it was sick. But it wasn't as if the bones she'd collected the other night *were* Ike, his essence, his soul. That part of him was in another place. A better place. She truly believed that.

What was left—it all depended on how she wanted to look at it. DNA. Material for forensic scientists. Evidence for the police. A problem for her husband and his sponsors at the Pentagon, because, of course, the wife of Dr. Richard Montague couldn't be someone who had bones in her trunk, no matter how innocent her motives.

It was *her* brother. She was the only family Ike had left. She could decide whether his death was something that needed to destroy other people's lives. He'd trust her to make that decision.

"My brother," she whispered to herself as she mounted the front-porch steps. She'd worn a lavender cashmere sweater today, although she could have gotten away with something lighter. But it was cool and damp out on the point, surprisingly still.

Inside the house, Lauren could hear Dolly Thorne running, yelling excitedly, "Lauren's here! Lauren's here!" In a moment, she was at the screen door, waving, even as Harley Beckett materialized behind her. Dolly jumped up and down. She was wearing a crown of glow-in-the-dark planets and stars. "Do you want to see Tippy Tail's kittens?"

Harl opened the door a crack. "What's up?"

"Nothing. I stopped by to see Andrew."

"Not here."

"I see." Even under the best of circumstances, Harl wasn't a great conversationalist. Lauren used to be intimidated by him, but she'd finally told herself that a man capable of restoring an eighteenth-century chair to its original beauty couldn't be that awful, no matter how surly or how many times he'd been shot. She smiled at him. "Well, I have a little present for Dolly."

Harl didn't like that. His eyes flickered with disapproval, but Dolly pushed open the door and shot out onto the porch. "A present for me?"

"It's just a little present. I made it myself." She'd glued multicolored sparkles to a bamboo plant stake, handed it to Dolly with a flourish. "I thought a princess might need a magic wand."

"Ooooooh! It's *beautiful.*" Dolly whipped it around, more like a sword than a magic wand. "Harl, look!"

"What do you say?"

She smiled up at Lauren. "Thank you, Mrs. Montague."

"You're very welcome."

"Do you want to adopt one of Tippy Tail's kittens? Harl says they all have to go to new homes."

"Well, I don't know, I haven't thought about it. I already have three poodles."

"I don't like dogs. I like cats."

Harl placed a protective hand on Dolly's shoulder. "Inside. Your dad'll be home soon." He shifted briefly to Lauren. "I'll turn the porch light on so you don't trip."

Talk about being shoved along your way. Lauren manufactured a cool smile. "Thank you."

But he and Dolly were already through the door. The light came on, as promised.

Lauren didn't want to leave.

She wanted Andrew to know what she'd done for him. Not the particulars. In general.

She popped open her trunk. The black garbage bag was still there. If the weather got hot, would it stink? She thought she could smell death but wondered if it was the nearby ocean, low tide, her imagination.

"Ike. Sweet Jesus."

They'd talked about dying when they were kids. He'd never wanted to go out quietly, in his sleep. He'd wanted to see death coming.

He had, she thought as she climbed back behind the wheel.

And that was something good to hold on to in this ugly business.

Moving the kittens was Harl's idea. He stayed with Dolly while Andrew rounded them up. The carriage house was pitch-dark, no stars or moon shining through the clouds, no streetlights. He had all the lights on out back at his place, but it didn't help. He wished he'd taken a bigger flashlight and imagined Tess here alone Friday night, hearing a cat yowling through the floorboards.

Tippy Tail didn't appreciate being moved. She clawed him, but he hung on. The kittens stayed asleep in their box.

He dumped them in the pantry, then had a beer in the kitchen with his cousin.

Harl pointed to the cut on Andrew's arm. "Damn cat do that?"

Andrew shook his head. "Barroom brawl."

"Do I want to know the details?"

"No."

Harl grinned. "I didn't think so."

They drank their beers, and Andrew told his cousin what he'd learned in Boston, which was nothing. "Everything checks out with Tess. There's no reason to suspect she made up this skeleton sighting just to rattle our chains."

"Anyone else's?"

"Whose? Ike's, to draw him out? Lauren's? Richard's? He's up for a Pentagon appointment. I don't see why Tess would care about that."

"Someone slips her a few bucks, tells her to think of something that'd undermine Montague's appointment." Harl shrugged, getting to his feet. "It could happen."

"Anything could."

"Yeah. We have to follow the facts." He rinsed his bottle and set it on the counter. "By the way, I called Rita Perez tonight. I'm volunteering at Dolly's school. I figure, hell, I can't have six-year-olds thinking I'm a frigging bank robber."

Andrew hid his smile behind a swallow of beer. "What're you going to do?"

"Help at snack time. Sounds like hell on earth, doesn't it?"

"School's out in a few weeks. If it's that bad, you don't have to go back next year."

Harl grunted as he made his way to the door. "If it's that bad, I'm not going back next week. Screw it. I just hope parents don't complain. I'm not your average first-grade volunteer, you know."

"I won't complain. I'm a parent."

"Yeah. Like you're your average father."

He left, and Andrew checked on the kittens. Tippy Tail was still agitated, but she was in the box, nursing her kittens, no sign she planned to abandon them. He made sure the doors were secured in case she decided to move them back to the carriage house.

On his way to the den, he thought about calling Tess and decided against it. Harl was right. They had to follow the facts, wherever they lead.

Lauren Montague had stopped by with a magic wand for Dolly. Harl said Lauren was pale, on edge. Because of the skeleton report? Did she suspect the remains were her brother's? If she did, why not sound the alarm with the police?

Was that what Tess wanted? What if she'd engineered the skeleton-sighting to prompt a police investigation into Ike Grantham's disappearance?

Then why not tell Andrew about the skeleton on Friday night?

Because, he thought, she needed Saturday night to make it "disappear." To make her it-got-stolen story work. No way would it have worked that first night.

The facts.

Andrew turned on the last of a ball game and sat in

his old leather chair, wishing he could focus more on the facts and less on the memory of Tess in his arms.

Tess figured she'd made four big mistakes. One, not taking Andrew down to the cellar on Friday to check out the skeleton. She'd needed a witness and confirmation.

Two, kissing Andrew in his daughter's doorway. Three, kissing Andrew on his back porch. Four, kissing Andrew in her kitchen.

Trying to throw him out of her father's bar hadn't been a mistake. That had been smart. The mistake—a little one, she'd decided—was how she'd gone about it. She'd operated on the assumption, however deeply buried under her anger, that he'd take the hint and leave once she'd started throwing furniture.

He hadn't.

But it was kissing him that was her big mistake.

"Mistakes," she muttered aloud. "Plural."

She sat on the couch with her laptop. She had her email archives on the screen and was waiting for a search on Ike Grantham to finish.

A list of eighty-seven popped up.

She was surprised. She wouldn't have thought they'd emailed each other that much. With a sigh, she set the laptop on the coffee table and went into the kitchen to pour herself a glass of wine.

Susanna called. "Gran says you drew blood."

Tess knew instantly she meant the brawl at Jim's Place. There would be at least a dozen different stories circulating through the neighborhood by now. "No such luck."

"You broke a bowl on his head?"

"The wall."

"A beer bottle?"

"Well, I did pour beer on him."

"That's good. I like that. And Davey had to go and intervene, didn't he?"

"Susanna, this is a serious situation."

"I know, I know. Dead bodies in the cellar and all that. It's a good sign this Thorne character was checking you out. It probably means he doesn't know how a bunch of bones ended up in the carriage house cellar, either." But she sucked in a sharp breath. "You're alone? You want to come here, stay with Gran, the girls and me?"

"And have your grandmother interrogate me about Andrew Thorne? No, thanks." Tess laughed, but heard the strain in her own voice. "I'm okay. Thanks for checking in."

"I still have friends in Texas I can call if you need a bodyguard."

Tess thanked her for her concern and hung up.

A bodyguard. Damn, she thought, and poured her wine.

The first email from Ike was a simple confirmation of their upcoming meeting on her work for the Beacon Historic Project. It was short, but the telltale Ike-slashing wit was there, if only a hint of it. "We watery-eyed rich Yankees love old houses. Only we call them historic. They're only old when they belong to fishermen."

Suddenly the intercom buzzed, and two minutes later her father was standing in her living room. "I parked on the street. I'm going to get towed?"

"Not if you don't stay too long."

"This place. You pay four times the rent for a quarter the space, and the parking stinks."

It was the same litany whenever he visited, which

wasn't often. Usually they saw each other in Somerville. "Did you get the mess cleaned up?"

"Yeah, it didn't take long. You owe me for that bowl you broke."

"Susanna's grandma thinks I broke it over Thorne's head."

Jim Haviland shuddered. "That old bat. She was old even when I was a kid." He glanced around her small apartment, nodded to her laptop. "You working?"

"Yes," she said, because it was easier than trying to explain about Ike's emails. She wasn't sure herself what she was looking for.

"Thorne leave?"

"He only stayed a few minutes."

Her father's eyes bored into her, as if to say he knew what could go on in a few minutes. "You falling for this guy?"

"Pop, I've only known him a few days."

"Like that matters."

Tess didn't answer because he had a point and she didn't want to lie. She didn't always tell him everything—she hadn't mentioned the skeleton—but she seldom lied outright. But to talk about her reaction to Andrew, her *relationship* with him, if it could be called that, was decidedly premature.

"He's got baggage, you know."

"Baggage? You mean his daughter? Is that what I was—baggage that you didn't want to inflict on another woman?"

He heaved a sigh, making it sound more like a growl. "That's not what I meant. And it wasn't like that with me and your mother. I wasn't the marrying kind to begin with. It took her to come along." He scratched his head with one hand, obviously hating having this conversation. "That doesn't mean I'm living in the past. I've had my women friends."

"Like who?"

"Never mind. For chrissake, that's not why I'm here. I'm just saying when you've been married before, you got a kid—it's not the same anymore. Don't fool yourself and think it is. You're not getting involved with someone who's never been through that."

"The investment banker," Tess said.

"Not him. Jesus, he was an asshole. He got an F on Davey's test."

"Davey's what?"

Her father was pacing, frowned at the picture of Ike and her. He looked back at her, distracted. "What? Oh, Davey. He's never told you about his test? He's got, I don't know, five or six questions he asks guys when they show up at the pub."

"Guys—you mean men I'm going out with. He doesn't ask every guy who comes into the place these questions."

"Yeah. Right. Nobody's done better than a B-minus."

Tess didn't know why, but she wasn't horrified. This was the sort of thing she expected from her father and godfather, the sort of thing her friends said didn't happen, couldn't possibly happen, she had to be exaggerating. "Has he given Andrew these questions yet?"

"I don't know."

"Tell him not to."

"What, you afraid he'll flunk or get an A-plus?"

"I'm not afraid of anything."

Her father pointed a thick finger at her. "That's your

problem right there. Maybe you should be afraid once in a while. Finding a dead body. Sleeping alone in that damn carriage house in the first place with ghosts and crap."

Tess refused to let him change the subject. "Pop, Andrew Thorne is an architect. He and Davey probably speak the same language. It's not fair."

"All the questions aren't about plumbing. Jesus. Davey knows you can call him about plumbing problems."

That was all she was going to get out of him. She understood. He'd had to see for himself that she was okay, not sitting on Beacon Hill in terror of whatever was going on up on the North Shore, perhaps even in terror of Andrew.

After her father left, Tess dialed Davey Ahearn's number. "You should give me your little test. See if I pass."

"It's a guy test."

"Davey! I'd hoped Pop was making this up. You really have five or six questions you ask men I bring to the pub? What are they?"

"None of your business. They cover the basics. Money, food, housing, career, kids. Sex."

"Damn it, Davey, I'm hanging up now. If I hit the subways right, I can be there in half an hour and beat you over the head with a rock—"

He was laughing.

She stared at the phone, realized he'd just had a hell of a good time at her expense. "Damn you," she said, and started to hang up.

But he turned serious and said, "Tess, if that was Ike Grantham you saw the other night, you need to watch yourself. Understood? We're talking murder, and you're playing with fire."

"Maybe I didn't see anything."

"Let's hope."

She hung up and returned to her laptop. Her screen saver had kicked in, and she tapped the space bar to bring up Ike's emails. She closed her eyes and tried to picture Ike smiling at her, reimpose his features—his smile—on the skull in the dirt. She couldn't imagine that he was dead.

But she could imagine that someone would want to kill him.

Twenty

❧❧❧

Richard walked on the path along the rocks, Lauren's poodles scrambling over his feet. He had a mad urge to kick them over the ledge one by one and watch their little white bodies smash on the rocks. The tide could carry them away. Lauren would be left wondering what had happened to them, the way she pretended to wonder what had happened to her brother.

She knew.

She'd always known.

That Richard had planned for this moment didn't lessen his shock at his wife's behavior. At least he knew she had Ike's body and not a stranger, an enemy.

But it wasn't *him* she was protecting, it was Andrew Thorne. Again, that this was part of his plan didn't ease his disgust.

A cold gust of wind penetrated his sweater, an old wool thing his mother had knitted him years ago. When he could get away with it, he didn't pay attention to what he wore. It was early, Lauren was still in bed, the sun still low on the eastern horizon, an orange ball reflected on the water. Beautiful, really.

In the end, Andrew would be blamed for Ike Grantham turning up dead in the carriage house cellar. Lauren, unwittingly, would see to that. Richard had put all the pieces into play over a year ago.

He walked out to the edge of a massive outcropping, the ocean and more rocks fifty feet below, gulls wheeling lazily.

The best scenario, still, was for Lauren to grind up her brother's bones and use them on her daylilies. Better yet, dump them at sea.

Once she said her goodbyes, perhaps she would.

Either way, he needed to sit tight and let things play out according to plan. Ideally, no one would have touched the carriage house until long after Ike's body had turned back to dust, and his disappearance would remain a mystery. But that hadn't happened. The timing of Tess Haviland's discovery was awkward—even suspicious—but that couldn't be helped. And it ultimately would make no difference. Richard knew he was too important for the Pentagon to pass up because of a little scandal involving the death of his wife's brother.

People often made the mistake of thinking because he was an academic, he was incapable of action. Violence. His work, however, had shown him just how incredibly ignorant most people were, and how dangerous it was to make assumptions based on stereotype and appearances.

"Dr. Montague!"

He turned, squinted at the path up toward the house.

A young man waved excitedly. "Over here! Can I have a word with you?"

A reporter. Richard should have expected as much, but felt every muscle in his body stiffen. He frowned, looking put upon but not afraid. Never afraid. The young reporter bounded down the path, and when he was within a distance that didn't involve shouting, Richard said calmly, "This is awfully early for an interview."

"I know. I figured it was the best time to catch you and your wife at home. I'm Al Pendergast."

Richard knew the byline. Pendergast was with the local paper, not one of the Boston papers. Ordinarily Richard wouldn't give him his time, and he supposed Jeremy Carver would want him to check with him first. But today, Richard already could tell, was one for breaking his own self-imposed rules.

"Walk with me," he said. "Ask your questions."

Muriel Cookson seemed annoyed when Tess entered the Beacon Historic Project offices shortly after lunch. With pursed lips, the receptionist informed her that Lauren Montague wasn't in. "I will tell her you stopped by."

"Actually," Tess said, "I was hoping to look at the archives on the Jedidiah Thorne carriage house. Lauren invited me to—"

"Yes, she told me." Reluctantly, Muriel Cookson directed Tess to the second floor. "Many of the files are quite old and delicate. If you need help, please ask."

Tess promised she would.

The archives were in a small room overlooking the harbor. She was immediately drawn to the view of boats and buoys, the sparkling ocean and endless blue sky. Yesterday's rain and clouds had pushed off over the Atlantic, leaving behind warm, summerlike air and light breezes. These were the images, she realized, that she associated with her best memories of her mother. They were why she'd taken Ike's offer of the carriage house—

not its history or its architecture, its rumors of ghosts or any urge on her part to restore an old house. She'd wanted it for its location. The ocean, the rocks, the beach, the gulls and the memories they brought back.

But reality surged back in, as inexorable as the tide. When he'd talked of the carriage house, Ike had made her believe in her fantasy. Then had come the tax bill, the stray pregnant cat, the kittens, the neighbors, the skeleton.

And now, she thought, reporters. They wanted to talk to her about her call to the police over her missing human remains. They'd left messages at her apartment and at her office, where, at least, she had Susanna. "You need to learn two words—*no comment*."

"They don't believe me."

"Of course they don't believe you. Tess, you don't even believe yourself!"

It was true.

She'd had trouble from the very beginning believing what she'd seen. Even before she'd charged up from the cellar, she'd backed off. It couldn't be. Not a human skeleton. Impossible.

Because it destroyed her fantasy. It didn't fit with her memories of her mother and her mother's tales of New England history, even the ones that included ghosts.

She set to work. The room was lined with old wooden file cabinets and shelves, with a big, scarred oak table in the middle of the floor. Simple furnishings compared to downstairs. In her work with Ike, she'd never been up here. "Lauren *loves* the archives. Not me. Boring as hell. A lot of musty, yellowed papers of no importance to anyone with a real life." He'd grinned, irreverent, the adolescent boy who could smile his way out of anything. "Lauren loves them."

Tess never had the arrogance to assume he didn't see through to her weaknesses, just as he did everyone else's. What had he told his sister about her, the graphic designer from Boston?

She familiarized herself with the archives in general, then focused on her carriage house. Information on it was filed with the Thorne family, among Beacon-by-the-Sea and Gloucester's earliest settlers. It didn't take long for Tess to see that Andrew hadn't been exaggerating when he talked about his ancestors.

Jedidiah Thorne had been a captain in the Civil War, wounded at Gettysburg, but fighting on until Appomattox. In a ragged manila folder, Tess found a brown-edged picture of him in his Union uniform in 1863, five years before he'd shot Benjamin Morse. He stared straight into the camera, unwavering, serious. He was tall and lean, with the same hard angles that were in his great-great-grandson's face.

She stared into his eyes, and she knew they were blue. Her pulse raced, blood pounding, her head whirling. She saw images of bodies littering blood-soaked fields, thousands of writhing men and corpses, dead horses and the living, grim-faced, unable to keep up with the horrors they faced. She could smell the smoke of the cannons, the stench of gangrene and death, and she could hear the cries of the dying, and the friends who'd lost so much.

And she saw Jedidiah Thorne walking among the dead and wounded, himself bloodied as he tended to his men, the other side's men. It was as if she were inside that image captured so long ago, seeing what he saw, touching what he touched. Boys, old men, young. Too many praying, begging. Jedidiah comforting when he could, but never looking away from what he knew he must see.

Hating it. The violence. Promising himself he wouldn't kill again, ever, even in self-defense.

He would die first.

Tess had to push the picture away and close up the folder. She was gasping for air, sweat streaming down her temples, between her breasts. She stumbled to her feet and found a washroom down the hall. With shaking hands, she splashed her face with cold water.

How could Jedidiah have killed Benjamin Morse after what he'd seen and done?

She returned to the archives. She was drained, as if she'd spent three days at Gettysburg herself. She wished there was a soda machine and gave a small, humorless laugh at what Muriel Cookson would say if she slipped down the street and fetched herself a Coke while she sorted through the files. She could use the jolt of sugar and caffeine, the tangible presence of the twenty-first century. A nice cold can of soda. She felt better just thinking about it.

The next folder contained a dozen pictures of the carriage house since its construction in 1868. Much better. Tess noticed the lilacs had been there from the beginning, and she sat back in her uncomfortable wooden chair, thinking about a handsome, serious young captain on a bloody battlefield, a stern man who would later build a house by the sea and plant lilacs—and who reminded her too much of the man she'd nearly made love to last night.

There was a separate folder on the duel. "I think

Benny Morse is the one haunting the carriage house," she remembered Ike saying. "He got what he had coming to him. Jedidiah should be resting well in his grave."

But he had no grave, Tess thought.

Thirty minutes later, Lauren Montague joined her in the small room. She was dressed in trim, elegant slacks and a silk sweater, a contrast to Tess's casual slim khakis and black cotton top. "The duel's fascinating, isn't it?" She came up behind Tess and peered over her shoulder at a yellowed, crumbling clipping of a newspaper article on Jedidiah's trial. "It's still something of a mystery why a pacifist like Jedidiah Thorne would even respond to Benjamin Morse's challenge, never mind actually shoot him. Morse was a bastard. Everyone knew it."

"Your brother told me he was a man who needed killing."

She smiled wistfully. "That sounds like Ike. But who are we to say who needs killing and who doesn't?"

"It gets at Benjamin's character," Tess said, "if not what should have happened to him."

Lauren pulled out a chair on the other side of the table and sat down. She was gracious and mannerly, so unlike her brother it was hard to believe they were siblings—and yet Tess could see touches of Ike in her, especially in her eyes and the shape of her mouth. But she wondered if Lauren tended to operate in his shadow, if she ever resented her brother's strong personality and outrageousness.

"I'm mesmerized by these files," Tess said. "Suddenly it all seems so real. Jedidiah Thorne, Benjamin and Adelaide Morse. She never remarried. She stayed right here in Beacon-by-the-Sea until her death in her mid-eighties."

"Apparently she was quite a shallow, vain woman. Most people believe she was rather pleased to have two men fight a duel over her."

"I haven't gotten the impression she and Jedidiah were lovers—"

"Oh, no, nothing like that. But she was the reason for the duel. She caused the two men to do what they did, and I think it gave her a sense of power over them. In the end, Benjamin was dead, and Jedidiah was in prison." Lauren leaned back, smiling enigmatically. "I wouldn't be surprised if she manipulated the whole thing to get rid of Benjamin."

"But she couldn't have been sure he'd be the one killed—"

"Couldn't she?"

"You mean she rigged the duel," Tess said.

"Why not? We would think of it as dishonorable and manipulative, but women had to use the means they had to effect a desirable outcome. Maybe Benjamin abused her—maybe she just wanted to be rid of him and convinced Jedidiah her husband was beating her." Lauren swung back to her feet and walked over to the window, staring down at the harbor. "Have you seen pictures of her? Adelaide Morse was a very beautiful woman."

Tess picked up a picture tucked into the file with the articles on the duel. Adelaide was dark-haired and unsmiling, but indeed, very beautiful. "Jedidiah didn't mount a defense at his trial. After he got out of prison, he never spoke about the duel."

Lauren glanced at her from the window, her arms crossed on her chest. "That's a Thorne trait, as you've perhaps already discovered. They have a long tradition of not giving a damn what other people believe about them. They operate from a code of honor all their own."

"But if Adelaide rigged the duel, if she used him to get rid of her husband, it makes no sense for Jedidiah to have continued protecting her—"

"Honor is seldom that practical."

"Well," Tess said, rising, "thanks for letting me use the archives."

"Have you decided yet if you'll keep the carriage house?"

She shrugged. "No, I haven't."

"You'll feel better when you know where Ike's taken himself off to." Lauren moved from the window, but she looked tired suddenly, slightly pale. "I understand. He's been doing this sort of thing most of his life, so I'm used to it. I forget other people aren't."

"He's not the only reason—"

But Lauren didn't seem to hear her. "The police want to find him. So do the people supporting my husband's appointment to the Pentagon. Whether Ike likes it or not, he will be found."

"That doesn't thrill you?"

"It's been a quiet year."

An awkward silence settled between them. Tess broke it, quickly returning files to their appropriate drawers. "Have any reporters called you? I've been avoiding them. It's embarrassing, calling the police to come find a skeleton and then having nothing there—"

"Was there nothing there?"

She thought of Susanna asking her that same question. What did she see that night? Was she sure? She saw a human skeleton. And she was sure.

But she didn't want to be. She wanted to have doubts. She wanted to be wrong. She'd rather have the police think she was the sort of woman who conjured up scary things in her attics and basements.

"I don't know," she said.

Lauren didn't seem satisfied. "Forgive me, Tess, but I think you do know, and you just don't want to admit it because it'll be complicated—because you're afraid what you saw was, in fact, my brother."

"If that's the case, then someone stole his remains."

"Because he was murdered." Her voice was soft, barely a whisper, and hoarse. "I don't blame you, Tess. I've been afraid to say those words aloud myself."

"Let's hope they're not true."

"Yes." Lauren started for the door, but stopped abruptly and looked back at Tess, composed, almost regal, with her straight, tawny hair shining. "And to answer your other question, yes, reporters have been calling, too. My husband's not very happy about the timing."

"Because of his appointment," Tess said. "Is it important?"

Lauren Montague smirked, a touch of humor sparking in her eyes, reminding Tess of her brother. "Everything Richard does is important."

Twenty-One

~~~~~~~~~~

Al Pendergast was working the ghost angle more than the Ike Grantham angle, because, he told Andrew, it was more fun. He liked the idea of a ghost of a convicted murderer trying to scare off a Boston graphic designer by putting a skull at her feet. "Maybe he goosed the cat or something to make her yowl," Pendergast said, plopping down in a chair in Andrew's office. "Would *you* have gone down in that cellar by yourself?"

"Have you talked to Tess yet?"

"No. Haven't caught up with her."

Pendergast seemed unconcerned. Andrew said nothing. The guy was having "fun."

"What about the duel? What's the Thorne family scuttlebutt on ol' Jed?"

Andrew kept his tone even. "We know nothing that's not already in the public record."

The young reporter made a face. "I tried to check the archives at the Beacon Historic Project. The old battle-ax at the front desk wouldn't let me in. The public library doesn't have much." He clicked his mechanical pencil a few times, an annoying habit. "I'm interested in how Jed died. Know anything?"

"He died at sea. There was a storm."

"Ah. No body."

"No traditional burial," Andrew corrected.

But Pendergast was off and running. "Your family pretty much went to hell after the duel. You grew up in a bad neighborhood in Gloucester, but managed to do well for yourself. How's it feel to own the family homestead, rebuild the family name?"

"That's not my purpose."

"Isn't it?"

Andrew looked at him. "Any other questions?"

Pendergast was smart enough to know the interview was over. "Your cousin, Harley Beckett. Is he at home?"

"He's picking up my daughter from school." Andrew decided not to warn the reporter. Let Al Pendergast find out about Harl on his own. "He'll be back in an hour."

The reporter left, and five minutes later, Dolly swooped into Andrew's office. "I'm mad," she announced.

"What are you mad about?" Andrew asked.

"It's *my* school, Daddy, it's not *Harl's* school."

"That's right, he volunteered today. How did it go?"

She was fuming, frowning with great flourish. "He made me drink my milk. He said I couldn't give my apple to my friend, I should eat it myself."

"Dolly, Harl's just trying to help Ms. Perez. Don't other kids—" Andrew stopped himself. Other kids didn't have Harl. "It was just his first day. He'll figure it out."

She huffed, the litany of Harl's offenses over-whelming her. "I hate him."

"You don't hate Harl."

"I do! He says I should lock Chew-bee in a closet. He's mean."

"Could Chew-bee get out?"

"Chew-bee can do *anything*."

"Maybe Harl's jealous of Chew-bee."

"What's jealous?"

"He thinks you like Chew-bee better than you like him."

"Oh, no! I *love* Harl!"

Tess wandered in, and Andrew gave up on getting any work done today. He noticed the shape of her and remembered the feel of her smooth skin, the taste of her. Dolly ran over to her. "Tess, I named the kittens. Do you want to hear my names? Harl says I should name the gray one Cement Mixer. That's *silly*."

"Cement's gray," Tess said judiciously.

Dolly rolled her eyes. "Daddy, do *you* think Cement Mixer's a good name?"

"I think whatever you pick will be fine. You know these are temporary names, right? The kittens' new owners will want to pick out their own names."

"I know," she said, and skipped back out to Harl.

Andrew leaned back and eyed Tess. "I gather you aren't getting any work done today, either."

"None. I tell myself projects are simmering in the back of my mind while I'm driving around, digging through Thorne family history for no earthly reason. I read through most of my emails from Ike last night." She was pacing, on edge. "He really was a jerk. If someone dumped him in the carriage house cellar and stole his remains after I took an interest in the place, what do I care?"

"So just say you imagined the bones."

"Right."

"Tess," Andrew said evenly, "if it was Ike, it's going to come out sooner or later. He can't stay innocently missing for much longer."

"I know." She sighed, coming to an abrupt stop within two feet of him. "The police are trying to find him."

"Maybe we should let them do their job. You reported what you saw. The rest is up to them."

"This can't be good for Richard Montague's Pentagon appointment," Tess said.

"No, I imagine not. He was angling for it when Joanna worked for him—"

"He'd probably like to dump me in the carriage house cellar for stirring up this mess. Well, I can't blame him." She focused on Andrew's office, giving it an appreciative once-over. "Nice. Pop and Davey would be hoping for a little more grease and dirt, but it's a good balance of working stiff and white-collar professional."

"It's functional."

She grinned. "That's what I mean. Shall I leave you alone so you can get back to work?"

"Give me a few minutes to wrap things up. I'll meet you back at the house."

"I thought I'd mop the carriage house floors this afternoon," she said, heading out. "It'll give me something to do while I try to shift gears. Do you really think the cops are taking this thing seriously now?"

"Hard to say. If Lauren balks, they could back off."

"And presumably they knew Ike."

Andrew nodded, picturing Ike Grantham standing in his doorway, ashen, shaken after hearing the news of

Joanna's death. He'd heard it first, even before Andrew. It was the only time he'd ever seen Ike truly shattered by what had happened to someone else.

Tess left, and Andrew headed home a few minutes later.

Not wasting any time, Al Pendergast was out back by Harl's workshop, trying to talk to Harl, who wasn't cooperating. "I don't talk to reporters. Personal policy."

"But I just have a few questions—"

"Nope."

Harl went into his shop and shut the door. Pendergast dropped his arms to his sides, turning to Andrew. "Post-traumatic stress disorder?"

"Maybe you should call it a day."

"I'd like to see where Miss Haviland found the remains."

"It's not my property."

Andrew stepped past him and entered Harl's shop. Pendergast didn't follow.

"Little prick," Harl said from under the rolltop desk.

"He's just doing his job."

"So was the SS."

That was a hyperbole, but Harl hadn't liked the way the local paper handled the bank robbery in which he'd been shot. He tended to lump all reporters in with the one who'd done him wrong. It made his life simpler. Sometimes Andrew envied his cousin his black-and-white views.

"Where's Dolly?"

"Up in the loft watching *The Three Stooges*." Harl scooted out from under the desk. "Two episodes, max.

She's still mad at me for showing up at her class. I thought kids liked adults they knew volunteering."

"Maybe she's secretly pleased."

"That's a secret she's buried deep, then, let me tell you. Although I don't know how long I'll last with these kids. I helped out at activity period. That's what we used to call recess. All those six-year-olds crawling over me. There's one, I swear, I'd like to tie a rock to her foot and dump her in the ocean. Save the taxpayers her upkeep when she goes to the slammer at sixteen."

"Jesus, Harl, I hope you don't talk like that in front of them."

He adjusted his white ponytail. "I'm venting." He made a face and shook his head. "That's what Rita Perez calls it. Venting. She says you have to get your frustrations out in the open in order for you to be nice to the little monsters. I'm with Dolly. I'd make them all bow and curtsy to me if I could get away with it."

"You're a lot of hot air, Harl."

"Yeah, *you* volunteer at Dolly's school. Then we'll talk."

Andrew grinned. "You're just doing it because you're sweet on Ms. Perez."

"She is an ex-nun, you know."

"What, you asked her?"

"Sure, why not? She left the convent five years ago. She says it wasn't her destiny. She has that chucklehead way of talking."

"Maybe you're her destiny."

"Watch it, Thorne, or Tess'll be finding another damn body in her cellar."

Andrew ignored him and collected Dolly, who was only persuaded to leave in the middle of *The Three*

Stooges because of the kittens. They were squirming in their box in the pantry, and one had its eyes open. Dolly covered her mouth to keep herself from screaming in surprised delight. Tippy Tail, who looked generally annoyed with motherhood, climbed out of the box and ate some of the food in her new dish.

"Can I pet them?" Dolly asked.

"Carefully."

She knelt beside the box and gently petted each of the squirming kittens, totally absorbed in what she was doing. "I forgot to tell Tess that we moved the kittens," Andrew said. "I should go over there. Do you want to go back to Harl's shop or play up in your tree house?"

"Can I bring the kittens up to my tree house?"

"I don't think that's a good idea."

She nodded sagely. "They might fall. There's no glass in my new window."

"Dolly, we're not putting glass in your window."

Harl was taking a break in the shade, and Dolly opted for the tree house. Andrew took the long way around the lilacs. The air was still and very warm, the lilac blossoms drooping, fading fast. He'd let them grow wild, creating an impenetrable hedge between his property and the carriage house. It wasn't just because of Jedidiah and ghosts. It was because of Ike, too. Andrew had moved on with his life and didn't blame Ike Grantham for Joanna's death, but that didn't mean he had to like the guy or want him living next door.

Tess, however, was another matter.

She was out on the kitchen steps with her new mop. "I should have gotten an old-fashioned rag mop instead of this sponge thing." She spoke without looking at him, a coolness to her tone. "The floors'll tear it up."

"Harl and I moved the kittens," Andrew said.

"I figured as much."

"I didn't think to tell you. We thought it best under the circumstances—"

"Yes, with the new neighbor finding skeletons in her cellar, I would, too. I understand."

She did, he thought, but that didn't mean she liked it. He eased around the back of her car and stood at the bottom of the steps. She was a physically fit woman, he realized, with a flat stomach, strong legs. He could see her charging over the rocks, racing into the ocean on a hot summer day.

"Tess—"

"You couldn't have Dolly sneaking over here to see the kittens on her own, not until we know it's safe. Even then. No one's here a lot of the time." She sighed and leaned the mop against the house, then walked down the steps. She raked a hand through her hair and squinted back at the carriage house. "What was I thinking, taking this place?"

"You tell me," Andrew said quietly.

She sighed again, more resigned. "Ike made me jump the gun on my dream of owning a place up here. I wasn't ready. That's what he does, I think—pushes people to do what they really want to do, whether or not they're ready."

"Call a Realtor. Put up a For Sale sign."

"Sure. Before or after the police find out Ike's not hiking the Australian Outback and bring in forensics to comb through the carriage house cellar?" She had her hands on her hips and was turned toward the carriage house, eyes still squinted, cheeks flushed from the heat and exertion. He could see where her shirt had stuck to her back. "It was Ike. Damn it, we both know it was Ike."

"Tess—"

She swung around at him. "He was *murdered.*"

"You can't stay here tonight." Andrew stood close to her, feeling her intensity. "You can't go back to your apartment, not alone. Stay at my place. Stay with your father."

"I haven't done anything."

"You found a dead body that wasn't meant to be found."

"Ghosts," she whispered. "I wish it had been ghosts."

"So do I."

The air went out of her, and her shoulders sagged, but only for a moment. She shot him a quick, brave smile. "You'll make dinner?"

"I'll even open a bottle of wine."

"Good," she said, rallying. "I hate making dinner after I've been mopping floors. And you forgot Tippy Tail's litter box. Trust me, Thorne, that's something you want."

"I think it was your brother-in-law in that cellar."

Richard listened to Jeremy Carver with outward calm, but inside, he wanted to vomit. He couldn't, not here in his own office. The North Atlantic Center for Strategic Studies occupied an attractive, low-key restored Victorian house in a pleasant section of Gloucester. Rumor had it a Thorne used to live here. Maybe that was his problem, Richard thought. He was haunted by Thornes.

"The police are investigating," Richard said. "Don't you think it's premature to jump to conclusions?"

"You're paid to follow the facts. I'm paid to jump to conclusions." Carver was standing, pretending to study the framed photographs on Richard's wall. They were all of the seacoast, none of himself. "I've learned to trust my instincts. So has Senator Bowler."

"What are you going to do when we find Ike kayaking in Tahiti?"

"Nothing."

"My appointment's finished, then. You're bailing."

"You're a brilliant man, Dr. Montague. You'll continue to do good work here, maybe more important work than if you moved to Washington."

"It's the media," Richard said, hating the croak in his voice. "You're bailing because reporters have been asking questions."

Carver turned to him, shaking his head profoundly. "No, Doctor, I'm bailing because Tess Haviland found a goddamn dead body in her cellar, and I think it's Ike, you think it's Ike, and your wife no doubt thinks it's Ike—and you're not doing a damn thing about it. You haven't done a damn thing since Ike disappeared."

Richard could feel the blood draining from his face. "Are you suggesting we had something to do with his disappearance?"

"I'm saying I think you're a couple of weird ducks. Let's leave it at that. I've asked around about your brother-in-law. He sounds like a flaming asshole. I can see you might not want to know where he is, but it's been more than a year."

"The police are investigating—"

"Now they are. Why not six months ago?"

Richard didn't answer.

Jeremy Carver stepped closer to him. "I'll tell you

why—no Tess Haviland, no skeleton in the cellar. That's why."

"She's a troublemaker."

"I don't think so. I've checked her out—so have you. Your crazy brother-in-law gave her a carriage house, and she's just figuring out what to do with it."

"Washington needs my expertise."

"It might, but Senator Bowler doesn't."

Carver left.

The door caught in a gust of wind from Richard's open window and banged shut. He jumped, as if the lid of his coffin had slammed down with him still alive, still determined to make a difference in the world.

Tess Haviland...goddamn you...

But there was time yet. Jeremy Carver was playing hardball with him, assuming Richard couldn't compete. But he could. He'd spent his entire adult life studying terrorism and the men and women who played that particular game. He had something to contribute. His work was *vital* to the country.

"You're a sniveling nerd, Richie. Admit it."

Ike.

God, he hated him. His only regret now was that Ike hadn't known how he'd tripped down the carriage house stairs. He hadn't seen who was responsible.

But at least he'd seen death coming.

That was something.

Twenty-Two

❦

Tess mopped up a mouse skeleton in a corner by the avocado refrigerator.

It almost did her in.

She was debating throwing the mop in the trash when her father called on her cell phone. "I just got off the phone with some jackass reporter from up your way. He wanted to know if you're nuts."

"What did you say?"

"I said you're an artist." But he barked out the words without humor, and she knew he was offended by the reporter's question. And worried. "He wants an angle on this skeleton thing."

Tess rinsed the mop out in the sink. The mouse skeleton basically dissolved and went down the drain, but she shuddered. She'd have to scour the sink next.

"What?"

"Nothing. What else did he ask you?"

"He asked about Davey and me checking the pipes. I don't know who told him we'd been up there. You?"

"I've avoided him so far."

"This guy wants to believe Davey and me would have stepped on these bones if they'd been there."

"That's what I want to believe, too."

"You'd rather be a nut than have seen what you saw?"

"No." She set the mop on the floor and dumped cleanser into the sink. A lot of it. "I'd rather it was a trick of the light and the conditions."

"Were we close to it?"

"I didn't see, Pop. My head and stomach were still off from having found it in the first place. You could have missed it."

"We *did* miss it, whether it was there or not. I wouldn't have stepped on a goddamn skull and pretended it was something else, a piece of wood or something."

"I know you wouldn't have."

"The police will be calling next," he said in a rough growl.

"Pop, my finding the skeleton, whatever it was, was a freak thing. I don't think I was meant to—"

"You mean you don't think that Grantham son of a bitch set you up."

She sighed, saying nothing.

Her father bit off another growl. "You're up there now?"

"Yes."

"I can't tell you what to do. You're thirty-four years old. Get this mess sorted out. Stay safe."

"Do you think this reporter was calling Davey?"

"Next on his list."

Which meant Davey would be calling. She finished cleaning the sink. The carriage house was quiet and empty, and she imagined a tiny mouse, scurrying across the vast floors on a cold winter night. She walked over to the trapdoor and knelt on the floor next to it, pushed open the wooden latch. It creaked when she lifted it, sending shivers up her spine. She leaned over and peered into the dark cellar, smelled the cool stone and dirt, the mustiness of it.

What if some poor homeless guy had camped out in the carriage house, fallen through the trapdoor by accident, broken his neck and simply not been found?

His body would have been clothed. He wouldn't have been in a position to shovel a couple of inches of dirt over himself. And he wouldn't have come back Saturday night and carried off his own bones.

Her cell phone trilled, giving her a start. She almost dropped the trapdoor on her fingers.

"I've got my .38 loaded," Davey said. "It's right here in the glove compartment. I can get it to you within the hour. I'm in my truck on the Tobin."

"Davey, for God's sake—"

"I took you shooting that time."

"That *one* time. I don't trust myself with a gun."

"You in the carriage house? Thorne with you? I don't know about him. I can see him snatching a body."

"The reporter—"

"Thinks you're fruitier than a fruitcake. I gave him the plumber's blow-by-blow of my tour of your cellar, told him I could have stepped on a skull and not known it, I was focused on the pipes." He grunted, disgusted. "Reporters."

"Thanks, Davey."

"Let me know about the .38."

Tess hung up, decided she'd done enough cleaning and headed out through the side door. The air was cooler now that it was dusk. She smelled ocean and lilacs, and she stood on the driveway a moment, letting the stillness envelop her. There was no wind. That was what the newspaper description had said about the morning of the duel in 1868—there'd been no wind.

A BMW pulled into the driveway behind her car. Richard Montague gave her a curt wave and climbed out, gravel crunching under his shoes in the stillness. Tess had only met him twice during her work for Ike and the Beacon Historic Project. He wasn't handsome or easygoing, instead radiating intelligence, logic and mental toughness, qualities, she could imagine, that Lauren might have found appealing because they were such a contrast to her brother.

"I thought you might be here." He tilted his head back, appraising her. His eyes were a light gray, incisive. "Your story about the other night has caused quite a stir."

"The reporter caught up with you?"

"And my wife." He gave Tess a wry, deliberate smile. "I also understand he spoke to Muriel Cookson. She's horrified."

"He tracked down my father, too. I've managed to avoid him so far."

"That's your good fortune." His good humor faded, and he averted his gaze from Tess. "The publicity has had an unforeseen consequence—an appointment I was expecting has been put on hold."

"That doesn't seem fair."

"It's the nature of the Washington beast, I'm afraid. I'm used to this sort of maneuvering and fear-based decision-making." He shifted his attention back to her.

"Would you mind telling me why you chose this particular timing to investigate the carriage house?"

Tess shrugged. "I received a property tax bill."

He laughed, more with incredulity than amusement. "To think my move to the Pentagon has been postponed, if not scuttled, because of the timing of a property tax bill. Well, it's hardly your fault."

"I didn't think through all the ramifications when Ike turned over the carriage house deed to me. So, I decided to figure out whether I wanted to keep it or not."

"Hence, your visit over the weekend."

"Yes."

He glanced at the carriage house. "It's in rough shape, isn't it? I haven't been here in years. I've driven by, of course, and Ike and Lauren both were fond of this place. It never was a good choice for the Beacon Historic Project, however, so I'm not surprised Ike unloaded it." He caught himself, smiled at her. "I don't mean it that way."

"That's okay. My father said more or less the same thing."

"Will you keep it?"

"I don't know. I'd like to be able to talk to Ike. I was supposed to do more work for him—that was our understanding. And I probably should know for sure what it was I saw the other night, even if it was nothing."

"I understand. Lauren and I feel the same way." He walked past her car to the end of the driveway and breathed in. "I love lilacs. Did you know Ike helped train Joanna here at the carriage house? I was surprised when Andrew bought the old Thorne estate. They'd been living in a house in the village. Frankly, after Joanna died, we all thought Andrew would move back to Gloucester."

Tess frowned, edging toward the lilacs. "Joanna trained here?"

"Hmm? Yes, Ike had rigged up ropes and a rock-climbing course. It wasn't elaborate, and it's not like this was their only training site. Joanna was very gung ho. It was good to see."

"Ike didn't go with her to Mount McKinley?"

"Oh, no. That was her dream not his. Look, everyone knows what Ike's like, and I don't pretend we got along—but he was a positive influence on Joanna Thorne. She worked for me, and I could see the change in her." He smiled wistfully. "Losing her was a terrible blow."

"It must have been." Tess tried to hide her uneasiness by tugging on a still-perfect lilac blossom, no hint of brown anywhere. "I think Ike felt guilty about what happened to her."

"As much as Ike can feel guilt, yes, I think so." She twirled the lilac stem in one hand, but gave Richard Montague a direct look. "You refer to him in the present tense."

He nodded. "I try to. Miss Haviland, normally I wouldn't engage in family gossip with an outsider, but because of the carriage house, you've been dragged into our affairs. I hope I haven't stepped over the line."

"No, I appreciate the insight. And I'm sorry about your appointment."

He waved a hand. "Under the circumstances, it's the least of our worries."

But it couldn't be easy, Tess thought, losing out, at least for the moment, on a Washington appointment because someone had reported finding a skeleton—which no one else had yet seen—in the cellar of a carriage house his wife's brother had once owned. He started back to his car, and Tess mumbled something about being glad to see him again.

"Likewise," he said over the hood.

Once he drove off, she couldn't wait to slip through the lilacs, Dolly-style.

Harl and Andrew were on the back porch, arguing over spaghetti sauce. "You can't put carrots in spaghetti sauce," Harl said. "That's a sin against nature."

"You grate the carrots. You can't taste them. They sweeten the sauce, neutralize some of the acidity of the tomatoes."

"Sugar does the same thing, and it's not a carrot." He wrinkled up his face at the idea. "You put onions in the sauce, you put garlic, you put mushrooms and peppers, maybe—once in a while—some olives. You don't put in carrots."

"I've put in carrots before. You've never even noticed."

Tess grinned at them and dropped onto a chair at the table, feeling some of the tension roll out of her. She'd tell them about her visit with Richard Montague, but later. "It's nice to hear someone talking about something normal."

Harl eyed her. "I suppose you don't make spaghetti sauce. You make *pasta* sauce."

"I do live on Beacon Hill."

"Watch it, Harl," Andrew said. "She gives as good as she gets."

She shook her head. "Not tonight. I'm not holding

my own with anything but a glass of wine." She smiled, adding, "Two. Two glasses of wine."

"Red or white?" Harl asked, getting to his feet.

"Red." She stretched out her legs and leaned back in her chair, feeling curiously at home. She winked up at Harl. "Red wine goes better with spaghetti sauce."

Lauren admired the perfect creamy yellow of the single daylily blossom in the flower garden just off the back porch. The gloom of dusk was settling in. The yardman had come today, the air still smelling of freshly cut grass. It was so normal and pleasant, reminding her of summer and running through the yard as a child, that she wanted to cry. She tried to be hardheaded and un-sentimental. She knew she had to keep her wits about her with a dead body in her car trunk. But she missed her family. She missed her parents. She missed Ike.

Ike.

The daylily was so beautiful, she wanted to lose herself in its shape and color, think of nothing else.

Her poodles rubbed against her ankles as if they sensed her mood. She couldn't let depression settle in. A tug of nostalgia was all right, but nothing more. Too much was at stake.

"There you are." Richard trotted down the porch steps, a drink in each hand. "I brought you a scotch, just in case. Hell of a day, I know."

She accepted the drink. "The police are stopping by tomorrow to interview me on Ike's whereabouts. It would be so much easier if I had a normal brother, but then—" She smiled, sipping the scotch. "But then I wouldn't know what to do with a normal brother."

"Ike's normal. Half the men in this country would

take off just the way he does if they could get away with it. He's got the money, no attachments." Richard shrugged agreeably, in a remarkably good mood considering his devastating news. Lauren wondered if it was the scotch. "A normal guy."

"You're joking with me."

"Lauren, everyone's on edge because of this Tess Haviland, not because Ike hasn't been heard from in a year. If she hadn't come around and claimed to find a skeleton, then have it disappear, no one would be thinking about Ike Grantham today. It's damn inconvenient, that's all."

His tone hadn't changed, remaining almost affable. Lauren walked up to the porch with him. She had to call the dogs, who liked wandering in the yard. So much for feeling her pain. They didn't give a damn about her.

She picked up the old, yellowed bound volume she'd been reading. Richard frowned at her. "What's that?"

"Adelaide's diary."

"Who?"

"Adelaide Morse. Benjamin's wife. Jedidiah Thorne's victim."

Richard shrugged, indifferent, and sat on a wicker chair. "I'd love for this to turn out to be a haunted-house scare. They happen now and again at the carriage house, don't they?"

"Yes, but never a skeleton—usually it's just strange noises, shadows, voices." She sat on the chair next to him with her scotch, the glass in a cold sweat in her hand. "I should put Adelaide's diary in the archives. In fact, I should give it to the project historians. I don't know why I insist on protecting her."

"Lauren, I'm not following you—"

"Adelaide. I'm protecting her."

"But she's dead!"

"She killed Benjamin. I almost told Tess the truth today."

Richard gave an exaggerated frown. "Lauren, what are you talking about?"

"She sensed it. Tess. It was as if Jedidiah and Adelaide were trying to speak to her through their pictures in the files and set the record straight."

Her husband simply stared at her.

She smiled. "Don't worry, Richard, you needn't call a doctor. I'm fine. It's just been a long day, and I've had so much to think about. I know Beacon-by-the-Sea history bores you."

"The study of history is vital," he said. "It helps us to understand why people do what they do today, and it can help us predict their actions in the future. But, Lauren, are you saying this story of the Thorne-Morse duel isn't true?"

"What is truth?" she asked, her eyes suddenly filling with tears.

His mouth snapped shut. "Perhaps I shouldn't have brought you that scotch."

"It's not the drink. I've been like this all day. Richard, Adelaide Morse was my great-grandmother's sister. My great-great-aunt."

"That's going back too far to make a difference."

"It did to my great-grandmother and my grandmother. My mother didn't care as much. She gave me Adelaide's diary." Lauren set her scotch down and ran her fingertips over the cracked old binding. "Benjamin was an awful man."

"He physically abused her—"

"No. No, he didn't. He was an awful man, but he never hit her. She made that up to manipulate Jedidiah. She knew he wouldn't keep silent, as so many of her friends would. And Benjamin responded just as Adelaide knew he would, by challenging Jedidiah."

Richard didn't say a word. He was staring at her, his gray eyes neutral, but she knew he was wondering if she'd gone out of her mind.

"She knew Jed would accept the challenge, but wouldn't fire on Benjamin or anyone else. He'd renounced violence after the war."

"He would stand there and let another man shoot him? That's ridiculous. And obviously it didn't work out that way—"

"But it did. Jedidiah gave Adelaide one of his weapons and asked her to get away, take a train west, leave Benjamin. He expected to die. But Adelaide—" Lauren picked up her drink again, relished the burning liquid coursing down her throat. It was unlike Richard to bring her anything more than an occasional glass of wine. "Adelaide shot Benjamin herself, just before the duel began."

"There were no witnesses?"

"No. Dueling was illegal in Massachusetts."

She could see his incisive mind at work and remembered he'd earned a Ph.D. from Harvard long before she'd met him. In so many ways, she knew very little about her second husband, which was only one of the reasons Ike had warned her against marrying him. He was silent, digesting her words. "Then perhaps Adelaide did Jedidiah a favor under the circumstances. If he wouldn't fire his weapon, she saved his life by killing Benjamin."

"But she let him go to prison."

"A small price to pay. She won her freedom, and she saved his life."

"That's how my grandmother and her mother looked at it."

"Adelaide?"

"There's no regret for her actions," Lauren whispered. "None. She says over and over again… *Benjamin deserved his fate.*"

Richard shot abruptly to his feet. "I'd burn that damn diary. If you don't want the whole story to come out, why keep it?"

"It's a reminder."

"Of what?"

"Of life's cruelties. We're not always faced with a good and a bad choice, a right and a wrong choice. Sometimes the choices are all bad, all wrong."

"Lauren, for God's sake—"

"What would you have done, if you'd been Adelaide?"

"I'd have found another way out. She could have left her husband without manipulating someone else into killing him." Richard spoke crisply, not harshly, and Lauren imagined him delivering his analysis on a terrorist cell in just such a tone. "But what's done is done. They're all dead now."

"Yes."

"If I were you, I'd burn the diary."

She smiled. "Yes, you would."

He rose, taking his scotch. At the door, he turned and faced her again. "You believe it was Ike in the carriage house cellar, don't you?"

"I know it was."

Twenty-Three

~~~~~

Tess had headed north prepared to stay the night. The carriage house was out, and she'd assumed Andrew's guest room was out, too, or at least not a good idea. One of Beacon-by-the-Sea's inns had seemed more sensible, but here she was, unpacking in the guest room, with a milk-glass vase of violets and dandelions on her bedside stand. Dolly had picked them.

"Harl says dandelions are weeds," she said at Tess's side. "I think they're pretty."

Tess laughed. "So do I."

"Will you read to me?"

"Sure, why don't you go pick out a book?"

"Two books," she said, and ran out of the room.

Tess sank onto the bed. She was wrung-out. Mopping floors had helped anchor her mind and keep her thoughts from spinning out of control. Dinner with Andrew, Harl and Dolly hadn't helped at all. They were a family, and no matter how comfortable she felt with them, she was the new neighbor.

Andrew slouched in her doorway, the shadows darkening his eyes and bringing out the angles in his face. "What are you thinking about?"

"That you, Dolly and Harl make a nice family." But she quickly shifted the subject. "Did anyone actually like Ike?"

"Did you?"

"In a way. I know he was self-absorbed, arrogant and totally narcissistic, but we got along. Then again, he was a client, not a brother, a friend or a neighbor. I didn't have to live with him." She winced, sighing. "I'm talking about him in the past tense. I can't help it."

"Ike's a strange case. His relationship with people— even his sister—was always on his terms, never theirs. He only was interested in helping Joanna because it made him feel good. What she wanted was irrelevant."

"He steamrolls people," Tess said. "One minute, I'm tallying up what he owes me, next minute I have the deed to a nineteenth-century carriage house he was positive I wanted."

"Tess!" Dolly shoved herself between her father and the door frame. "I'm ready. I picked out two books."

Andrew placed the palm of his hand on her head and squeezed playfully. "Tess is tired. She can read you two *short* books, but that's it."

Tess brushed against him on her way out with Dolly. Even the brief contact gave her a jolt of awareness. He seemed to know it, feel it himself. But Dolly grabbed her by the hand and dragged her into her room.

Before they could settle in and read, Tess had to help her dress up one of the stuffed animals and have pretend tea.

"Do you think Snowflake or Snowball is a better name for the white kitten?" Dolly asked, carefully sipping thin air from her china tea set. "She's not *all* white. She's got some gray parts."

"Snowflake," Tess said decisively. "Snowball would be better for a furrier cat."

Dolly frowned in thought, then nodded. "That's what I was thinking."

Tess smiled. Dolly had been thinking no such thing, but she was trying to seem very grown-up, as Tess had when Davey Ahearn would come over and she'd show him how she'd stopped the kitchen-sink faucet from dripping. She wondered what might have been different if she'd had a woman in her life. Davey's two wives had never taken much interest in her, and her father had kept any romantic interests he'd had after her mother's death completely private.

Mercifully, Dolly had picked out two *Madeleine* books for Tess to read. They were very short, and their intrepid heroine was a good reminder for her, too. She could feel Dolly's warm, sturdy little body snuggled in next to her, as if Tess had been reading books to her forever.

She couldn't resist. She reached down and picked up *The Hobbit* off the floor, opened it to the Winnie-the-Pooh bookmark and read softly, until Dolly fell asleep on her arm. Tess extricated herself and tiptoed out of the room.

Andrew was standing in the hall, ghostlike. He caught her by the hand and pulled her into the guest room, quietly kicking the door shut. He captured her against it, raised one arm to run his fingertips over her mouth. His lips followed, brushing lightly. "I thought you'd never finish reading."

"*The Hobbit* does go on."

"Tess." He still had one hand flat against the door, his forearm straightened at shoulder level. With his free hand, he snaked his fingers into her hair. "Why do I want you so much?"

She tried to smile. "Deprivation."

"Is that a knock on me or you?"

"Neither. It was a joke."

But she was having difficulty talking, and he pressed in closer, letting his fingers trail down her neck, over the curve of her shoulder, down her arm. Their mouths met again, hungrily this time, neither holding back. Tess felt desire, deep and full, well inside her until she thought she'd burst just from their kisses.

"I've thought about you," she whispered, barely able to get the words out, "all day."

His fingertips skimmed across her breasts, and she sank a bit on the door. He didn't relent. They kissed again, his control ragged. He spoke near her mouth, his eyes searching hers. "What about at night?"

"All night, too. When I wasn't thinking about—"

"Hell."

She knew she'd broken the spell. Perhaps she'd done it deliberately, if not consciously. But he didn't draw back. Instead he put his free hand against the door, trapping her between both his arms. There was no threat. If there had been, she knew what to do. Davey had taught her. But there was simply determination, strength and a tenderness that made her heart stop.

"When I make love to you, there won't be any talk of goddamn skeletons in the cellar." His voice was low and intense, a mix of intelligence, discipline and experience. He was reticent by nature, she realized, only because he chose his words well and expected people to listen. His eyes, darkened now to a midnight blue, held her in place as surely as his arms. "And my six-year-old daughter won't be down the hall."

"But Dolly lives here—"

"She has aunts, uncles, grandparents and Harl. But she's not the problem. She'll never be a problem."

"Not for me," Tess said quietly. She leaned against one of his outstretched, muscular arms. "It's Ike."

"It's not just Ike."

"It's the skeleton in general, too, whatever, whoever it is or was."

"Tess."

She frowned at him, with his eyes narrowed, his jaw set in that serious, uncompromising way that reminded her of Jedidiah Thorne. They were a rough lot, the Thornes, and had made their mark on the unpredictable North Atlantic over the centuries. Andrew was one of them. She had to remember that, father of a six-year-old though he was. "You have something else in mind?"

"It's Davey Ahearn, too," he said. "And Jim Haviland."

She scowled. "That's ridiculous."

"Is it?"

She saw he was serious. She had to laugh. "Andrew, Davey and my father are what they are. Get used to it. I have."

"You're sure?"

"Positive. They're a part of my life, and as much as I bitch and moan at times, I wouldn't have it any other way. But the men in my life might, because of crazy ideas—"

"Not so crazy," Andrew muttered.

"Fast-forward yourself thirty years. What kind of relationship do you think you'll have with Dolly?"

He didn't hesitate. "Whatever kind of relationship I want."

"Exactly. I rest my case." She ducked under his arm and went over and plopped down on the bed, noticing that Dolly's dandelions had already wilted. The violets were still in good shape. She smiled, and looked up at Andrew. He was aroused, clearly frustrated. "But point well taken about skeletons and Ike. And Dolly."

"Forget it. We can lock the damn door—"

But she shook her head, knowing what he wanted and thought was right. Knowing what she wanted. She licked her lips, deliberately sensual. "No, our first time... I don't want to hold back."

He stared at her a moment, then growled, "Hell," and left, shutting the door firmly but not loudly behind him.

She shot to her feet and ran to the window, breathing in the sea breeze, the smell of the ocean, the memories that seemed to hang over the rocks and sand.

"Oh, God, Mom."

It was the voice, not of a six-year-old, but of a woman almost the same age as her mother when she'd died. So young. How had she known so much? How had she been so wise? *"Live well, Tess. Love well. That's what matters most."*

She loved well, all right, she thought with a rush of sarcasm. She was hyperventilating, bursting with a turmoil of emotion that seemed to press against her chest, rob her of air.

Meet a man on Friday. Lie to him and argue with him about skeletons on Saturday and Sunday. Fight with him on Monday. Fall in love with him on Tuesday.

Yeah, she loved well. She just wasn't smart about it. Never had been. Love made no sense to her whatsoever. There was no logic, no trusted instinct she could rely on for direction.

Just this feeling of panic. And yearning. And somewhere deep inside where she couldn't quite reach…an incongruous sense of calm.

She turned from the window, wishing she had her white-noise machine. She scanned a bookshelf, coming up with a frayed copy of *Emma*. That was something. Jane Austen on the bookshelves. It had to be a positive sign. A man didn't have to read Jane Austen himself, but having a book in the house signaled an open mind. An ability to compromise. An understanding of different tastes and sensibilities.

Then again, he hadn't renovated this room yet. He might come in here, throw out all the Jane Austen and put in how-to books on things like building your own gazebo.

For no reason at all, she smiled and opened to page one. At least, she thought, nobody'd be sneaking around stealing dead bodies out of old cellars in *Emma*.

Andrew gave up on sleep around 1:00 a.m.

He rolled out of bed and headed downstairs, noting the lights were out in the guest room. He checked on Dolly, fast asleep with about a million stuffed animals.

The lights were on in Harl's shop. Andrew walked out across the dark, dew-soaked lawn. He made sure Harl knew it was him coming, not anyone he'd require a baseball bat against.

They sat out on the Adirondack chairs in the dark. A half-moon and stars shone overhead, and they could hear the tide coming in. "You working on the rolltop?" Andrew asked.

Harl nodded. "I'm treating that thing like a museum piece. The people who own it don't care. They just want it to look good and not fall apart. They're going to use it for bill-paying." He looked over at Andrew, his white beard and white hair standing out against the darkness. "Tess Haviland keeping you awake?"

Andrew didn't answer.

"You need a woman raised in a bar that makes the best chowder in Boston and serves college students and working stiffs both. She's the kind of woman Joanna would have wanted for Dolly. She told me, you know. She said she wanted to be stronger, more self-reliant, for Dolly's sake." He stretched out his thick legs, this much talk more than Harley Beckett would ever consider easy. "Joanna couldn't make herself happy, never mind you."

"It wasn't her job to make me happy."

"That's part of the problem with you and women. I'm not saying I'm any expert."

"Good."

But Harl was on a roll. "You were always too independent for Joanna. She wanted more control over you. She was smart, and she was a damn good woman, but I think she figured she could control a mountain better than you. Tess is used to independent men. She can hold her own."

Andrew stared over at his cousin. "You've been doing a lot of thinking, Harl."

"Up yours, Thorne. You want to self-destruct, send this woman back to Boston, go ahead."

"Her relationship with Ike—"

"Maybe it was a real friendship. Ike never had friends, and not just because he was a pain in the ass. He was rich, he had a lot of energy, he could do things.

People projected stuff onto him, fed off his optimism. I mean, he could home in on a person's weaknesses, and he was self-centered—but he was arrogant enough to think he had enough energy and charisma to go around."

Andrew settled back in the old Adirondack chair and gazed up at the shagbark hickory, the stars and moon shining through its branches, creating black silhouettes against the sky.

"I wonder if Ike had a premonition he'd need Tess to find him," Harl said.

"And that's why he gave her the carriage house? Not Ike."

"It could have been an unconscious premonition. They were friends, and he knew if something went wrong, Tess had just the kind of bulldog personality that'd get the truth out on the table, make everyone see what was what." Harl nodded, pleased with his theory. "I think about Jedidiah. Who knows what happened at the carriage house that day? Maybe the truth's never come out, justice has never been served."

"He had years to tell his story."

"Maybe his sense of honor stopped him. You know those nineteenth-century types."

"You could have a point."

"Or I could be full of shit. I need to get some sleep if I'm going to face six-year-olds tomorrow." He got heavily to his feet. "Forget what I said. I talked too much. Must be the ghosts."

He went back into his shop, but Andrew didn't move. He listened to the ocean and stared up at the hickory, the stars and the moon. For all he knew, Harl was right about everything. Joanna, Ike, Tess, Jedidiah. And the ghosts.

Twenty-Four

~~~∽◦◦∽~~~

Tess tried to sleep in. She thought it would be easier
if the Thorne household went on their way before she
got up. Then she could shower, have a cup of coffee on
the porch and figure out what to do with her day. She
definitely wanted to slip down to Boston and check her
email archives. She'd gone through her saved emails
from Ike, but not the ones from her to him.

Not that she intended to do any actual graphic design work. If the distractions up north continued, she'd
be so far behind she'd never catch up. And her reputation would be in ruins. It wasn't just a question of doing
good work—it also had to be done on time. What she'd
found in her cellar on Friday night wouldn't help clients
facing their own deadlines.

She sighed at the ceiling. She could hear Dolly singing a made-up song in her bathroom, something about
kittens.

The Beacon-by-the-Sea police, Tess thought, needed
a greater sense of urgency about her skeleton report.
They were supposedly looking for Ike, but not with any
apparent energy or enthusiasm. She could try lighting

a fire under them. As Susanna, who knew such things, had said, the police didn't like missing bodies. Much easier if hers was a ghost or a figment of a highly creative imagination.

"No kidding," Tess muttered sarcastically to herself.

It was only seven-fifteen. What time were Andrew and Dolly on their way in the morning?

Dolly burst in. "The kittens' eyes are open!"

Tess just managed to squash a startled yell. "They are?"

"Dolly," Andrew said from the hall, nearby, "you should always knock. Tess might have been asleep."

Not a chance, she thought.

Dolly was too excited to waste time on apologies.

"Sorry. Do you want to see the kittens? They're so cute!"

Andrew had the grace not to appear in the guest-room doorway. Tess didn't know what she'd have done if he had. She felt exposed as it was, out of her element. Dolly had a scraggly stuffed cat tucked under one arm. Tess sat up in bed. "I'll meet you in the pantry once I've gotten dressed."

Dolly skipped out, leaving the door open behind her.

Andrew closed it.

So much for sleeping in, Tess thought, the brief image of him in his work shirt enough to eliminate any prospect of sleep or even calm. She quickly got dressed, a cool ocean breeze floating in through the open window as she pulled on jeans and a fresh shirt.

Down in the kitchen, Andrew had a mug of coffee poured for her. Dolly motioned excitedly, but silently, from the pantry.

Indeed, all four kittens had their eyes open. They

were still tiny, but their fur was softer, less matted-looking, and even Tippy Tail seemed more pleased with the situation.

Dolly whispered, "Daddy says I can hold one if I'm careful."

She scooped up the gray one—Cement Mixer—with two hands and held it against her cheek, her eyes shining at Tess. "She's so soft!"

Harl came in through the back door. Dolly had to show him the kittens, too. He grunted, which seemed enough for the six-year-old, and she ran out to get ready for school. There was some discussion over taking the magic wand Lauren Montague had given her. Harl and Andrew didn't think that would go over well with Dolly's teacher.

Tess stayed out of it. Dolly handled herself well with the two men, and they seemed to know just how far they could go with her without overpowering her.

Harl said, "I'm still in training as a teacher's helper. Will you give me a hand today?"

That thrilled her. "But I don't want you coming to my school *every* day, Harl, okay?"

"Yeah, I know. Kids need a chance to give away their celery sticks without some big old adult hanging over their head."

Andrew, Tess noticed, kept his opinion on the subject to himself, allowing his daughter and cousin to have their own relationship.

"I'm off to Boston for the morning," Tess announced abruptly. "I need to check in at the office, but I don't imagine I'll stay long."

She decided not to mention checking more emails, since the first batch of archives had produced little. She was probably just spinning her wheels, digging into the history of the carriage house, reading emails between Ike and herself—making herself feel as if she was doing something when she wasn't. But what else was she supposed to do? Stay at the carriage house and mop more floors? Sit on the police until they got busy?

"Keep in touch," Andrew said.

"I named all the kittens," Dolly told her in the sort of non sequitur Tess had come to expect. "Cement Mixer, Snowflake, Midnight and Pooh."

Tess made a face. "Pooh?"

Dolly giggled. "I know Winnie-the-Pooh's a bear, but Daddy says it's okay."

He repeated his mantra. "Dolly, we're not keeping the kittens. You know that, right?"

She rolled her eyes, not answering. Squelching a smile, Tess headed out.

Traffic on Route One was miserable, and she got caught in a backup for an accident, then another one for construction. She parked on Beacon Hill, raced to her office and took the stairs to the fourth floor two at a time. She didn't know why she was rushing, but she couldn't stop herself.

Susanna Galway calmly looked up from her computer. "I've been sitting here making money for hours. You look as if you've been digging up more skeletons. Some reporter keeps calling, and I keep putting him off."

Susanna looked gorgeous, as always, and probably had been making money for hours. Tess glow-ered at her and dropped into her chair. "What do you think the odds were of my ending up with a carriage house next door to a motherless six-year-old girl, a burned-out cop and an architect-contractor?"

"Seeing how Ike Grantham gave it to you, very good."

"They were a factor, then."

"This is just now occurring to you?"

"No," Tess said, slightly annoyed. "It occurred to me sitting in traffic."

Susanna shrugged, ignoring Tess's irritable remark. "I think Ike was worried about more ghosts than Jedidiah Thorne."

Tess had worked this out, too, and knew what Susanna meant. "My mother."

Nothing more needed to be said, and Susanna returned to her work. Tess checked messages. Most could be put off for another day, but one could not. Fortunately, it only required five minutes to take herself off the hook. Then, without mentioning to Susanna what she was up to, she checked her email archives for messages from her to Ike.

There were forty-nine.

One was on the day of the meeting when he'd stood her up. She opened it.

Three o'clock is perfect for our meeting. Don't worry if you're a little late—enjoy your last walk-through at the carriage house. I'm not sure I'll let you in after I renovate! Of course, you might not want to come near the place—have I told you I love gingham and chintz? Okay, have fun, and don't get into a duel with your future brother-in-law. One ghost haunting the carriage house is plenty.

She'd forgotten that he'd been meeting his future brother-in-law—Richard Montague—that day. It was one of a thousand insignificant exchanges she'd had with Ike, and there'd been no reason to attach any importance to where he'd gone that morning. After all, he hadn't been *missing*.

But he was now, Tess thought. She just hadn't realized it until the past few days.

Maybe he'd never made it to the carriage house. Maybe he'd left town before his meeting there with Richard Montague.

Tess checked ten more emails, refusing to let her thoughts rush ahead, and as she read, she remembered the easy banter between Ike and herself. It wasn't just on his end—it was on hers, too, but without the slashing wit, the thrill of poking at other people's weaknesses.

Ike had loved Joanna Thorne, and he'd believed Richard Montague, who was about to marry his sister, Lauren, was partly responsible for Joanna's malaise. The woman had worked for him, and anyone who worked for Richard Montague had to be as consumed with getting him to Washington as he was. She hadn't made all the connections until now, perhaps because she hadn't known the players, perhaps because she'd been so occupied with sorting out her own life and hadn't paid proper attention to what was going on with Ike.

The reference to Joanna working for Richard was in a note from Ike copied at the bottom of one of Tess's emails to him. She hadn't kept the original.

Whether he was a client or perhaps even a friend, her relationship with Ike, she now saw, had been a guilty pleasure. She hadn't really known the people he'd trashed with his cutting, often very funny wit. Now she felt like a coconspirator, although she couldn't bring herself to regret their relationship. He'd never meant people to take him seriously. He was an overgrown adolescent who believed everyone should forgive his excesses because he was a good guy at heart. Tess had never expected anything from him—Ike Grantham was what he was.

But, she thought, he really hadn't liked Richard Montague at all.

She sat back, her head pounding. "Susanna, yesterday Richard Montague told me he hadn't been to the carriage house in years." Her voice was steady but hollow, the strain evident. "That was a flat-out lie. He and Ike were supposed to meet there a few hours before Ike stood me up."

"There could be an innocent reason."

But Susanna's voice was flat and serious, and Tess knew they shared the same fear. "What if Richard Montague was the last person to see Ike alive? Wouldn't he want to tell the police, especially now, given the circumstances?"

"Maybe Ike never showed up."

Tess swallowed, her throat dry and tight. "Maybe he did."

Susanna swore under her breath.

"They meet, they argue over Lauren and Joanna—"

"And Ike ends up buried in the cellar."

Tess looked over at her friend. "Am I getting ahead of the facts?"

"Way ahead." Her green eyes leveled on Tess. "But who cares? You're not a cop. Go sit on the Beacon police, Tess. Make them talk to this Montague character. Look, another month or two of Ike Grantham and

I might have been driven to dump him in a dirt cellar myself, but—" She inhaled. "Damn it, you don't get to murder people."

And there it was, Tess thought. You don't get to murder people.

She printed out a copy of the pertinent emails and charged out, promising Susanna she'd check in later. "Don't tell your grandmother or *anyone* who's ever stepped foot in my father's bar about this development, okay? I could be off track, and it was hard enough explaining falling on top of a skeleton in the first place."

Susanna nodded, but managed a grim smile. "Davey and the gang would never let you live down accusing someone of murder based on an email."

"God, it is thin, isn't it?"

"Go. Let the police talk to Montague and find out if he has a simple explanation."

"I hope he does. Matter of fact, I'm still hoping it *was* a ghost I saw."

Susanna said nothing, but Tess knew—they both knew.

Ike Grantham was dead.

Andrew found Lauren in her herb garden with her poodles. The little dogs were running through the grass, looking as if they'd collide, but never did. Lauren stood on a narrow gravel path among the herbs—Andrew recognized oregano, several kinds of thyme, sage, all getting going for the season. The seaside mansion and extensive grounds reminded Andrew that Lauren Grantham Montague was a wealthy woman. It was easy to forget, and maybe she wanted it that way. She didn't have drivers or guards at a gate or even full-time household help, but she came from money—and a lot of it.

If she or Ike wanted to disappear, or to make someone else disappear, they could do it.

"Dolly would enjoy the poodles." Lauren spoke without looking at him, her gaze on the dogs. "You should bring her by sometime."

One of the dogs scrambled over Andrew's foot. He ignored the tight ball of tension in his gut and concentrated on why he was here. But he let her have her moment of pleasantries. Why not? "I'm sure she'd get a kick out of these guys. She's an animal lover."

Lauren turned to him, her eyes red-veined, as if she hadn't slept in days. She smiled without feeling. "Most princesses are."

Her comment irritated him. Her idea of being a princess and Dolly's were so different. Lauren didn't have a clue about how he or his daughter thought. It wasn't because she was rich. That was too simple, too black-and-white. She established her own ideas for who people were and what they believed, why they did what they did, to suit herself. She'd take one fact about them and run with it, creating a whole panorama out of one tidbit. He'd seen her do it even with antiques she brought to Harl. She'd mix fact with fantasy, project herself and her own perceptions and beliefs, and turn a Windsor chair into a grand story.

Bottom line, she tended to jump to conclusions about people.

Andrew suspected she had about him.

"Tess Haviland's skeleton is for real," he said.

She didn't seem surprised at his abrupt comment.

"She thinks it's Ike. That's the police's nightmare scenario. They're hoping he turns up."

"What about you?"

She shrugged. "It would be horrible if it was Ike. I'd suffer personally, of course, but so would the project, my husband, you. Richard's Pentagon appointment is already in jeopardy, just at the whiff of something wrong. And you. You're right next door. Can you imagine if it turns out that Ike Grantham was killed in the Thorne carriage house?"

"You sound like a reporter reading the news. He's your brother."

She tossed back her head, annoyed. "I know who he is."

Andrew didn't back off. "You know more than you've admitted."

She kept her head back, her eyes half-closed as she stared at him. "Do I?"

"Lauren, whatever pieces of this mess you have—maybe you've put them together wrong, come up with the wrong answers."

She scooped up one of the dogs and held it, scratching under its chin. "I think I like dogs better than people." She pressed her cheek to the top of the dog's head, her eyes filled with tears. "You don't respect me, Andrew. You never have. You've never appreciated what I do for you—or anyone else for that matter. You're very independent that way, you know."

He didn't respond. A light breeze had stirred, bringing out the smells of grass and soil, flowers. It was a beautiful spot, no old Adirondack chairs, no overgrown lilacs, no Harl.

Lauren set down the dog and walked a few steps

onto the path. The herb garden was planted in a classic star pattern, with a gazing globe at the center. "I haven't seen or heard from my brother since last March. He was supposed to meet Tess that afternoon in Boston to discuss a new design for the project's webpage. They often met up here, but not that day."

The dogs had followed her onto the path and were getting into the herbs. Lauren herded them out of the rosemary. "Stay on the paths, kiddos, or I'll put you inside." She squatted and replaced dirt one of them had scratched up. "He was stopping at the carriage house first. He told me at breakfast. We'd argued."

"About the carriage house?"

She shook her head and rose, brushing the dirt off her hands. "No, about his living arrangements."

Andrew knew what she was talking about. A frequent subject of gossip in town, the Grantham living arrangements were one of their more obvious eccentricities. When he was in town, whether for an extended period or a few days, Ike lived in the family mansion with his sister. It apparently was never a problem with her first husband. He and Lauren had traveled frequently themselves, and his family owned a place on Cape Cod. After their divorce, with their daughter away at school, it was just Ike and Lauren again, brother and sister, in the Beacon-by-the-Sea house where they'd grown up, an arrangement that apparently had suited them.

But Andrew guessed all that changed when Lauren decided to remarry. "Richard didn't want Ike staying here?"

"He wanted me to buy out Ike's share, minus all the work I'd had done, the maintenance, the taxes I'd paid.

If not for me, the termites or the tax man would have gotten this place. Ike never lifted a finger or contributed a dime. Richard didn't want to be unfair to him, but Ike was furious. You know how he was—is." The correction was halfhearted, and she gave a quick, sad smile, as if she didn't expect Andrew to believe she thought her brother was alive. "Rules and details like mowing the lawn and paying property taxes were for other people, not him. He was above that sort of day-to-day trivia. That's all well and good, I told him—then he should hire someone to handle the tasks that bore him."

"I don't recall you two arguing in the time I've known you."

"We never did, but Richard made me see how my brother was taking advantage of me—and had been for years and years. All our lives, really."

Andrew walked onto an offshoot of the main path, two of the dogs scooting past him. He was suddenly aware of the stillness and beauty around him and expected this would be hard to give up. And Ike would feel entitled to it. That was the way he was.

But Andrew stuck to the main issue—Ike's actions on that day in March. "Why was he headed to the carriage house?"

"Oh, he was being ridiculous. He said he never should have given it to Tess, he should have kept it himself and renovated it as his Beacon-by-the-Sea home. He was trying to pretend nothing I said mattered."

"The carriage house isn't on as grand a scale as this place—"

She waved a hand angrily. "Ike was just blowing smoke. He'd never give up this place without a fight, without making me feel as if I were stabbing him in the back. He'd fight me every inch of the way. I never told Richard, but according to our parents' will—he could win."

"They stipulated you both owned the property or neither did?"

She nodded, almost embarrassed. "Basically. It was a way to manipulate me from the grave. They knew Ike wouldn't live up to his share of the responsibilities, so they made sure I'd have to keep sweeping up after him the way they did. It's not as if I couldn't afford to." She turned and started back down the path toward the lawn, walking slowly, pensive more than outraged. "Richard was having none of it. I didn't want him to know how I rated with my parents."

"What did you do after you and Ike argued?" Andrew asked.

"I went to the office. Ike got all the prestige there, too, without having to do any of the hard work. He did what he wanted to, what amused him. I was furious with myself for putting up with it. It was as if Richard had taken off the blinders, and I have to say I didn't thank him for it. It's an awful feeling, knowing you've been a doormat for your brother, that your own parents expected that of you."

Andrew headed on a parallel path back out to the lawn, the poodles there ahead of him, finally collapsing in the shade. "You must have hated him at that moment," he said.

"No, that's just it." She smiled over at him, tears spilling out onto her cheeks now. But her voice was steady, as if she was unaware she was crying. "I loved my brother. I take him as he is, faults and all, the whole package. All I really wanted, I realized, was the same from him. Acceptance of my bad points, appreciation for my good ones."

"So, you're sitting in your office, fuming, but finally you figure—the hell with it, I need to patch things up with Ike, explain to Richard my brother's a part of the package and move on." Andrew glanced over at her. "You don't wait. You head to the carriage house."

"Yes." Her voice was distant, and he could feel her transporting herself back in time, to that March day. "It was very cold. I remember being impatient for spring. March is my least favorite month, but last year it was just interminable. But I walked over. I wanted the cold air to whip the last of the resentment out of me, I suppose."

"What time?"

"It was before lunch. About eleven, I'd say."

She spoke in a monotone, and she began shivering. Andrew stepped closer to her. "Then what?"

"I didn't see his car. He must have walked. He was always so physical, and he'd have wanted the exercise after our argument. I knew he was there." She crossed her arms on her chest, pressed them against her. "I climbed up the side steps."

She stopped, her face going ashen, the shivering worse. Andrew knew he had to keep her in that moment, talking. "Did you go inside?"

"Not then."

"You saw something," he said.

Her eyes met his. He could see her swallow. "I saw you."

"You're sure?"

"You were going through the lilacs. You had on that

old denim jacket of yours. I called you, and you didn't answer."

"Did you see me, Lauren, or did you see my jacket?"

"I saw *you*."

He didn't argue, still wanted her in that moment. "What did you do after you didn't get an answer?"

"I went inside."

"Into the carriage house," he prodded.

She nodded, her eyes dry now, dull. "There was water…and an awful smell. Lime. Flesh. At first I thought it was my imagination—"

"You thought it was the ghost at work."

"Yes, the ghost. That's what I thought. But I knew…" She looked at him, focused on him. "I knew better."

"Lauren—"

But she didn't stop, and he saw what was coming, felt it. "I knew you'd killed my brother. Because of Joanna. I didn't blame you. Ike shouldn't have gotten involved."

He didn't react outwardly. Carefully, he took her back to that day last March. "When you were at the carriage house, did you see Ike?"

"No." She shook her head. "Not then. The trapdoor was wet. It—it was unlatched. I latched it again and left. I never went back."

"You went back this Saturday," Andrew said quietly.

"Yes, when Tess finally showed up. I couldn't bring myself to act any sooner. I wish I'd waited until later in the evening, but Richard—" She paused to swallow, her breathing light and rapid, her voice strangely calm. "Richard would have noticed and asked questions. Andrew, I didn't want you to realize what I knew. I just wanted to take care of Ike for you."

Jesus, Andrew thought, but maintained his outward

control. "You collected his remains from the carriage house cellar."

"So you didn't have to."

"Where are they now?"

With one hand, she brushed back her straight, shining hair and leveled her eyes at him. They were clear and sad, but also, Andrew decided, a little smug. After all, she'd risked a lot to do him this favor. "I'll show you. We'll need to decide what to do with them."

We. Andrew gritted his teeth. Had someone tried to frame him? Or was connecting him to the jacket just a leap of logic on Lauren's part? She got a glimpse of denim and filled in the blanks.

She started across the lawn and glanced back at him, not breaking her stride. "Ike always wanted to be buried at sea." She smiled almost peacefully. "I think we can arrange that, don't you?"

Andrew decided it was time to go on record. "Lauren, I didn't kill him."

But she ignored him, whistling for the poodles. They roused, stretched and trotted after her with less energy than when they'd romped in the herbs.

"Coming?" she asked, the wind picking up, whipping tawny hairs into her mouth.

Andrew nodded. "Sure."

She took him around front to the driveway. Her car was parked in front of his, and he winced as she went to the trunk. "Hell," he breathed, watching her pop it open.

She gasped. *"No!"*

Andrew saw from where he stood. The trunk was empty.

This woman had been carrying her brother's remains

in her trunk for the past three days, thinking Andrew had killed him.

She spun around at him. "Is this your idea of a *joke?* He was in a black garbage bag. I put him there myself. I made sure I had all of him. I didn't want to leave behind a finger or something for the police to find. You know, with DNA testing, these days you can't just leave that sort of thing lying around." She was talking rapidly, her composure eroding fast. "My God in heaven. What kind of person would steal a bag of *bones* out of my car?"

What kind of person would have them in there in the first place? Andrew reined in an urge to get in his car and get the hell out of there. "Lauren, we need to call the police."

She frowned at him. "What?"

"I didn't kill Ike. You don't need to protect me."

"But I—I saw you."

"It wasn't me."

She blinked. "What?"

He was losing her. The stress of finding her trunk empty was too much. "Where's your husband?"

"Richard? He's at work."

Andrew didn't think so. Richard Montague was shorter than he was and thicker through the chest, but he could have easily grabbed the denim jacket off its hook on the back porch and thrown it on, just in case someone saw him at the carriage house and Ike's body was discovered sooner rather than later.

Even later—now, over a year later—his simple precaution was paying off.

"Lauren, did you tell Richard you were going to the carriage house to talk to Ike that morning last March?"

She rallied. "Yes, we talked right after I got to the office. Why?"

Because it meant Richard had planned for her to think Andrew had killed her brother, in case she showed up. He'd guessed how she'd react. He was an expert in that sort of thinking. It also meant killing Ike wasn't an accident Richard covered up, but a deliberate act.

"We need to call the police," Andrew said. "And we need to find your husband."

Twenty-Five

━━━◦◦◦━━━

Richard needed a murderer.

He parked his car in the carriage house driveway. He had the outlines of a plan—a daring plan, because daring was called for—and he needed to be direct. To hide his car was to invite the wrong sort of question.

He was an innocent man. He needed to act innocent.

He got his Walther .9 mm out of the glove compartment. Lauren hated guns, so he'd never mentioned the one he kept in his desk at his office. It was against company policy, but he'd sneaked it in piece by piece.

He tucked the weapon into his waistband and got Ike's bones out of the trunk. With the bag tightly sealed, no smells could escape, yet he could smell it, anyway, knew it was the memory of over a year ago. He hadn't expected blood. Ike must have caught his head on a loose nail on his way down the carriage house stairs.

But there was the smell of the lime, too, it and the dirt cellar floor, Ike's body, all wet and slick from being hosed down. He'd had to speed decomposition, move things along before warm weather set in.

He'd burned Ike's expensive clothes and tossed the

ashes into the sea. Much easier than getting rid of a body. He'd cleaned up inside as best he could.

He hadn't worried that much about someone discovering Ike's remains in the cellar. He'd taken precautions. But he hadn't counted on Lauren stealing them. He thought he could weather having a brother-in-law turn up dead, but having his wife involved was something else altogether. That smug bastard Jeremy Carver would never stand for that sort of scandal.

No, he couldn't just dump Ike's remains at sea. He needed to produce a murderer. An ending to this sordid affair. The work he did was far too important to risk that he might end up in any way tarnished by Ike Grantham's death.

He ducked through a small gap in the lilac hedge, the trash bag snagging on a branch. The smell came through, musty and earthy. His stomach roiled.

He could hear the little girl—Dolly—singing in her tree house. He moved quietly across the lawn to Harley Beckett's workshop. The door was open, and as he crossed the threshold, he removed the Walther from his waistband and leveled it at Harl, who was already reaching for a baseball bat.

"I wouldn't," Richard said.

"Yeah, you wouldn't—you've got a goddamn gun. What do you need with a baseball bat?"

But Harl's hand was suspended midair, his eyes focused on Richard, his white ponytail hanging over his left shoulder. Richard set the bones on the floor. "With Tess Haviland's report of a skeleton, I've reluctantly come to the conclusion that you had to be involved. You live right here on the other side of the lilac hedge.

You're a burnout. There was no love lost between you and my brother-in-law. But before I went to the police with such an explosive accusation, I thought I should check it out myself. Armed, of course."

"Just don't touch the kid. You hear me? Touch her, and I'll haunt you forever. It won't be pretty."

Richard smiled and shook his head. "Such a romantic." He motioned toward the door with his gun. "Shall we? I'm afraid I need you at the carriage house."

"Hide the weapon. I don't want Dolly to see it. I'll cooperate."

"Just move," Richard said, "and pray."

The little girl didn't stop singing as Richard followed Harl back through the lilacs. Beckett seemed to relax once they were onto the carriage house driveway, out of view of the tree house. He glanced back at Richard, his eyes knowing. "No way I'm coming out of this alive?"

"Unfortunately, no," Richard said. "No way. It's not personal. In my work I've learned that sometimes one must make sacrifices for the greater good."

"The greater good here being saving your sorry ass."

"The world needs me."

"Yeah? You know what I say? Screw the world."

Richard smirked. "That's what all the burnouts say. Let's go inside, shall we?"

Harl started up the kitchen steps.

"You're a brave man," Richard said. "There's a role in the world for simple, uneducated, brave men with a clear sense of duty."

"It's called cannon fodder."

"Gallows humor?"

Beckett didn't answer.

Once inside, Richard had him unlatch the trapdoor

and lift it. "I know you're going to try something. In fact, I'm counting on it."

But what Beckett did, Richard hadn't counted on. He said, "Fuck you," and dove headfirst through the trapdoor. He might have been diving into the ocean.

Richard fired, striking Harl in the hip as he disappeared through the opening. His second shot hit the wall. He heard Harl land with a sickening thud on the dirt floor below, without a cry of pain, a moan or even so much as a sigh.

Richard stood over the dark opening. Maybe Harl had broken his neck. A headfirst dive was risky and awkward—unexpected. But if he'd gone through the trapdoor feetfirst, Richard would have had a better chance of hitting a vital organ or shooting him in the head. It didn't matter, provided Richard could credibly claim self-defense.

What a moronic move on Harl's part, Richard thought, frustrated, as he got down on his knees and with his free hand, unlatched the ladder. He had to make sure Harl was dead. The only way his plan would work was if he could claim to have killed Harley Beckett in self-defense.

Though who would believe Beckett's version of events over his own?

The ladder dropped to the floor.

This was very risky. If Harl was alive and functioning, Richard would be exposed on the rickety ladder.

Best to go around to the bulkhead, he decided.

He tucked the Walther into his waistband, observed that he wasn't breathing hard at all and headed for the kitchen door.

A little girl popped through the lilacs. "Have you seen my cat?" she asked.

* * *

Tess pulled up in front of Andrew's house and jumped out of the car. He wasn't at his office. She'd stopped at the Beacon Historic Project offices to check on Lauren Montague, but she wasn't there, either. Tess wanted to talk to both Lauren and Andrew about her visit to the police.

They were looking into Ike Grantham's disappearance. They weren't happy with what they'd found—or, more accurately, *hadn't* found—so far. They thought perhaps she had seen a skeleton on Friday night, after all.

"We wish you'd called us then," Paul Alvarez had told her.

"I wish I had, too."

She pounded up the front steps, but the door was locked and no one answered the bell. She went around back, calling for Harl and Andrew both.

Harl's workshop door was open. Tess picked up her pace, calling for him as she ran over to the outbuilding at the far end of the yard.

She saw the black trash bag and knew what it was. To be sure, she tucked a finger in where it was torn and peered inside.

Bones.

Ike.

It was after school. Harl would have picked up Dolly by now. Had they gone somewhere together?

"Dolly!"

Tess ran out of the shop, climbed up into the girl's tree house. There were stuffed animals and her tea set and books, and a plate of chocolate chip cookies.

"Dolly!"

She could hear panic edging into her voice, assaulting her system. She half climbed, half jumped out of the tree house. She had to call Andrew, but she'd left her cell phone in the car.

Tippy Tail leaped out of the rhododendrons. Tess was so startled, she thought she'd die on the spot, but she didn't scream.

Someone had put the garbage bag in Harl's shop.

Not Harl, she thought.

If Tippy Tail had escaped from the pantry and her kittens, Dolly would be on the case. *Find her,* Tess told herself. *Then call the police.*

Or call the police first?

She was already at Dolly's gap in the lilac hedge. A fat blossom brushed against her face as she started through to her yard.

A black BMW was parked in her driveway. A painful jolt of adrenaline shot through her. *Richard.* Tess took a step backward, knowing she had to call the police now, first, but she heard Dolly say, "My name's *Princess* Dolly."

Tess went dead-still.

Oh, God.

Her only advantage was that they hadn't seen her. She had no choice. She had to back out into Andrew's yard, and she had to call him, and she had to call the police. She couldn't take any chances. Not with a six-year-old, she thought. Not with Dolly.

"And I'm *not* going into that dirty old cellar!"

She was there in the lilacs before Tess could move, and the little girl gasped in surprise. "Tess! Tell that man I don't have to do what he says. Have you seen Tippy Tail? And I can't find Harl." She was talking rapidly, ready to cry. "Will you help me find Tippy Tail and Harl?"

Richard Montague came up behind Dolly. "Hello, Miss Haviland."

Tess grabbed the little girl, pulled her through the lilacs and shoved her toward the house. "Run, Dolly! Run! Go get your dad. Hurry!"

"But what are you—"

"Go! It's an emergency. Get your dad. Call 911. Tell them Richard Montague's a—a—"

Dolly's eyes widened in terror. "Is he a bank robber?"

"Yes!" Tess hung on to every shred of control, refused to look back through the lilacs, although she knew what was happening. Dolly was moving toward the house. "Show me how fast you can run!"

Dolly started screaming and running.

"Oh, for God's sake." Richard Montague leveled a very black gun at Tess through the gap in the lilacs. "Obviously you're in this with Harl."

Tess feigned complete surprise, as if Montague couldn't have heard her instructions to Dolly. "Look, I don't know what you're talking about. Is Harl with you? I can't believe he left Dolly alone."

"Come through the lilacs, Miss Haviland." She really had no choice. While she had her doubts whether he'd shoot her—how would he explain it?—he just might. "Fine," she said, impatient, ignoring the twist of fear in her stomach, "let's get this straightened out. I don't like people pointing guns at me."

When she landed on the carriage house side of the lilacs, Richard Montague stepped back. He looked ragged, gray-faced. And calm, she thought. Arrogant.

"I don't usually underestimate people," he said, "but I'm afraid I underestimated Harley Beckett."

"Harl? Come on. He works on furniture and takes care of a six-year-old."

"And you," Montague added, as if she hadn't spoken.

"Me? Not to worry. People underestimate me all the time. It comes with the turf. When you're a graphic designer, the artists all think you're not a real artist and thus not one of them, and the nonartists all think you're a real artist and thus not one of *them*." She sighed, her instincts operating almost without her consent. "Please put the gun away. I'm not in cahoots with Harley Beckett."

"He's manipulated everyone, my wife included. He killed Ike. I found his remains in the trunk of Lauren's car. I brought them here—I was furious, I admit. I wasn't thinking."

Tess doubted Richard Montague ever stopped thinking. "You confronted him?"

He nodded. "I should have called the police."

"But you didn't. What did Harl do?"

"He told me he wanted to confess. We walked over here together, but that was another manipulation. He jumped me, and my gun went off—"

"My God." Tess could feel herself go pale, her breathing get shallow. Her throat and chest felt tight. "Were either of you hurt?"

"I wasn't."

"Dr. Montague—"

"You've done well, Tess, but now—" He shrugged, resigned. He motioned at her with his gun. "Let's go inside, shall we?"

* * *

Richard didn't love her. He'd never loved her. He loved the *idea* of her. Her money. Her family name. Her house on the ocean. Ike had seen through him from the beginning.

She should have known. He saw through everybody.

Lauren ducked under a low-hanging branch and sank onto her favorite teak bench under a canopy of climbing roses. They wouldn't bloom until mid-June. She wondered if she'd be around when they did.

What did the police do to a woman who'd tried to cover up the murder of her brother, even if she was protecting the wrong man?

Would she be arrested, tried, found guilty of something and thrown into prison?

If she'd testified against Andrew, he could have been convicted, like Jedidiah Thorne, of a murder he did not commit.

But, of course, Andrew would never lose control. She should have known.

Two poodles climbed onto her lap, the third snuggled next to her. She sank her head back and closed her eyes, smelling the roses that weren't there as she waited for the police to come for her.

The police were on the way.

Andrew gripped the wheel of his truck and drove along the ocean road. The tide was up, the wind brisk. He had his windows rolled down and was breathing in the ocean smells, letting them calm him. He would get home. He would find Harl and Dolly.

Harl wasn't answering his phone, but he did that on a regular basis.

But not today. He'd answer today. He had to.

Andrew hit redial on his cell phone one more time. A little farther and he'd be there.

Dolly.

He jumped on the brakes and was out of his truck before the picture fully registered in his brain. His daughter. She was running down the side of the road, red-faced, her sturdy little legs eating up pavement.

He scooped her into his arms. She was sweating, unable to talk or cry.

"I've got you, baby, I've got you."

"The bank robber," she choked out. "The bank robber."

"I know, I know."

She gulped. "Tess."

He wanted to tell her it would be okay, but he didn't know it would be. He carried her to his truck, kept her on his lap as he climbed behind the wheel and pulled the door shut.

"Are they at the carriage house?" he asked softly, trying to sound calm, in control, to hide his own terror.

She nodded, holding on to him tight.

Then his house was safe.

He dialed the police and told them Richard Montague might have hostages at the carriage house.

His truck moved forward, down the road. Dolly's sweat soaked into her shirt. And his own.

She began to cry openly. "Daddy, Daddy, Tippy Tail's *gone.*"

"She'll come back, Dolly. She won't leave her babies."

And his heart wrenched, Joanna's voice playing back

to him. *"I'll be back, Dolly. I would never leave my baby."*

Ah, Joanna, he thought. *You died too young, and I'll be forever sorry for that.*

But every fiber of his being, right now, with his daughter in his arms, was with Tess. He couldn't lose her.

He pulled to a stop in front of his house.

Harl staggered in front of the truck. A baseball bat dangled from one hand. He was ashen-faced, his entire front covered in dirt, his face smeared with it.

And blood. It was on his hands and arms, and Andrew saw the dark, wet spots on his jeans and black POW-MIA shirt.

As Andrew opened the truck's door, Harl grabbed Dolly. "Go," he told Andrew. "I just crawled out of the carriage house bulkhead. Montague's there. Go before the son of a bitch—" But Dolly was staring at him, wide-eyed, and his voice softened instinctively. "I've got you, sweetie." His eyes, pain-wracked but totally focused, leveled on Andrew. "Don't wait. Go."

Andrew took the baseball bat and went.

"I think that cat wants to move her kittens back here." Tess spoke matter-of-factly, ignoring the panic that was trying to work its way through her, ignoring the gun. Richard had told her it was a Walther .9 mm. She'd told him she didn't know guns. "Did you shove Harl through the trapdoor the way you did Ike?"

Richard had quit his it-was-Harl act. He was thinking—plotting his strategy, she knew—before he killed her rather than after. He had the trapdoor open already.

"Don't you think you should make sure Harl's dead first?"

She thought that would buy her some time. If he wasn't dead—and she prayed constantly he wasn't—he might have a chance to do something to help their critical situation. And if he was dead, she knew he wouldn't want Richard Montague to get away with another murder.

If he did, they could haunt the damn carriage house together. Her, Harl and Jedidiah.

Don't get giddy. Stay focused!

"Tess! Montague!" Andrew was yelling from the driveway in that hell-to-pay voice. "The police are on their way. For God's sake, Montague, cut your losses. Harl's alive."

In that split second between thinking he had the upper hand and realizing he didn't, Richard Montague gave Tess the opening she'd been waiting for. It was a gesture, a momentary loss of concentration, but she saw it, knew it.

And she gave him a slicing, unequivocal kick to the testicles, just the way Davey Ahearn had taught her.

Montague dropped the Walther down the trapdoor and sank forward in agony, and Tess followed with another kick, throwing him off balance. He stumbled, falling into the dark opening, grabbing the ladder with one hand as he cursed and spat.

She stomped on his hand.

In a fight, her godfather had always told her, you don't show mercy. But you fight to get away, period.

Montague let go, but before he could regain his balance, Tess slammed the trapdoor shut, latched it and ran out through the kitchen.

The police were massing in her driveway, lights and sirens off.

But she landed in Andrew's arms.

"Perfect timing," she said, her voice catching.

He managed a ragged smile. "Always."

Twenty-Six

It was chowder night at Jim's Place.

Davey Ahearn was on his stool at the end of the bar, and the Red Sox were playing an away game with an expansion team he didn't consider worthy of the big leagues. Tess didn't even know who it was. She was concentrating on her chowder and her argument with her father.

"The carriage house is on the state historic register," she said. "I can't do a deck with a giant hot tub. Besides, that's tacky."

"Almost getting yourself killed—that's tacky."

It had been a month. Four weeks of no skeletons, beautiful spring weather, and time with Andrew and Dolly. First, they'd made sure the six-year-old was okay. Rita Perez was a huge help, and Tess could see Harl was falling in love with the ex-nun. She'd done her part, too, because she'd once been a traumatized six-year-old girl and could talk to Dolly in a way the little girl understood.

But Dolly was resilient and creative, and a step in her healing, Tess thought, was moving from the world of royalty to oceanography. She was loading up on stuffed penguins, whales, dolphins and sea otters. But cats were still her favorite, and she'd even managed to talk her father and Harl into keeping one of the kittens, the gray one, Cement Mixer. Tippy Tail had settled in and no longer ran off for long stretches.

Tess had settled in, too, if not in Andrew's house at least in his life, and that both scared and excited her. It meant walks on the beach with him, wine on the back porch, fixing dinner together, working in the yard together, coming up with ideas for the carriage house together. And dates. Once Dolly was in good shape, Tess had pointed out that uncovering a murder and stopping a murderer didn't count as a date.

She'd spend nights in the guest room or at her apartment, never at the carriage house, never in Andrew's room, not until one night when Dolly was off with Rita Perez, Harl and the rest of the Thorne family in Gloucester, celebrating his release from the hospital.

Tess remembered every slow, delicious move Andrew made that night in his bed as they made love, the feel of his rangy, muscular body, the heat of his kisses, the look of his eyes in the dark of his bedroom. She remembered quaking with him, losing herself with him.

But thinking of such things in her father's bar could only lead to trouble. "If not for Davey, you know," she said, "I might have ended up dumped through that trapdoor myself."

Her father shook his head. "Damn, I never thought I'd hear my daughter tell me she was alive today because Davey Ahearn taught her how to kick a man in the balls when she was twelve years old."

"Best time to learn," Davey said.

Jim Haviland took her empty bowl and refilled it, not waiting to be asked. He'd also made chocolate cream pie, her favorite, because he knew she'd be here tonight. Tess understood. It was his way of telling himself she'd come through this mess intact. She was alive. Richard Montague was awaiting trial, and Lauren, both shattered and relieved by the truth of what happened to her brother, had her lawyers working out a plea bargain for her role in covering up Ike's murder.

A slim, yellowed volume had turned up in Tess's mail at work. Adelaide Morse's diary. There was no note, but Tess knew it must have come from Lauren. She'd read it in one sitting. Jedidiah Thorne was innocent. He didn't kill Benjamin Morse, yet he'd refused to mount a defense at his trial—because the evidence against him was too overwhelming and he couldn't win without a confession from Adelaide? Or because of that peculiar sense of Thorne honor Tess had come to know so well? She'd given the diary to Andrew. He could correct the public, historic record. Or not.

"I don't know how you can draw up plans for that damn place," her father said. "I'd tear it down."

"I can't. It's on the historic register."

Davey grunted. "One match. That's all it'd take."

"Look, I don't expect you two to understand, and I'm not sure I do myself, but something happened…" Tess sighed, scooping up more chowder. It was thick and creamy, a pat of butter melting into the clams and potatoes. "About a week after the police took Montague away, I'd been to see Harl in the hospital. He was trying to break out, but Rita Perez, Dolly's teacher, was there. Anyway, I stopped back at the carriage house."

"By yourself?" her father asked.

She nodded. "The bad guy was in jail."

"Up to me, you'd never go out alone again," he grumbled. "So, what happened?"

"I was standing in the big room, picturing Ike falling to his death, Richard Montague shooting Harl as he dived through the trapdoor, me fighting him off. I could see Dolly running through her yard, screaming in total panic. I could feel my chest squeezing, a panic attack coming on."

"I don't believe in panic attacks," Davey said. "I think that's a bunch of pop-psych bullshit."

Tess cast him a silencing look.

"Go on," her father said.

"Then—I know this is going to sound weird—but it's what happened. I felt this warmth surround me, this incredible sense of peace, and I knew it was Jedidiah and Ike…and Mom," she said. "They were there, all of them. And I knew it would be all right."

For two seconds, Davey and her father were silent, and she thought for once in her life, they might actually understand her creative imagination.

Then Davey snorted. "Hell, I wish I had me some ghosts today to tell me it was all right, I could open the trap on that sewer line and all those weeping-willow roots would just melt away. Uh-uh. Broke my goddamn plumber snake on them."

"I was going to get rid of my trapdoor," Tess said, "but I don't think so. I think I'll keep it around for you, Davey. You bug me, and I'll give you a good kick to the testicles—"

"Balls," he said. "Testicles sounds too medicinal."

"I'm not even going there."

"Chowder night, the Red Sox and a discussion of

ghosts and men's privates." Andrew slid onto the stool next to her and grinned. "My kind of place."

Tess felt a surge of warmth and glanced over at Davey, wondering if he'd noticed. But she didn't care. She smiled at Andrew. "How long have you been here?"

"An hour."

"An *hour?*" She glared at her father. "You knew? Is this some male thing, you not telling me he was here? Because it has to stop."

He shrugged. "You've got eyes. You can see who's here as well as I can."

"I was preoccupied."

"With fantasizing about turning a haunted carriage house into a graphic design studio," Davey said. "Geez, Thorne, I'm glad you came forward before my eyes glazed over in boredom. You're the architect. You like this stuff."

Tess kept her focus on Andrew. "Susanna's helping me with a five-year business plan. It's torture for me, but she's having a ball."

"Do you think you can skip chocolate cream pie?" he asked, his voice low, deep, sexy.

"Well, it better be for a good reason—"

"Jesus Christ," Davey said. "You want me to paint you a picture?"

She almost choked.

Her father was grinning. He produced a small stuffed animal from somewhere behind the bar and tossed it to Andrew. "Give that to Dolly. Tell her it's a blue penguin. I picked it up at the aquarium the other day."

Tess was shocked. "Since when are you sneaking off to the New England Aquarium?"

"Since I've had a membership for about a million

years. You don't know everything about me, you know."
He turned back to Andrew. "The blue penguins are
those little guys."

"Thanks. She'll love it." He caught Tess by the arm,
sending jolts of sexual energy right through her. "Now,
do I have to start a brawl, or are you coming?"

They made it to her apartment, but not as far as her
bedroom. She said something about having a drink, and
next thing, they'd fallen on her couch, toppling stacks
of folded laundry as they tore off the clothes they were
wearing.

She felt warm and fit in his arms, her skin smooth
and so damn tempting. Andrew knew he'd never get
enough of her. Never. With mouth, tongue and teeth,
he blazed a trail down her throat and stomach, lower
and deeper, wanting to love every part of her, feel her
shuddering with pleasure and heat.

But she had ideas of her own, as she always did. Her
mouth, tongue and teeth did their own erotic torture,
until restraint became impossible.

When they came together, the ferocity of his need
was overwhelming. He forced himself to hold back, but
she pulled him in deeper, harder, matching his rhythm.
Their bodies, minds and souls seemed to melt together,
separate, melt again. The release came suddenly, in a
blinding, nonstop rush.

Stillness settled in slowly, tentatively. He eased between her and the back of the couch, and she slid in
close to him and laid her palm on his chest. "I can feel
your heartbeat." She spoke softly, as if she didn't want
all of Boston to hear her. "I think it was Jedidiah who
put the idea of giving me the carriage house in Ike's

head, don't you? A proper ghost would know we belonged together."

"We do, do we?"

"Yes. Absolutely. You, me and Dolly. And Harl. I'm talking to him about moving his shop to the carriage house. He'd have more space. It'd be better for both of us, I think." She sighed, contented. "This will be so much fun."

Andrew smiled at her. She was a strong woman, and she never stopped. That mind was always going. "Work and living arrangements can be worked out. Let's go back to you and me belonging together."

"We do, you know. I think I've known it, on some basic instinctive level, for the past year, and that's why I was reluctant to take possession of the carriage house. I knew I'd have to go through the fires of hell before I could have a man like you. And I did. We did." She smoothed her palms over his shoulders, her eyes fixed on his. "I love you very much, if that's what you're asking."

"I wasn't asking—I was trying to tell you the same thing." He kissed her softly. "I love you. I want to be a part of your life forever, wherever it takes you."

His cell phone rang, which meant it was Dolly. He rummaged on the floor for it. "Yeah, honey, what's up?"

"Honey?" Harl grunted. "I haven't been called that since I was six months old. Hey, Dolly just threw up. No fever. She's fine. Just wanted you to know."

"Should I come get her?"

"Nah. It was a mechanical thing."

"What did you feed her?"

In the background, he could hear Rita Perez insisting Harl tell him about the sardines. Harl sighed. "She wanted to try sardines. She didn't like them, so she washed them down with some other stuff. Chips and things. You know. Kids."

"I'll be there in the morning. Give her ginger ale. If she gets worse, call me."

Harl swore under his breath. "You'd better get here. She's heaving again. Man. I *told* her the Chinese food would put her over the top."

The line went dead.

Andrew looked at Tess, who was grinning. It was good to see. All the tension of uncovering Ike Grantham's murder had gone out of her. "We have to run up to Gloucester. Harl doesn't do sick kids."

But she was laughing.

He feigned a glower. "And what's so funny?"

"You, me, Dolly and Harl. And Rita Perez. Pop and Davey." She sighed as she rolled off the couch and picked clean clothes out of her scattered laundry. "My life couldn't be better."

He smiled. "Neither could mine."

He crawled into his clothes, and when they walked out into the warm Boston night, he felt it, just the way Tess had described her experience at the carriage house. And he knew.

All his ghosts were at peace.

* * * * *

From *New York Times* bestselling author

CARLA NEGGERS

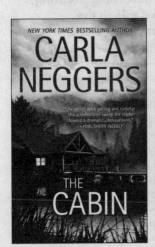

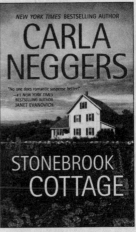

Greed and vengeance disrupt the quiet stillness of the Adirondack mountains...

When everyone is keeping secrets, it's impossible to know whom to trust...

Available now, wherever books are sold!

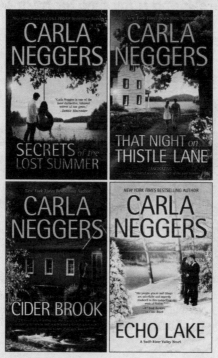

New York Times bestselling author

CARLA NEGGERS

returns to charming Swift River Valley, where spring is the time for fresh starts and new beginnings.

Kylie Shaw has found a home and a quiet place to work as an illustrator of children's books in little Knights Bridge, Massachusetts. No one seems to know her here—and she likes it that way. She carefully guards her privacy in the refurbished nineteenth-century hat factory where she has a loft. And then California private investigator Russ Colton moves in.

Kylie and Russ have more in common than they or anyone else would ever expect. They're both looking for a place to belong, and if they're able to let go of past mistakes and learn to trust again, they just might find what they need in Knights Bridge…and each other.

Available now, wherever books are sold!

CARLA NEGGERS

32990 THE WHISPER	___ $7.99 U.S.	___ $9.99 CAN.
32926 KISS THE MOON	___ $7.99 U.S.	___ $9.99 CAN.
32824 COLD DAWN	___ $7.99 U.S.	___ $9.99 CAN.
32773 THE MIST	___ $7.99 U.S.	___ $9.99 CAN.
32608 THE ANGEL	___ $7.99 U.S.	___ $8.99 CAN.
32586 TEMPTING FATE	___ $7.99 U.S.	___ $7.99 CAN.
32419 CUT AND RUN	___ $7.99 U.S.	___ $9.50 CAN.
31779 HARBOR ISLAND	___ $7.99 U.S.	___ $8.99 CAN.
31743 ECHO LAKE	___ $7.99 U.S.	___ $8.99 CAN.
31669 THE CABIN	___ $7.99 U.S.	___ $8.99 CAN.
31615 STONEBROOK COTTAGE	___ $7.99 U.S.	___ $8.99 CAN.
31603 DECLAN'S CROSS	___ $7.99 U.S.	___ $8.99 CAN.
31588 CIDER BROOK	___ $7.99 U.S.	___ $8.99 CAN.
31453 HERON'S COVE	___ $7.99 U.S.	___ $8.99 CAN.
31420 THAT NIGHT ON THISTLE LANE	___ $7.99 U.S.	___ $9.99 CAN.
31393 THE WATERFALL	___ $7.99 U.S.	___ $9.99 CAN.
31368 SAINT'S GATE	___ $7.99 U.S.	___ $9.99 CAN.

(limited quantities available)

TOTAL AMOUNT	$	_____
POSTAGE & HANDLING	$	_____
($1.00 for 1 book, 50¢ for each additional)		
APPLICABLE TAXES*	$	_____
TOTAL PAYABLE	$	_____

(check or money order—please do not send cash)

To order, complete this form and send it, along with a check or money order for the total above, payable to MIRA Books, to: **In the U.S.:** 3010 Walden Avenue, P.O. Box 9077, Buffalo, NY 14269-9077; **In Canada:** P.O. Box 636, Fort Erie, Ontario, L2A 5X3.

Name: _____
Address: _____ City: _____
State/Prov.: _____ Zip/Postal Code: _____
Account Number (if applicable): _____

075 CSAS

*New York residents remit applicable sales taxes.
*Canadian residents remit applicable GST and provincial taxes.

MIRA®

www.MIRABooks.com

MCN0216BL